He h

C.

Pretty much all the workers in eyeshot had dropped whatever they were doing and stood to stare. Ricky vaguely gathered that, because he had a pretty strong case of tunnel vision himself.

Krysty turned back toward the water. She put her hands up behind her neck and fluffed her glorious hair. Suddenly it seemed to expand into an incredible mane of fire. Ricky knew that was because her hair actually moved of its own accord, though fortunately there was no way the watchers could know that.

She put her hands behind her back and hooked her thumbs in the elastic of her waistband. She paused a moment that way, as if in contemplation.

"Oh, my God," somebody whispered, "she's really gonna do it…."

Then everybody in the room except Jak Lauren yelped and screamed as a sound like thunder broke the air.

Other titles in the Deathlands saga:

JAMES AXLER

DEATH LANDS®

Motherlode

A GOLD EAGLE BOOK FROM

WORLDWIDE®

TORONTO • NEW YORK • LONDON
AMSTERDAM • PARIS • SYDNEY • HAMBURG
STOCKHOLM • ATHENS • TOKYO • MILAN
MADRID • WARSAW • BUDAPEST • AUCKLAND

First edition November 2013

ISBN-13: 978-0-373-62623-6

MOTHERLODE

Printed in U.S.A.

Ours is a culture and a time immensely rich in trash as it is in treasure.

—Ray Bradbury,
Zen in the Art of Writing

THE DEATHLANDS SAGA

This world is their legacy, a world born in the violent nuclear spasm of 2001 that was the bitter outcome of a struggle for global dominance.

There is no real escape from this shockscape where life always hangs in the balance, vulnerable to newly demonic nature, barbarism, lawlessness.

But they are the warrior survivalists, and they endure—in the way of the lion, the hawk and the tiger, true to nature's heart despite its ruination.

Ryan Cawdor: The privileged son of an East Coast baron. Acquainted with betrayal from a tender age, he is a master of the hard realities.

Krysty Wroth: Harmony ville's own Titian-haired beauty, a woman with the strength of tempered steel. Her premonitions and Gaia powers have been fostered by her Mother Sonja.

J. B. Dix, the Armorer: Weapons master and Ryan's close ally, he, too, honed his skills traversing the Deathlands with the legendary Trader.

Doctor Theophilus Tanner: Torn from his family and a gentler life in 1896, Doc has been thrown into a future he couldn't have imagined.

Dr. Mildred Wyeth: Her father was killed by the Ku Klux Klan, but her fate is not much lighter. Restored from predark cryogenic suspension, she brings twentieth-century healing skills to a nightmare.

Jak Lauren: A true child of the wastelands, reared on adversity, loss and danger, the albino teenager is a fierce fighter and loyal friend.

Dean Cawdor: Ryan's young son by Sharona accepts the only world he knows, and yet he is the seedling bearing the promise of tomorrow.

In a world where all was lost, they are humanity's last hope....

Prologue

"Come on, Spider!" Monkey hissed in an urgent undertone.

"I am, I am," his sister said in her long-suffering voice.

The music of a piano floated tinnily up to her as she laboriously scaled the drainpipe running down the back of the four-story gaudy. The metal was cold with spring night-time chill; she wore fingerless gloves because she needed the sensitivity and grip only bare skin could provide.

She climbed without looking down. The rear of the ville's biggest and most important building, which occupied a full block all to itself in the middle of the central intersection, was a dark jumble of houses, streets, alleys and small, dusty yards. Which of course were why she and her brother were climbing up that way.

Because the rear was dark and not many people went there at night, and auxiliary buildings like storage sheds and the annex where most of the gaudy sluts lived gave easy access to the windows above ground floor, the back windows were inviting targets. That in itself would have made the twins wary—if they hadn't known for a fact they were rigged with mechanical cunning alarms. Where their boss had learned that fact they had no clue; she hadn't told them. Despite the way that made Spider's curiosity itch, she hadn't asked how Madame Zaroza knew.

That wasn't part of their job. They had been stealing things for a living long before they'd become traveling show freaks. They knew the drill.

Monkey perched on the end of the steeply peaked roof's ridge beam, clinging like his namesake and peering down at her with his huge eyes. Like hers, his torso was bulked by a heavy sweater. Though to an outsider's eyes she was built the same as her twin brother, with the same unnaturally long legs and arms and short torso that gave them, justified or not, the stigma of mutie taint in the eyes of many norms, they were quite different. She was smaller and skinnier. He was stronger—surprisingly strong, for his slight body and stilty limbs. She was smarter.

Spider made her way to the top. He shifted back as she approached. He knew she didn't like to be helped, even when she needed it.

The roof was metal corrugated into square-section ridges and troughs. It was wicked slick and treacherous, but both twins knew what they were doing, and had smeared sticky pine resin on the pads of their long, strong fingers to help them grip.

Monkey scrambled backward, watching. Spider raised a hand to shoo him, and he turned and scuttled on along the treacherous peak as if down a mostly intact sidewalk.

She followed with only slightly less ease. She was a little concerned he might get overconfident. One slip and he'd shoot down the slippery side and off into the street, where the likes of them could expect no sympathy from the people of the ville. Much less under circumstances that offered no easy innocent explanation.

Which was simple, because their purpose wasn't innocent.

They were there to steal a thing. An Artifact, Madame Zaroza told them. It was a thing someone else had offered to pay highly for. That was all they needed to know.

It wasn't enough for Spider. For either of the twins, actually. Though he wasn't very bright, Monkey had his own curiosity. His was more physical: he liked to get into things, see them, pick them up and feel them. His sister's curiosity was more intellectual. She wanted to know *why* and *what for.*

Right now what mattered was *how.* But that part, at least, they had wrapped.

If they could get in the front window unobserved.

That was the sticky part. As they approached the front of the gaudy called the Library Lounge, voices yammered up from the street. Monkey reached the end, peered cautiously over, then withdrew and slid down a few feet to one side to brace himself on the concrete housing for a metal chimney pipe.

Spider took her turn peering down. While she was careful—she'd learned the price of carelessness not long after she learned to walk—she wasn't very worried about being spotted. Nobody ever looked *up.* Especially drunks.

The street was well lit by lanterns. A couple hung from hooks over the gaudy entrance. More dangled from streetlights west along the main drag of Amity Springs. A couple customers stood and drank in the yellow light-spill in front of the gaudy door. They chatted in slurred voices with one of the male gaudy sluts who stood outside smoking a joint of wolfweed.

"What are you waiting for?" her brother whispered. "We'll get caught."

"We will if you don't shut up," she said sternly.

Nonetheless she turned her attention back to the job. Doing well for the mistress of the traveling show that had sheltered and employed them the past two years meant doing well now, here. A drunk lurched homeward down a side street, supported by a child who seemed to be a gaudy-house helper. He vanished behind a general store as she watched.

She glanced down. A single window opened into the attic at the building front.

Spider gestured her brother forward. With practiced motions he moved toward her as she rummaged in a snapped compartment in her web gear belt. When she found what she sought, Spider nodded at him.

He grasped her ankles while she worked her way down over the eaves of the roof. Then with him securing her, Spider took the glove off her left hand and smeared more resin on her palm from a little tub from her belt. She leaned in and planted the palm against the center of the window until it stuck. Then, setting her jaw determinedly, she began to score the glass with the old diamond ring she had taken from her pouch.

She made sure to hold it tight. Not only was it vital to their present assignment, Madame Zaroza trusted them with it, though it was valuable. Precious stones were once again becoming trade items in Deathlands. She didn't dare lose it.

Perhaps the worst part of that would be it would inevitably cause suspicions that they had stolen it. Madame wouldn't beat them. She never beat her people, even her freaks, nor suffered anyone to mistreat them. But she'd be disappointed, and they couldn't hack that. And if they lost the trust of their boss and their fellow troupe members, they'd have to leave. And *that* was something Spider couldn't bear to think about.

Pressing as hard as she dared for fear of breaking the glass with the attendant noise, Spider scored a circular hole. It seemed to take forever.

When it came loose, she felt it shift in her hand just in time to pull it out while rotating her palm upward. The resin only stuck to the glass so much. Mostly it gave her time to react before gravity had its way. She popped the ring in her mouth for safekeeping.

She signaled for her brother to pull her up.

He did, as if she weighed no more than a rag doll.

She put the ring in her palm and carefully put it away.

Monkey disappeared over the edge, while Spider stashed the cut-out glass circle at the angle where the chimney came out of the drain-channel roof. Then she crept back to the end of the roof.

"Come on," she heard her brother say. "It's open."

This time she swung herself down to the little sill of the window. Her brother had reached inside to unlatch it. Now he reached out to help her inside.

After the cool rooftop air the attic seemed musty, dusty, and almost hot. Though there was no internal illumination—nor were the twins eager to give away their location by lighting any lamps—the starlight and backscatter lantern light through both front and back windows allowed them to see well enough. They both had good night vision.

The attic was crowded with dusty trash, nondescript boxes and busted furniture. For all her natural curiosity Spider spared it barely a glance beyond what was needed to assure herself there weren't any surprises lurking in there to spring out at them. The goal was near; her blood ran high.

The center of the attic was clear. Just enough to allow the trapdoor into the bedroom beneath to swing open.

At a nod from Spider, Monkey did that. Spider picked her way around the trap and hunkered down next to her brother to peer through. A waft of lilac-scented air hit her in the face as she did so.

As expected, the bedroom was dark—the delicate curtains on the window weren't enough to block even feeble light, even had they been pulled. Again, there was more than enough light for Spider to see by.

What surprised her was how luxurious the room wasn't.
If I was a big-time gaudy-house owner, she thought, I'd do
way better than this.

She was getting ready to slip down into the deserted
room when she heard a key clatter in the lock.

Her brother froze. She gently pressed the trapdoor closed
to barely a slit. Then she pressed her eye to it. Monkey did
likewise.

The doorknob turned. The door opened, and a two-
headed giant entered the room.

Crouching at Spider's side, Monkey literally put a hand
over his mouth to stifle his exclamation of surprise.

She shot him a fast sidelong frown. Did you forget we
were told about him, too, you simp? she thought furiously.

Still, it was alarming seeing such a creature in the flesh.
Especially so much of it. Just because she and her brother
were muties—or at least that was what most people said
they were—didn't mean they didn't find some muties scary.

This one would've chilled Spider's blood if he'd had
one head.

The mutie quickly scoped out the room, both heads
scowling suspiciously. The way the two heads moved in-
dependently of each other creeped Spider out totally.

After a final dubious glance at each other, and a quick
scratch of the back of the left head, the monster pulled back
and shut the door. A moment later Spider heard heavy boots
clumping away down the hallway a floor below.

Monkey started to open the door. She held it firmly and
shook her head furiously at him. What if it's a trick and he
comes right back? she mouthed.

But it apparently wasn't. The terrifying two-headed man
didn't return.

Finally satisfied it was safe, Spider nodded. Taking her

brother's hand, she let him lower her far enough to drop to the little throw rug in the middle of the floor with no noise.

She caught Monkey when he dropped down. He wasn't heavy.

She set him down, so as to make no noise. They looked around the room.

Monkey wrinkled his nose at the well-packed shelves occupying most wall space that wasn't given over to window.

"Books," he said. "Stupe."

"Books aren't stupe," replied Spider, who could read and liked to and was proud of the fact. "Books are how you know things."

"Know by doing," Monkey said with a sniff.

Some of the shelves had vases with dried-flower sprays in them. Spider thought they were pretty.

She went to the bed. It had a brass frame. From the way it glinted in the dim light from outside she reckoned it was frequently polished. Or at least recently.

She dropped down to hands and knees by the bed, hoisted the frilly dust ruffle and peered beneath. She could make out a square shape on the floor.

"Come look," she told her brother. "You see better in the dark than I do. And I don't want to strike a light."

He joined her, looked and grunted.

"Looks like it," he said.

He pulled it out. It was a metal strongbox.

"That's it," Spider said. She already had her lock pick set open. That she did by feel, not sight. After a few moments fiddling at the padlock, biting her underlip to help her concentrate, the lock popped open.

The twins looked at each other.

"We're not supposed to look," Monkey said.

"We should. Got to make sure it isn't empty."

"Too heavy."

"Then we need to make sure we're not toting a box full of bricks out of here, don't we?"

He looked dubious, but he did not look away as she opened the lid. Cautiously, in case of booby traps.

For a moment they both squatted on their heels, staring inside the open box in wonder.

"*Shiny,*" Spider said.

Chapter One

"We're here to bring order to this here lawless valley," the rangy man with the greasy blue bandanna tied around his head declared. "We're here to save you from the prevailing anarchy."

"Nice work," J. B. Dix said.

Ignoring the drama playing out not fifty yards from Ryan Cawdor and his companions, he nodded and waved the apple he'd just taken out of his pack at the covered wag stopped at the crude barricade across the dirt road. It was little more than a pair of ruts, cut by wag wheels and deepened by wind and occasional rains. *Very* occasional, if Ryan was any judge.

"Looks like they scavvied motor wag springs for the suspension," the Armorer went on. He was a slight man who always wore a scuffed and battered brown leather jacket, along with the hat and a pair of wire-rimmed spectacles.

The occupants of the wag had dismounted onto the road to stand facing the four coldhearts, except for the driver, who still sat in the box behind the four-mule team that pulled it. He was a Mex-looking kid, not too unlike Ricky, and seemingly much younger than the rest despite the fact he wore a spade beard the way the other two males did.

The one confronting the coldhearts with hands on broad apron and long-skirt-covered hips was a matronly woman with a scarf tied over her head. Ryan couldn't see her hair color from behind, as he led his small group trooping along the road behind the stopped wag. But from her sturdy build, her voice, and her manner, he guessed she was well into middle age.

"What do you mean by blocking our progress, young man?" the woman demanded.

"It costs to bring the power of government to do good to this benighted Basin," the blue bandanna man declared. "So we'll need to know whatcha got in the wag so's we can assess the proper fees."

Ryan steered left around the stoppage. The road led down between dwindling hills from bare mountains to the east. A stream ran down the right side. It apparently provided irrigation for a number of farms, since Ryan's one blue eye could make out broad green swatches against the tan of the broad, flat, hill-ringed Basin below and in front of them.

By habit the companions spread out into a loose vee formation when they left the road, such as it was. J. B. Dix and Doc Tanner walked behind Ryan, then Krysty Wroth and Mildred Wyeth. Bringing up the rear came Jak Lauren and the newest member of the crew, Ricky Morales. None of them had weapons in their hands. Yet.

But as they started over the dusty clumps of bunch-grass beside the road, one of the three coldhearts standing behind the barricade while their leader argued with the matron spotted them.

"Hey!" he shouted. "What the nuke do you think you're doing?"

"Walking," Ryan replied. "Minding our own business."

Blue Bandanna fixed a furious glare on them. He had a bristling red beard and an often-broken nose. He put fists on hips and made no move for his holstered handblaster.

His three pals promptly aimed their longblasters at Ryan.

"That's not neighborly, pointing those things like that,"

he said calmly. "A move like that's liable to be taken as unfriendly."

He kept walking as if nothing was happening, crossing the clumpy ground to pass wide of the barrier, which consisted mostly of a wood beam like an old telephone pole propped across some obviously weighted-down oil drums. The three coldhearts tracked them with their re-made blasters.

"In the name of Diego and the Crazy Dogs, I'm placing you under arrest!" Blue Bandanna yelled. And Ryan could just envision spittle flying from his mouth.

"Your funeral," Ryan said.

He sensed quick motion from behind and to his right. Something arced against the painfully blue sky, heading toward the roadblock.

"Down!" he shouted.

Following his own command, Ryan threw himself forward with his face in a clump of grama. His well-stuffed backpack landed on his back like a full-grown man. He had already been hauling up his Steyr Scout longblaster, which rode his back barrel-down on its sling.

The wag driver screeched, "Gren!" and cowered on the driver's box. The quartet of coldhearts stared up at the round, dark object descending toward them with terrible purpose.

Then they scattered as if a bomb had already burst among them.

Ryan was watching over the ghost ring sights of his carbine, beneath the longeye-relief Leupold Scout scope when what the dark-skinned kid had called out as a gren bounced once off the hard-packed road dirt and rolled out of sight.

The three spade-bearded men from the wag had also bit the dust. Only the stout woman stood, her hands on double-wide hips, shaking her head at these goings-on.

"Come up with your hands empty and in the air and we'll all walk away from this nonsense without any more holes in our carcasses," Ryan called.

"Fuck you, nuke-suckers!" screamed the coldheart leader. He reared up with a battered .44 Magnum Smith & Wesson blaster in hand.

Ryan's longblaster roared and kicked his shoulder with its butt. When he brought the weapon back online from the recoil, the action was jacked and a fresh 7.62 mm cartridge from the 10-round detachable box magazine was locked up tight in the chamber. He saw a deeper red patch dead center of the boss coldheart's sun-faded red plaid shirt. A cloud of red spray hung in the air behind him. He sort of folded back into it, lying back on his own calves. His heavy blaster dropped from lifeless fingers.

A second coldheart, the bearded, hang-bellied one who'd spotted them, came up roaring and blasting shots from a lever-action carbine at his waist. How he expected to hit anything like that, a good twenty-five yards from his nearest target who was lying in cover and was in fact Ryan, was a mystery to the one-eyed man. He shifted his body to twist his aim onto the Crazy Dog to take him down before he got lucky.

Then the man's head jerked back. He had a new dark eye over his right one. Another dark cloud appeared behind him. He seemed to melt straight to the grass as if his skeleton had dissolved instantaneously.

The other two coldhearts had leaped to their feet, as well. But they were rabbiting off across the lumpy grassland as fast as their boots would carry them.

"Show off, Mildred," Ryan said. He got to his feet, still holding the Scout to his shoulder and pointed more or less at the fleeing Crazy Dogs. There was a chance, however hair-slim, one of them would suddenly change his mind and want to turn and fight.

Ryan had not kept dirt from hitting him in the eye, nor kept his motley band of friends from such a fate, by taking chances. Even slim ones. When they were avoidable, anyway.

"It worked," Mildred said.

The coldhearts were already bounding dots in the distance, like fleas on a bunched-up blanket. Ryan lowered his Scout but didn't sling it as he walked up to the wag.

The menfolk were picking themselves up off the ruts, dusting off their homespun shirts and canvas pants, retrieving their hats and trying not to look sheepish. They failed miserably.

The matron watched Ryan approach without favor.

"Menfolk," she declared. She didn't spit, but she might as well have.

"You're welcome, ma'am," Ryan said. "What's your story?"

"Those ruffians were trying to hold us up!" stated the tallest of the menfolk. He was a spindly sort, with a thin nose and long upper lip over a sand-colored beard, and a pair of round glasses perched in front of squinty blue eyes. "They were pretending to be the duly constituted authorities. An outrage."

"Yeah," Ryan said. "I kind of gathered that."

He turned his own single blue eye to the woman. He calculated she was the one in charge. She certainly showed the most presence of mind, if not the most ace sort of judgment.

"We were perfectly capable of handling the situation on our own, young man," she said. She had round cheeks reddened by weather, and small, hard brown eyes. He couldn't see her hair for the scarf; her brows were brown. "I was preparing to reason with those people."

"Coldhearts behind leveled blasters don't see much need for reason," J.B. said from behind the barricade. He had his backpack off, his M-4000 shotgun slung, and his Uzi in one hand.

He stopped and with his free hand picked up the apple, still unbitten, which he had hurled at the coldhearts. Straightening, he examined it through his glasses, dusted it off on his shirt and bit into it with a crunch.

"That's the way it is," Ryan agreed.

"And what are your intentions?" Hands on hips, fierce brows furrowed, she swept the gathered group with an almost tangible glare of disapproval. "Do *you* plan to rob us? Or worse? I warn you, I shall sell my chastity dearly."

"We intend no harm to you, madam," said Doc, whose courtly nineteenth-century manners seemed to defrost the stout woman's expression by half a degree or so.

"Your appearance is certainly not reassuring," she said. "An assemblage of scruffy ruffians, old men, a mutie, women who seem to be no better than they need to be, and a beardless boy, all apparently led by a starved-looking wolf of a man with a most unholy gleam in his one good eye."

"Well," Mildred said from behind Ryan, "you can't really argue with her assessment."

Ryan smiled. They were a double-strange looking lot, even for the Deathlands: a twentieth-century physician, who was a sturdily built black woman with her hair worked in beaded plaits; a knockout redhead; a seeming doddering wrinklie; a little, deceptively harmless-looking dude in a hat and a battered jacket; and a round-faced Latino kid. He was glad Jak was hanging back and keeping his blood-colored eyes skinned for more trouble—not really listening to the exchange, for such didn't interest him. He was an albino, and tended to take vehement exception to being called a mutie. Ryan didn't contradict the woman, though.

They did have a mutie in the bunch. It just wasn't the one any outsider would think.

And he himself, he knew, was a somewhat daunting specimen: tall and lean in his faded jeans and long coat, with a shag of curly hair as shiny black as a raven's wing, and one keen blue eye set deep in a craggy face with a black patch over the left eye socket and a brow-to-jaw scar that ran across it.

He also knew that, in all honesty, he was as scary as he looked. But he truly meant this group of people no harm.

"What do you know about this bunch?" he asked with a sideways nod at the two coldhearts who were currently cooling to ambient temperature.

"I believe they identified themselves in your hearing as Crazy Dogs," the woman said. "They have recently moved into the area from parts West, which I gather had grown uncomfortably hot for them. They have found a relatively prosperous region to infest, here in the Río Piojo Basin. But the baronies within the valley proper are too powerful to trifle with directly, and the farmers and settlers stick together to defend themselves."

"Amity Springs isn't rightly a barony, Maw," a stout, red-bearded man said. "They claim not to be, anyways. Call themselves a free ville."

"Well, *that* woman is certainly their baron, regardless what she chooses to call herself," the woman said. "Indeed, both main baronies are run by women."

"You come from a ville up in the mountains?" asked Krysty, walking up. She nodded her flame-haired head at the bare, jagged range to the east, which she and the rest had come from as well by a different path.

The woman's brows lowered suspiciously, but she answered civilly enough. "Yes. New Zion. We are Latter Day

Saints. I have come to Amity Springs with my husbands to sell items we have made in our shops."

"'Husbands'?" queried Mildred, who'd come up with the others.

"Why, yes," the woman said. "I told you, we are Mormons."

"Well, I knew Mormons used to practice polygamy," Mildred said. "But, see, I thought—"

"You think too much, Mildred," Ryan said. "What can you tell us about this Amity Springs? You say they don't have a baron?"

"They claim not," the woman from the wag said. "But the town is dominated by the Dark Lady, the proprietor of the Library Lounge."

"We should pay the place a visit, Maw," said the third of the men afoot. He was a gangly young man with a weedy blond beard and an excess of forehead.

"You are *not* entering that den of iniquity, Nephi!"

"But, Maw! I only want to—"

"I know what you want to do, young man!" She sniffed and turned back to Ryan.

"If you've no further reason to detain us with your questions, we are burning the good Lord's daylight, with miles yet to travel."

"Just one more question," Ryan said. "You know if this… non-baron is looking to hire steady blasters? To deal with the coldheart problem, say."

"I'm sure *I* don't know what goes on in the mind of such a person. But the ville of Amity Springs is known for sheltering all manner of vagabonds and outlanders. You and your friends should fit in quite nicely there."

Chapter Two

"Welcome to Amity Springs, my friends!"

Ryan turned his eye to the man who had hailed them as he came bustling forward. He was somewhat baggy and built low to the ground, like a badger. He wore shabby clothes, not very clean, and had a multi-day growth of beard on his round face. His black hair was unkempt and looked as if he simply grabbed a chunk when he thought it got too long and sawed it off with a pocketknife. As he approached, Ryan saw he had dark-olive skin and black Asian eyes.

Fists on her generous hips, Mildred said, "This doesn't look like that prosperous a ville to *me*."

She turned her scowl on the man. "Case in point."

The speed of the man's approach and his body language gave Ryan no sense of alarm. Nonetheless he kept his hand convenient to the butt of his 9 mm SIG-Sauer P-226 hand-blaster, because he generally did.

"The place doesn't live up to the billing that Mormon lady gave it, for a fact," he said.

They had walked a few blocks between sagging ramshackle buildings, built not so much of scavvy as planks probably rough-hewn from timber from the mountains that seemed to surround the large Basin. Most of the buildings they had seen, except for obvious shacks, sheds and outbuildings, were two stories at least. Some stood three, none too securely, to Ryan's eye. Board sidewalks fronted many of the structures, at least on the main street that the track they'd followed from the eastern hills had turned into.

Now they stood at the edge of a public square. The buildings here were a bit more pretentious: larger and a little less precarious-looking. A fair number of people were around, pushing carts of tools, pulling carts of goods. Down a side street somebody on a ladder was hammering at a façade, the woodpecker tapping reaching Ryan's ears a heartbeat after the actual strokes.

"Curious," Doc said, mopping his face with a grubby handkerchief from an inside pocket of his long black frock coat. "One would think that Latter Day Saint lady would have been at few pains to compliment the town, given her evident disapproval of its having a woman at the helm."

He was tall and skinny, his eyes as pale blue as Ryan's. He looked every second of sixty-five. Yet his actual age, in terms of years he'd lived through, wasn't that much greater than Ryan, who was approaching forty.

"I hope you enjoy your stay in our fair ville," the local said, half stumbling up. As he got close, Ryan realized that wasn't because he was drunk, as he'd first thought, but because the guy was lame.

"I'm Coffin. Perhaps I can interest you in my wares?"

"What are they?" Krysty asked.

"Coffins!" he said proudly.

"Not in the market," Ryan replied. "Anyway, I don't care much what happens to chills. Even my own. *Especially* my own, come to think."

"We're not reckoning on dying here, any too soon," J.B. stated.

Unfazed, Coffin turned to Krysty. "What of you, ma'am? Surely you're more concerned with the eventual repose of your mate."

"Why would I want to prevent my lover's body from once more becoming one with Mother Gaia?" she asked.

"Ah. You are cultists! Well, all are welcome here in Amity Springs. We have learned to be most tolerant of everyone, since the Dark Lady has come among us."

"Yeah," Ryan said. "Well. About that—we hear she runs this ville."

Coffin cocked his head to one side, which made him look mostly as if he were trying to drain water surreptitiously out of one ear.

"Well, she doesn't exactly run Amity Springs," he said. "And then again, she doesn't exactly *not.*"

"Great," Mildred said. "Just our luck. The first person we meet is the village idiot."

"Can it, Mildred," Ryan growled. "This Dark Lady's the person we need to see. How do we get to the Library Lounge?"

Coffin turned and flung out an arm. "It's right before you, the grandest structure in all Amity Springs!"

Ryan frowned. It was grander than most, he acknowledged: three broad stories with what looked like an attic beneath a pitched metal roof. A one-story annex winged off from one side. The front was painted white, well weathered, with lamps hanging from ornate black iron holders to either side of a large door with a lot of colored-glass inserts. A pair of life-size lions, probably concrete casts, incongruously flanked the entryway.

It was impressive, in its way. It just didn't look a lot less sorry-ass than the rest of the place.

"Right," he said to Coffin. "We'll take it from here. Thanks."

"Don't thank me," he said. "I reckon you'll be good for business."

Beside the door was a placard reading Welcome to the

Library Lounge, Amity Springs' Finest Entertainment Establishment. Beneath it was a smaller sign, neatly hand-lettered, that read Please Ring Bell for Admittance. Since that was five words more than most people in the Death-lands could read, fifteen if you counted both, Ryan reck-oned that at least folks in the ville had more education than was common. Or at least liked to pretend as much.

The bell in question was small, brass, and dangled from a bracket right over the sign. Ryan gave it a good ring.

The door opened fast. An angry two-headed giant filled the doorway, holding a normal-looking man in the air with one hand.

"LEMME GO!" the captive yelled. He kicked his cracked and dusty cowboy boots frantically. The heels swung a good six inches off the bottom of the doorframe. The giant held him out at the length of one inhumanly long arm—hold-ing him by a bunch of the back of his shirt, Krysty saw—so that he couldn't kick the monster, by accident or design.

Ricky Morales's round olive face went ashy-pale, and he swung up his DeLisle carbine with the barrel fattened by its built-in noise suppressor.

"Blaster down," Ryan ordered sternly.

Ricky turned wide black eyes to him. "But—"

"You heard me."

J.B. stepped up beside the kid and gently pressed the bar-rel down with two fingers. Ricky didn't resist. Perceiving in the crew's newest member a fellow born tinkerer, with a shared love of weapons and fiendish booby traps, J.B. had taken the youth under his wing as more or less his protégé.

For his part Ricky idolized the Armorer. Almost as much as he did Ryan.

"I said let me go, you rad-blasted mutie!" the man screamed, spittle flying from his fury-reddened face. He looked young, not much older than Ricky—a year or two older than Jak, say.

The mutie shook him up and down furiously. "I'm not a mutie, you diseased buffalo sphincter!" roared the right-hand head in a voice of thunder. It was the better-looking of the two, if such a term was applicable. It had a broad jaw and a shock of black hair.

"He displays a highly unusual combination of erudition and vulgarity," Doc said. "Admirable, in its way."

"We're conjoined twins," the other head said calmly. "It's a common error. Don't blame my brother Michael too much. He has a sensitive soul, especially on that subject."

That head was much the less presentable, with a bald-ing pate that seemed to come to a point, a furrowed brow and snaggled teeth. Yet its voice was soft.

"I don't give a shit, you freak! You got no right to lay your nuking hands on me!"

The giant carried his uselessly struggling burden into the street. Krysty saw he had apparently done so to give way to a second figure, considerably smaller but possessed of undeniable presence.

"You violated the rules of my establishment, Chad," a woman said with a languid wave of her long slim cigarette holder, which Krysty observed held a long, thin black ciga-rillo. "Actions have consequences. You need to learn that."

"What? That gaudy slut had it coming! She talked back to me!"

The woman's face, its pallor already marked and accen-tuated by the chin-length black hair that framed it, went as white as Jak's.

"You do not call *my* people that!" she said.

Chad had some comeback to that, but it got lost in the general sputtering and gobbling as the giant shook him up and down again, much harder.

"Nor do you lay hands on them if they tell you not to," the woman said. She was dressed all in black, from the bow in her hair, down to her pinafore-like dress, elbow-length fingerless lace gauntlets, knee-high stockings and shoes. "That is what you're being ejected for. The abusive term merely compounds your offense."

Chad's eyes bugged out and he flailed his arms in a hopeless attempt to get at the hand that was shaking him. Finally he managed to choke out, "P-please, sto-oo-oo-p!"

"Do you promise to behave yourself?" the woman said.

"Y-y-yes-ss, mumm-umm-am!"

The balding head had turned to keep one eye on the gaudy owner. The other, Krysty noted, was still positioned to keep watch on the band of newcomers. The better-looking head continued to admire the giant's handiwork in shaking Chad.

"You may stop, Mikey-Bob," the woman said.

"Mikey-Bob?" Mildred repeated incredulously but quietly.

Chad hung from the giant's fist like an unconscious puppy. His jaw hung slack, his tongue lolled out and his eyes had rolled up in his head.

The woman in black put her hands on her hips. "Well, young man? I hope you've learned your lesson."

Chad raised his head. He managed to twist his mouth into a leering smile.

"Why don't you suck my dick, you bi— Uh! Uh!"

Mikey-Bob had started shaking him again. This time the giant's efforts made his earlier exertions seem like playful fooling around. Krysty actually wondered if the unruly customer's neck might snap.

"Is it time to smack him, D.L.?" asked the sparse-haired, homelier head.

"I believe that it is, Bob," she said.

With surprising coordination for a guy with two heads, Mikey-Bob let Chad's shirt go with his right hand while fetching a straight-armed slap to the side of his head with the other. Chad sailed fifteen feet into the middle of the street and landed hard, in a crumple. He had his ass in the air and his face pressed to the hard-packed yellowish dirt, as if he were trying to imitate a plow.

With an air of immense satisfaction, Mikey-Bob dusted equally immense hands together. "Good riddance," Mikey said.

"—to bad rubbish," Bob finished.

"Regular stand-up comedian, these two," Mildred muttered.

The woman turned her attention to Ryan.

"You look interesting," she said, leaning a hip against the door and kind of slouching into it. "Who might you be?"

"Ryan Cawdor," he replied.

He quickly introduced the others, finishing with Jak, who stood a little apart from the others, in part watching out for the approach of possible danger, in part watching the shenanigans with obvious amusement.

As he did, Krysty became aware of a muted bubble of conversation coming out the open door past the woman, and the sound of a piano being played. It wasn't the usual off-key clinking you heard from a gaudy. It was smooth and well-modulated. Classical music, she thought in surprise.

"And you're the one they call the Dark Lady?" Ryan asked.

"Indeed they do," she said.

"We heard tell you might be looking to hire a crew of blasters," Ryan said.

She smiled. She had high cheekbones, a thin nose, and big black eyes outlined in kohl. Her right eye was accentuated even more by looking out of a painted-on black Eye of Horus. She was quite a strikingly lovely young woman, Krysty saw. Though she seemed to be careful to smile with her black-painted lips pressed firmly together.

"I am," she said.

"Come into my parlor."

Chapter Three

"So," Dark Lady said. She sat back in her gilded-armed chair with its velvet cushions and crossed one slim leg over the other. "What exactly is it that you and your friends do, Mr. Cawdor?"

"Lot of things," J.B. said. "But mostly they come down to trouble."

The office was small enough to feel crowded with Ryan and his companions inside, even with the giant bulk of Mikey-Bob looming in the hall outside the open door.

The room's most remarkable feature was the floor-to-ceiling shelves filled with books, mostly hardbacks with age-cracked backs, as well as vases holding sprays of fresh lilac that crowded the room additionally with their fragrance. But they came as no surprise to Ryan at this point, given that the main barroom of the gaudy likewise featured cases filled with hundreds of volumes. That *had* surprised him, as well as Doc, who had earned a genuine smile from the Dark Lady upon his exclamation of pleasure at seeing all the books.

As they had made their way to the office, the companions had seen perhaps a dozen customers sitting around talking or flirting with the gaudy sluts. These were of both sexes, though predominantly female; they were on the whole younger, fitter, and brisker somehow than the type Ryan was acquainted with. It was almost as if they wanted to be here doing this. Or at least were okay with it, whether ace or not.

They had made their way through the main saloon. The bartender, a long, narrow-faced man with long lank light-brown hair, had glanced up from polishing a mug with an amazingly clean-looking rag.

"Think I see what's going on here," J.B. had said softly at Ryan's back. "The whole shabby look of everything outside's mostly a front. Folks here don't want outlanders knowing just how well they're doing."

"They seem to draw in a power of trade from some-where, though," Ryan muttered back.

DARK LADY RETURNED to the business at hand, leaning back in her gold-armed chair, dragging in smoke.

"So," she said, letting blue smoke slide out and up in front of her pale face. "Do you mean, get into trouble, Mr. Dix? Or do you mean, make trouble for other people?"

J.B. shrugged. For an answer, he took off his glasses and began to polish them with a handkerchief.

"Both," Ryan said, taking up the slack for his friend. "Emphasis on the latter. At least, given our preference."

Dark Lady smiled. Again, she seemed to take care to keep her black-painted lips covering her teeth.

"I quite understand," she said. "You do seem to show a degree of erudition unlooked for in—let's say, a man of your appearance, Mr. Cawdor, in all candor."

Ryan grinned even broader. Their hostess's already-pale face seemed to turn a shade paler. He realized he was prob-ably giving her what Krysty called his wolf smile.

"We'd rather take other people by surprise than the op-posite, ma'am," he said.

He felt strong hands grip him by the shoulders from behind. Recognizing Krysty's touch at first contact, he relaxed slightly and sat back in his own chair. She was letting him know that his tact was slipping, in her own very tactful way.

"Do I take it that you have trouble of your own you'd like help resolving, Dark Lady?" Krysty said.

"I see no reason to be coy about it," the woman said. "Yes. A situation has come up, and you look to be just the people to help me solve it."

Krysty laughed. "I'm going to take that as a compliment."

"Oh, yes."

Ryan tried to keep his expression stone-like, but he couldn't help noticing that the Dark Lady had let her cool reserve slip slightly out of place. Perhaps she wasn't as in control of the situation as she liked to pretend. Or mebbe not so much in control of herself.

"I must tell you I don't much like violence," Dark Lady said.

"We don't, either," Mildred replied. "But we're very, very good at it."

Dark Lady looked at her as she inhaled on her cigarette holder. The motion made her already rather hollow cheeks look positively gaunt.

She nodded. Just a touch abruptly, as if she had come to whatever decision she had visibly just made against her own better judgment.

"I have recently suffered a theft," she said. "I would like to hire you to recover the...item."

"What exactly is this item?" J.B. asked.

"It's a metal box, perhaps fourteen inches wide by ten inches deep and six inches high." As she spoke, she gestured with her hands to frame the dimensions.

"And the contents of the box, Madam?" Doc asked.

"Let's say you have no need to know that," she said.

Then she smiled. It was a surprisingly engaging, open-mouthed smile. But she still was double-careful to keep her teeth covered.

"And don't call me madam," she added.

Ryan emitted a soft grunt. So she actually had a sense of humor.

"Are you sure you can't tell us anything about the contents of this box?" Ryan asked. "Seems like it could be important."

"Needless to say, it's an item of some value," Dark Lady said, waving her cigarette holder a little too carelessly to be credible.

"But it could be important for us to have at least some idea what the box contains, Dark Lady," Krysty said. "We want to be sure we bring back the right thing."

"Oh, you'll know," Dark Lady said. "And if you do perchance bring back the wrong item, I will pay an added fee for you to try again. Within reason, of course."

"Yeah," Mikey grunted. "Nothing like trusting a bunch of random coldhearts from the outlands."

"For once I am compelled to agree with my brother," Bob said. "I *hate* that feeling. It's not a double-smart call, Dark Lady."

"About that fee," Ryan said.

They dickered. For all the little-girl-lost Ryan had thought to glimpse when her cool façade slipped, the gaudy proprietor proved hard as a blaster barrel when it came time to bargain. Then again, so was Ryan Cawdor. They were down to their last supplies and needed the jack from the Dark Lady. So the companions' services didn't come cheap. And in the end, Dark Lady was rather generous.

"There is one stipulation," she said, leaning back in her chair blowing smoke out her fine and narrow nose. "There must be no chilling. Indeed, I insist that violence be kept to the absolute minimum."

"We may find our opposition forces our hand," Doc said.

"Yeah," Ryan said. "You aren't paying us enough to wind up staring at the stars."

"I think what our new employer is saying," Krysty said sweetly, "is that the people she suspects of stealing her... property are not of a violent character."

Dark Lady nodded. "That's right, Ms. Wroth. They cannot afford to be, in their situation. Moreover, their lack of violent disposition is precisely the reason they have sought the employee they have."

"Ace on the line," Ryan grumbled. "All right. We'll do our best not to chill anybody."

Dark Lady thought about that a moment. "I will pay a slight bonus if you return my property without hurting anybody," she said, with an emphasis on "slight." "But do not try to deceive me. I assure you, I will know."

Ryan held up his open right hand. "All right, I believe you."

He leaned forward again. "Now tell us what you can about these robbers you want us to rob from."

Chapter Four

"A mutie traveling circus," J.B. said dryly, shaking his head. "The last one nearly killed us."

A couple hundred yards away the wags of Madame Zaroza's traveling circus showed a few yellow gleams of lights. They were mostly panel trucks, pulled up in a rough laager a bit over half a mile outside the ville of Amity Springs. Ricky, who had been expecting tents and lights, even if not currently on, was disappointed.

"Dark night!" Ricky heard J.B. exclaim—softly, because the Armorer was always in control. "Don't pop out of nowhere like that, Jak. Almost blasted you."

Ricky glanced around to see his friend, crouching on his haunches and grinning in the starlight like a white coyote.

"No sentry," Jak reported in that weird abbreviated way of his. By now Ricky understood him as well as the rest of the group did. "Quiet. Mebbe thirty inside."

"You find where this Madame Zaroza's likely to be?" J.B. asked.

Jak nodded. "Center wag," he said. "Got lights."

"So the others are circled around it?" Ryan asked.

"Yeah."

Sotto voce, Ryan asked Jak a few more questions. Jak answered in monosyllables volubly.

"Right," Ryan said with decision a few moments later. "Here's how we play it…"

He led his companions in a wide circle around the camp,

counterclockwise to the northwest. Ricky realized he meant to avoid taking the obvious approach from the ville.

For a few moments they hunkered down in the crackling-dry grass. Ricky used the opportunity to catch his breath and try to still his heart. He was in good enough shape after a few months of tramping the Deathlands with his new family. But he still tended to tense up at the nearness of action. It wore him right straight down.

"You fit to fight, son?" J.B. asked him.

The Armorer was not what anybody would call a sensitive man, but he had a surprisingly perceptive way to him. Especially for somebody who mostly acted as if he was more comfortable working with machines and gadgets than people.

Like Ricky himself.

He nodded. He didn't trust himself to speak without panting.

Ryan gestured for Jak and Ricky to lead off to the wag circle. The rest stayed behind crouched in the concealment of the grass. Before he took off Ricky couldn't help noticing that Ryan had *his* longblaster in his hands, ready to roar.

Running bent over, the two young men quickly crossed the hundred yards or so to the wags. They were camped in a wide area of bare dirt. From the looks and firmness it had been trampled clean of vegetation and packed down by the boots of ville folk avid to watch the show. That and the performers, likely, as well as whoever set up and took down the stages and signs or whatever they used.

I wish I could see the show, he thought. *At least what they do.*

They made it with no sign of detection, or any sign of life within the wag circle except the lights from the central mobile home. Breathing hard through his open mouth, Ricky pressed his back against the box of the show wag.

He realized—or his mind, over-revving, finally took note of something he'd been seeing but had been too mentally busy to take in—that the circled wags had paintings on the side of them. Not just the sign—Madame Zaroza's Caravan of Curiosities—but images, fabulous images: a lizard man like a giant scalie but with a protuberant muzzle almost like a dog; an enormously fat woman; a pair of what looked like kids just younger than Ricky, a boy and a girl, with arms and legs of exaggerated length.

And then the woman. He had spotted her on the next wag over. Without thinking, he drifted over, ignoring a soft chirp of inquiry from Jak. He did keep presence of mind to glance between the wags as he passed the gap, to make sure no one was lurking on the inside to leap out at him.

No one was.

She was magical, even painted there on the box of a blunt-nosed cargo wag in colors he could tell were bright even by starlight. Her hair was so golden, streaming down the sides of the bed or cloth-covered table or whatever it was she lay on on her back. And her nipples were clearly in evidence poking up the fabric of the evidently flimsy nightgown she wore. The unknown artist's skill hadn't been great—Ricky didn't know a thing about painting, but he did know *workmanship* when he saw it, or didn't—but he managed to show that just fine.

He got so worked up by the picture that he took little notice of the giant beast-man shape looming over the painted lady in the background—whether threatening her or protecting her being left considerably more to the imagination than the contours of her lovely body.

"Quit gawking, kid," he heard a familiar voice growl in an undertone. "We're not here to sightsee."

Ryan trotted up, straightening after a hunched-over dash

across the clear space to the wags. He held his longblaster in both hands, but as he slowed he slung it.

The others, Ricky realized in sudden chagrin, had already come up to cluster by the other wags. Pursuant to their employer's wishes, which Ryan had decided to humor for now, they had no weapons in hand and consequently looked even more paranoid than usual.

"What the Hell's wrong with you, Ricky?" Mildred demanded.

"I believe you moderns call it 'adolescence,'" Doc said with a smile half dreamy, half humorous.

"Great. It's the perfect time for testosterone poisoning to strike." She glared accusingly at Doc. "You probably think it's funny, you old coot."

"Indeed."

She turned away in disgust. *"Men."*

"Pipe *down,* everybody," Ryan said.

He pointed first at Jak, then at Ricky. "You and you, go scout the wag in the middle."

Jak insisted on going first, and Ricky followed hard on his heels.

The circle left about twenty yards of open space between the outer wags and the side of the mobile home. It was huge, at least to Ricky's eyes, covered with paintings of stars and planets, galaxies and nebulas and other fantastic things. Ricky only knew what the stuff other than stars was because his parents had insisted he read old books as part of his education growing up.

He wondered what Jak made of the paintings—which again, even in the darkness, the yellow glow spilling out curtained windows did little to alleviate, he could tell were colorful to the point of gaudiness. He wasn't sure Jak's mind even registered them. He was so tuned to immediate survival, and the natural world in general, that his disdain for technological artifacts, including signs of civilization, struck Ricky sometimes as bordering at least on deliberate obliviousness.

He joined Jak beside the trailer. Its interior was obviously heated somehow. He could feel the warmth beating from its thin-gauge metal sides. He fought the desire to press his body against the painted panels and suck up the warmth. The others seemed to find the high-desert spring evening no more than pleasantly brisk. He, Tropics-raised, found it freaking *cold*. He shivered when he remembered their sojourn in Alaska.

Jak flicked his ruby eyes toward Ricky. He nodded.

His pale hands made a complicated series of gestures, which Ricky, after a beat, understood to indicate that Ricky should look for a way into the trailer. The albino wasn't much for talking, but he did love his hand signals. By constant exposure, Ricky had learned to interpret them with at least as much ease as he did Jak's notoriously abbreviated speech.

Oh, he thought. He wants me to pick the lock.

He grinned. For all of his love of gadgets, growing up in Nuestra Señora had offered little opportunity to practice lock-picking. His home ville had seldom bothered to lock its doors. But his new idol and mentor, J. B. Dix, had proved willing to teach Ricky the art. For his part, Ricky was an avid student.

The problem was that the only door in the site was up front right beside the driver's seat, which, naturally, would likely be watched, if not alarmed. As quietly as he could, Ricky stole to the rear of the vehicle and peered around. While there was a sort of rack affixed to the back, there was evidently a cargo hatch back there.

Uncertain how to proceed, Ricky glanced back at the outer circle of wags. Ryan was crouched behind the trailer hitch of the wag with the image of the sleeping woman on its side, and he gestured peremptorily for Ricky to proceed.

He seemed to be getting pretty hot, so Ricky swallowed his misgivings and decided to proceed. He duck-walked around the corner of the mobile home.

A massive weight slammed onto his back and shoulders. His vision was blacked out an instant before he landed face-first on the cold, hard ground.

Chapter Five

"Fireblast!"

Ryan saw a shadow-shape like a giant, limb-deprived spider drop suddenly onto Ricky's back.

His first thought was that things were already out of control and it was time to forget about Dark Lady's instructions. He'd learned early on that it was easier to get forgiveness than permission. And hardest to get either when you had dirt hitting you in the eyes.

But he'd no sooner thought of reaching back over his shoulder for the pistol grip of his Steyr Scout longblaster than he felt the blaster being grabbed from behind. It was rudely yanked away. The sling spun him half around as if he were a mutie child's rag doll before it slid off his arm.

Nightmare loomed behind him. His flash impression was that he'd been attacked by a scalie. But a scalie taller than he was and much broader through the shoulders. And with something wrong with the head—for either a scalie or a man.

He fired a straight right hand into the misshapen scaled face. It had a muzzle, he saw now, more like a dog's than a lizard's, and two eyes mounted on the face's front like any human or other predator's. In the bad light they still looked disturbingly human-like.

His fist connected on the left underside of the chin. That was the "button," and it tended to overload people's brains and cause them to temporarily go blank, or rattle their brains around hard enough in their brainpans they got concussed and blacked out.

The weird lizard man's head barely rocked back on what Ryan now noticed was a massive neck. The creature had lips, too. They pulled back in a smile from alarmingly pointy teeth.

Ryan went for the grip of his panga. Before he could so much as start to tug the broad blade out of its sheath the lizard man shot out a black-taloned hand twice the size of his own in a straight palm to his sternum. The blow hit so hard that Ryan's one-eyed vision blacked out for a split second as his heart skipped a beat.

When he came fully back to himself he was flying through the air. Not for long. He hit the ground so hard the breath was knocked out of him.

Around him was shadowed chaos, screams and curses. Something—many somethings—were grappling with his friends. He caught a glimpse of Ricky, in the middle of the laager beside the lit-up mobile home, teetering in circles and flailing uselessly at a shadowy form that seemed to envelop his head and shoulders.

At the same time Jak was menacing a second dark figure with a big trench knife. This mutie appeared to be mostly arms and legs, though only two each despite its own marked similarity to an arachnid. It was dancing around Jak, juking left and darting right.

Then it screeched, "You stay away from my sister!"

It threw itself on its hands, flung its long supple legs in the air, and kicked Jak square in the snow-white face. The albino sat right down. Ryan thought it was more of surprise than because he'd been knocked on his butt.

Nuke this, Ryan thought. He snapped up to his feet.

To find himself eye to snout with the lizard man.

He punched the creature hard in the columnar throat.

Usually that was a kill-shot, dooming the target to slow strangling death from a collapsed trachea. This was like hitting a steel pipe.

The lizard man smiled wider. "You don't get it, do you? Give it up."

Ryan smiled. Then he kneed the monster in the balls.

Or tried to. The lizard man pivoted his hips, fouling the blow with the great muscle of his right thigh. He knew a thing or two about fighting.

The lizard mutie slammed both palms into Ryan's chest and sent him flying back.

So THIS DUDE in a top hat and a coat with crazy mustachios just like Snidely Whiplash comes up to me in the dark, Mildred thought.

That happened. Plus he fixed her with a burning gaze, raised both hands in a silent-movie spooky gesture, and intoned, "Look into my eyes, dear lady!"

She punched him in the face instead.

He reeled back in surprise. Mildred took quick stock of her friends. J.B. was sparring with an enormous fat woman. She looked as if she could crush him simply by falling on him. Mildred wasn't worried. J.B. was a smart fighter.

Krysty was wrestling with a balding man in tights. It didn't look like near a fair fight, either: perfectly proportioned though she was, the tall redhead looked as if she was twice his size, and she was strong for a woman to boot. Doc was flourishing his ebony cane in the fur-covered face of some kind of beast-man mutie. The creature was powerfully built and had pointy ears on the top of his head.

What have we gotten ourselves into? Mildred wondered. *Oh. Right. A traveling mutie show.*

She raised her fists and closed in on her assailant. The

man looked to be middle-aged and none too robust. She figured she didn't need a blaster to take him.

Movement caught her eye. Fearing a blindside assault, she glanced around to see Ryan fly through the air and slam right into the obese woman confronting J.B. Ryan literally bounced off her and landed on the ground in a heap. The woman turned on him triumphantly as J.B. nipped out of sight around her own bulk.

Mildred turned her attention back to the man in the ludicrous top hat. He flung an arm at her. Powder gusted into her face.

Poison! she thought in horror. She tried not to hold her breath.

But it was too late. She'd already gotten a noseful.

And promptly erupted into convulsive sneezes.

RYAN LAY ON the ground struggling to catch his breath. He didn't have any cracked ribs, he thought. But he didn't feel good.

He saw Krysty putting a wiry little guy in a hammerlock, then she yelped, and the man sprang lithely away from her.

Ryan came flying up off the ground to race to Krysty's aid. He feared the man had stabbed her with a knife.

He was propelled forward by a belly-bump from the huge fat woman the lizard man had tossed him into.

This is going fifteen kinds of out of control, he thought, on his back on the ground again.

He saw something spin end for end out of the night and knock Doc's swordstick whirling end over end from his hand with a clatter.

"A bowling pin? By the Three Kennedys!"

He reached inside his frock coat. "I fear you leave me no choice—"

Something flickered in dim starlight. There was a *thunk,* then a knife pinned the sleeve of Doc's coat to the painted side of the wag.

"Right," Ryan grumbled. "That's it."

He saw Krysty flipped over the skinny guy's shoulder to land flat on her back. He was already reaching for the butt of his P-226 in its shoulder holster.

He heard a scream of outrage and fury from Mildred. Still flat on his back he turned his head to see her grappled from behind by what looked like the Wolfman from an old-days movie poster. She had her ZKR 551 revolver in hand; one furry paw had her by the wrist and her gun hand thrust straight up over her head.

The .38 cracked off with a bright yellow flash.

Ryan's handblaster came out. He pointed it at the center of the vast chest of the lizard mutie, who was looming over him like a colossus.

White light dazzled him.

He cranked out three fast shots. They were completely blind. His ears rang from an explosion so sharp and savage he barely heard the 9 mm blaster go off.

Ryan wondered if he was shot. He felt no pain, except in his stinging eye, which saw nothing but shifting purple-and-orange blurs. He'd been shot before and knew a person didn't always feel it—at first.

The SIG was wrenched from his hand. Still unable to see anything other than what now looked like giant balloons floating inside his own eye, he grabbed at the hilt of his panga. Instead his own arm was grabbed and yanked clear. He felt the broad-bladed knife being pulled from its sheath.

His arm was released. He sat up.

Slowly a semblance of vision returned. He still had big balls of color floating in his vision field, and the night, which had been lit by stars and the glow from Madame

Zaroza's Winnebago, looked dark as four feet up a coal miner's ass. Around him he heard his friends moaning. He became aware of shapes on the ground, and others standing over them.

Then he could see well enough to start confirming his worst fears: all his friends were on the ground, and all their enemies were standing over them.

"Okay," growled the immense lizard mutie. "Time to give these rubes a stomping to remember us by."

"Hold on, everybody," a calm and quiet voice said.

Everyone froze. Ryan turned his head toward where the voice had come from.

It was J.B. The Armorer stood between the back of one trailer and the snout of a parked motor wag. He had his fedora tipped back on his high forehead. A placid half smile was on his face and the muzzle of his Smith & Wesson M-4000 shotgun was aimed at the small of the back of a stocky, middle-aged woman with flowing skirts and big hoop earrings.

"Playtime's over," J.B. called. "All you folks just sort of step back now."

"Don't do it!" she commanded brusquely. "Don't give in, no matter what happens to me. You know what happens when you give in to the rubes."

"Sorry, Z," the hairy dude said in a surprisingly high and piping voice. "No can do. These people play for keeps, and we know that without you we're nothing."

She looked around at the rest. "Anybody?"

She slumped. "Oh, well. It was worth a try. And the Beauty said they didn't mean to hurt us if they could help it."

"We didn't really mean to hurt you people, either," the lizard man said in a deep, rasping rumble. "Just rowdy you up some. We can't let the rubes think they can get away with picking on us, you know?"

Picking himself up, Ryan paused and cocked a brow at him. "Yeah. You know, I think I do."

"So, no point in standing out here in the cold," Madame Zaroza said. "Thanks for giving your best, everybody. Go back to bed. And you people—" she looked hard at Ryan to make clear whom "you people" meant "—might as well come on in and enjoy a nice pot of tea."

Chapter Six

"For a bunch of performers," Ryan said, "you sure took us down pretty quick."

"You got the advantage of us in the end," said the wiry man with the hair cut short to his narrow skull and the vest full of knives.

"By cheating," the enormous lizard mutie rumbled.

"That's enough, boys," Madame Zaroza said. "That's behind us now. Anyway, we never give a mark an even break. Why would these folks do any different?"

Seated in a wooden chair across from her, Krysty noticed that the room, which was the style for mobile homes, combined the functions of kitchen, dining room and living room, had even fussier décor than Dark Lady's office, and was a lot more packed with stuff: bobble-head dolls, Ouija boards, what looked like a crow's skull. Scented candles burned on bookshelves, one stuck to the top of a skull that looked mostly human but not quite. The lamps were oil-burners with lacy shades stuck over their soot-stained glass chimneys with brass harps. They gave off a pretty decent light.

"What exactly are you people, anyway?" Ryan asked. He sat perched at the edge of a green overstuffed chair as if afraid that if he relaxed, comfort would swallow him and he'd lose his keen edge.

"Just what you see, sir," Professor Finesse said from behind the counter in the kitchen area. He was a courtly middle-aged man with exaggerated mustachios and a fawn suit coat over a white shirt with a frilled front and a string tie. His top hat, which matched his coat, rested crown-down by the sink. "A troupe of performers, making our way across the Deathlands."

Ryan grunted.

With a bit of a trill a rangy orange tabby jumped up on Krysty's leg.

"Belphegor," Madame Zaroza said sharply from her chair. "You be good, now."

Krysty smiled at her. "He's not bothering me."

His claws bit slightly through the faded blue denim of her jeans. She didn't mind; she could tell they were not all the way retracted. He wasn't trying to hurt her, or even clinging on. It was obviously just the way he was.

"Thank you, Draco," Madame Zaroza said to the enormous lizard mutie, who had just poured her a cup of steaming tea from a big white-painted, cast-iron teapot.

"Might as well call me Gordon," Draco said, moving on to pour for Mildred.

"Tut, tut, Draco," Madame Zaroza said, wagging a finger. "We've got marks here. We don't use real names."

He frowned. His face had fewer mimetic muscles than a normal man's, but he managed to get a lot of mileage out of them. His eyes were amber-colored and actually had lashes. They were oddly pretty, Krysty thought. Especially by contrast to the dull green- and gold-scaled rest of him.

"I thought that, under the circumstances—"

She gave him a look. He shut his big saw-toothed jaw with a clack.

With surprising delicacy for his bulk and build Draco pivoted to pour for Krysty, who stood with her back to a bookshelf between J.B. and Ryan. Though spacious for a recreational vehicle, the room was crowded. Jak, naturally, insisted on restlessly prowling around outside, searching for threats. Ryan, Krysty, J.B., Mildred, Doc and Ricky were all inside. As was most of the traveling show troupe they'd encountered in their scrum outside. The show folk had not obeyed their boss's instruction to go to bed, and she hadn't pressed the issue.

Krysty had no idea how Madame Zaroza managed to find fuel for the giant Winnebago, much less her other motor wags. No doubt it was converted to burn alcohol, and probably other fuels, as well, like a lot of wags were these days.

"Are these people marks?" asked the double-long limbed boy. He and his obvious twin sister stood together behind Madame Zaroza. Their dark eyes were wide in dark-olive faces.

"Everybody's a mark, properly considered," Madame Zaroza said. "Even these folks. Though not now."

She dragged in smoke, then pensively let it out. "Right now, looks like we're the marks for *them*."

"Are you coldhearts?" asked the spider-limbed girl twin. She seemed more thoughtful than her brother.

"Mebbe," Madame Zaroza replied, "but I wonder. Tall, dark and dangerous there is too good-looking for a coldheart. Come to think of it, so's the redhead. Women who look like that don't *stay* looking like that long running with coldhearts. Unless they get kept more or less intact to sell on to slavers."

"I assure you, Madame Zaroza," Doc said in his most formal tones, "we are no coldhearts."

"At least not your usual run of coldhearts," Mildred said.

"So what is your gig?" Madame Zaroza asked. "I'm guessing this isn't a straight jack-up? Because we'd have gotten to the point by now."

"Not exactly," Ryan said. "You got something that doesn't belong with you. We're here to take it back."

She nodded. "Well, Sleeping Beauty warned us you were coming for that, yes."

"'Sleeping Beauty,'" repeated Ricky, who stood behind Ryan. "That's the lady in the painting? On the side of the wag?"

"Yes."

"And you said she said we didn't mean you any harm, too. Is she a doomie?"

"Well, you're sure full of questions, aren't you? Yes, she is."

"Indeed, Madame Zaroza," Doc said. "I cannot help noting that a high proportion of your performers appear to be muties."

"I'm not," said the fur-covered man, who answered to Squatsch. In the light, the pointed tufts sticking up from either side of his skull proved to be hair. His ears were normal in size, shape and placement, though covered with the same dark fur as the rest of him except the pink palms of his hands. "I've got a condition called hypertrichosis."

"I'm not," said the slight man in tights. "I'm Stretch—what they used to call an India Rubber Man in the carny trade. I was born flexible and trained myself to the rest."

"Masked Max—yeah, he takes his mask off sometimes—is a skilled knife thrower and nothing otherwise out of the ordinary," Madame Zaroza said, nodding toward the man with the vest sewn with many pockets or flaps with flat hiltless knives stuck inside. "Although he can also juggle, and he throws a mean bowling pin, as well—as I believe your older friend discovered."

With great gravity Doc mock bowed in his chair. He never spilled a drop from his teacup.

"Professor Finesse, who dosed your other friend with his

patented sneezing powder and then stunned you all with one of his Patented Double-Wide Flash-Bangs, is a whitecoat, exiled from the lab community he grew up in back East."

The man in the fawn coat bowed. "In many ways," he said, "my life, should my background become known, would be in more perilous straits than those of our mutant brothers and sisters."

He straightened and smiled at their clump of visitors. "No hard feelings, I trust."

Mildred glared and sniffled. Ryan shrugged.

"Ace trick," he said. "Worked. That time."

"I also perform stage magic and conjuring. And of course my patent medicine will display remarkably curative properties to a diversity of ailm—"

"Can the sales pitch, Prof," Madame Zaroza said, lighting a cheroot. " Our twins there are Spider and Monkey. They'd been with us a year before we found out their given names were Moss and Hilary."

"Are you muties?"

"Ricky!" Krysty said sharply.

"Sorry."

Moss—Krysty thought he was Monkey, but wasn't sure—alternately glared defiantly and dropped his gaze. His sister seemed more comfortable with the strangers.

"We don't know," she said in a clear voice. "All we know is we're different. We've been on our own since we could walk and not welcomed anywhere, until we fetched up here."

"I don't suppose I could convince you this is all makeup," Draco said. He had laid aside his tray and rested his finely scaled forearms on the breakfast bar.

"He's a mutie. Sleeping Beauty, I told you about. And Catseye, of course. She's our lookout."

The last was a tiny young woman, who looked to be

little more than a child, who crouched in a corner staring at the intruders half curiously, half fearfully from beneath brown bangs with a pair of golden eyes that were easily twice as large as a norm's. And their pupils were indeed vertical black oval slits, like a cat's.

"What about you?" Mildred asked.

Madame Zaroza shrugged. "I'm just the head freak-wrangler," she said. "I ride herd on this crazy outfit, run the shows, do some sleight of hand, run a few scams on the side, do what I can to keep everybody fed and safe and the wags running. Otherwise my job is Woman of Mystery." She said the last pointedly.

"As to why we could handle you so fast," Masked Max said, "it's the same reason I can throw knives and Stretch can put his heel behind his head when he's standing up— practice."

"It's hard enough on my people being muties and freaks," Madame Zaroza said. "My traveling show just barely gives them a pretext to be accepted among norms, and that's lim-ited in degree and duration. Even here in Amity Springs, and that's an accepting place."

She sighed. "Or was. So we don't dare hurt any of the locals. Nothing permanent, anyway. You see?"

"Yeah, well…" Ryan said. "What I *saw* was that you people were ready enough to put the boot in when you had us down."

Chapter Seven

Madame Zaroza sighed theatrically. Krysty felt some of the sudden tension bleed out of the crowded room.

"We can't afford to let the rubes feel like they can pick on us with impunity, either," said Squatsch. His voice was surprisingly high, given his size. While he was shorter than Ryan, he was thicker and his fur made him look bulkier still. "So we got plenty experience in beating them down and teaching them a good lesson, without leaving more than bruises."

"You see our dilemma," Madame Zaroza said. "Anyway, though Sleeping Beauty warned us, and Catseye watched you the whole way, kept me informed of your kids creeping around my mobile home and everything, you didn't give us time for a better plan."

"That wasn't rightly our intent," J.B. said with a slight smile.

A woman came into the already-overstuffed room from the passage to the rear that no doubt led to the bedroom. She was a small but curvaceous woman with long blond hair framing a pretty face. Also she was entirely naked.

Ricky uttered a squeak like a stepped-on mouse.

"S.B.," Madame Zaroza said, "you're naked."

Sleeping Beauty, who this evidently was, yawned and stretched.

"You make me wear clothes all the time, Z," she said. "It's not comfortable."

"Yes," Madame Zaroza said. "When marks are around. As they are now."

"No," the blonde said sleepily. "These are Dark Lady's friends. Tol' you."

"Employees."

"Whatever. I'm hungry."

Masked Max, sans mask, reached to a kettle of washed but unpeeled and uncooked potatoes on the stove. He picked one up and without looking lofted it over his head toward the naked woman.

Without even opening her blue eyes fully, Sleeping Beauty reached up and caught it one-handed. The movement made her full breasts dance in a way that made Ricky's eyes stand straight out of his head. Her pink nipples played hide-and-seek with her long gold ringlets.

Without a further word she turned and padded back the way she'd come. Krysty looked over to see Ryan frankly admiring the play of her well-rounded naked buttocks as she walked. Good thing I'm not the jealous type, she thought.

As if sensing her attention—or unusually self-conscious—Ryan's lone blue eye flicked toward her. They traded smiles.

Madame Zaroza shook her head. "She's a sweet girl, and an ace draw," she said. "But she got no more sense than a week-old blue-tick hound pup. She sleeps a good twenty, twenty-two hours a day, like lazy old Belphegor there."

She nodded at the orange tabby, who had settled, purring, on Krysty's lap.

"So," Ryan said, "where's what you took from Dark Lady?"

The woman cocked her head at him. "Did she tell you what it is?"

"No," Ryan said.

She laughed. "I have no earthly idea, either," she said.

"And I looked at it. Baron told me not to, of course, and of course I did. Just like I told those fool kids not to look, and of course they did."

Moss dropped his eyes and shuffled his feet. "We did not!" his sister exclaimed in outraged tones.

"Don't lie to me, little missy," Madame Zaroza said. "It's not like I won't know."

"Well—" It was the girl's turn to sidle her big long-lashed eyes and scuff her foot. "I might've peeked. A little."

"She picked the lock," Madame Zaroza said matter-of-factly. "Same as I did, the moment I got alone with it once they brought it back here."

"So, what is it?" J.B. asked. Krysty knew he was not much given to abstract curiosity—not like Ryan was, much as her man tried to pretend he wasn't. But the Armorer was clearly hoping it would be some kind of wizard gadget.

Madame Zaroza snorted a laugh. "No clue," she said. "Couldn't describe it to you if I cared to try. Only thing that really matters to me or you, for that matter, or so I reckon— is that somebody's willing to pay for it." She yawned and rolled her shoulders.

"But your quest for the Great Whatsit is in vain here. I already passed it on to the person who hired the job done."

Ryan's eye narrowed to a slit of blue fire. "Are you trying to put something over on us?"

The room got tense. Before taking his blaster off Madame Zaroza, J.B. had insisted his friends' weapons be returned to them. Though their longblasters were in a trunk outside, where Jak could keep an eye on them, everybody had his or her handblasters and knives.

"Pull back off the trigger, there, sport," Madame Zaroza said. "I know better than that. Mebbe my children here think we could get the better of you a second time tonight. I don't. We got paid for delivery. Even ten times that wouldn't be worth getting even one of us chilled. Least of all me."

"Don't tell them, Z," Draco said. "Mebbe they ain't such bad sorts for locals. Mebbe they ain't coldhearts. But they're still rubes."

"I already agreed to," she said. "And, scammer or not, I'm as good as my word. Especially to a bunch of chillers like this. Anyway, I don't owe my principal anything more than delivery of the goods."

She tipped her head briefly to one side. "Rad-blast it, I doubt the principal would mind if I told. But I'm going to. It was Baron Sand, up to Arroyo de Bromista."

Ryan looked at Krysty. She nodded. As far as she could tell, the woman was telling the truth. She didn't have any kind of power that'd let her tell—not mutie stuff. But both of them trusted her intuition and her judgment.

"All right." Ryan stood. "Reckon you might want to shift away from Amity Springs, and keep clear for a while."

"Reckon we will," Madame Zaroza said with a rueful smile. "We're already ready to roll. It's why we break down the show every night and pack it in. Never can tell when we may need a sudden change of location for our health."

Ryan rounded up his own troop with his eye. "It's time we shook the dust of this place off our heels," he said. "Our employer won't like the taste of what we've got to tell her any better, the staler we let it get."

"Tell D.L. I'm so sorry," Madame Zaroza said in a dull voice.

"D.L.?" Ryan asked.

"Dark Lady. Tell her sometimes there's such a thing as conflicting loyalties. You know? Uh—she will."

"Why not?" he asked.

She relaxed visibly.

"But won't this Baron Sand get hot, you ratting him off like this?" Ryan asked.

"Baron Sand won't care," she said with a secretive and, Krysty thought, somewhat sad smile. "I think I can assure you of that."

"Doesn't sound much like most barons we've encountered, ma'am," J.B. said. "The harder cases they are, the tenderer their sensibilities tend to be about that kind of thing."

She laughed.

"You've just pretty much defined Baron Sand, my boy. Not a scrap like any other baron you've known. Expect surprises."

"Back so soon?"

It was Mikey, the more ingénue, snarkier head of Dark Lady's titanic mutie right-hand man, calling out as Ryan and the companions walked through the swing doors. He—and of necessity his brother—stood behind the bar, where they appeared to have taken over the role of bartender for the evening. Right now he was mainly occupied washing glasses.

"Looks dead in here," Ryan said, looking around the mostly empty barroom.

The scattering of customers went back to their muttered conversations or lonely beers. The three or four gaudies, which had looked up alertly if not necessarily eagerly when the door opened, visibly lost interest when they recognized the new hires.

The giant shrugged.

"Amity Springs is known for nothing if not its solid bourgeois values," balding Bob said. "Everybody works, and goes to bed at night."

"And if they've left here, definitely to sleep," said his brother with a dirty snicker. That earned him a dirtier look from his twin. "Unless a bunch a outlanders are in town, the place drains out early."

"Where's your boss?" Ryan asked.

"Asleep," Bob said.

"She said to report in when we got back," Ryan said. "Go get her."

Mikey sneered. "You're not my boss."

"We could just go up ourselves," Ryan said. "Or stay down here and make enough noise it'd be triple sure to wake her."

"My brother's just being obstreperous," Bob said wearily.

"Isn't that a fancy word for a two-headed freak," Mikey said.

"You know it, too. You're not as big an ignoramus as you like to pretend."

Before his twin could respond the balding head looked toward a pretty woman with café-au-lait skin, a brown ringlet hanging in her face from a pile of hair pinned atop her head, and a frilly dress with a blouse cut low enough to display everything short of nipples. She was playing solitaire on a table to one side of the bar.

"Ruby," Bob called. "Run up and tell D.L. her, uh, independent contractors are here."

She looked at him with sleepy eyes and pouted briefly with bright-red painted lips. Then she stood and trotted up the stairs.

THE GAUDY PROPRIETOR slouched in her chair with her chin sunk to her clavicle and listened as Ryan rendered his report by the light of a low-turned lamp. She made no comment or even showed sign of reaction until he mentioned the person who paid for the theft—and now had possession of the object she'd sent them to bring back.

"Baron Sand," she repeated, with a certain fastidious distaste. "I should've known."

"So what now?" Ryan asked.

For a moment Dark Lady kept her head down. She looked oddly vulnerable like that. The shadows hollowed her cheeks to the point of gauntness and made her eyes look huge. Like a lost little girl, Mildred thought.

When she looked up her expression was resolute.

"I hired you to bring back a certain object," she said crisply. "I still want it. Nothing has changed."

"Where is this Baron Sand to be found, exactly?" Ryan asked.

"On Arroyo de Bromista. It's about two miles northwest of here, nestled against the ridges that ring Santana Basin on that side. It should be no more than a bracing hour's walk for travelers as seasoned as you."

Ryan rubbed his jaw. Mildred heard his coarse blue-black beard bristles crackle against his palm.

"Yeah. You mean for us to go now? Tonight?"

"By no means," she said. "You shall sleep here. I have already had rooms prepared. Nothing is likely to have changed by the morning."

She looked from one of them to the other with her dark, haunted eyes.

"You would not find it easy to sneak into the Baron's Casa de Broma."

Ryan grunted. "Come to that," he said, "we didn't find it so rad-blasted easy to sneak into the bastard freak show, either."

Chapter Eight

They spent the night in several fairly comfortable rooms on the Library Lounge's second floor. The gaudy did not attract much morning custom, it turned out. And not surprisingly the gaudy sluts of both sexes slept late, as apparently did their employer.

The only person in the barroom when Ryan led his friends down the stairs just after dawn was Mikey-Bob, both of whose heads were unusually taciturn. Without speaking a word he served them a breakfast of scrambled eggs, ham, boiled beans and chunks of sourdough bread. Then he retreated into the kitchen.

"I guess they're not a morning person," Mildred said.

They lingered over mugs of what tasted surprisingly to Ryan like real coffee. That was a rare and expensive trade item. He judged the gaudy, at least, had to be doing even better than he'd initially thought.

He drained the final drop from the fired-clay mug and set it back down on the tabletop. Then he stood, picked up his Steyr from where he had it leaned against the wall beside his chair and swung out the double doors.

The morning sun wasn't far up the bright sky, but its light on his face was nearly hot. It was shaping up to be a fine high desert day.

A fair number of people were on the street when the seven companions set out. Some walked briskly on errands or pushed handcarts with goods in them. A pair of laughing children chased a small blue-dotted dog with one blue eye and one brown across the street in front of them, laughing. A medium-size guy in an apron swept off a wooden sidewalk beneath a sign that read V. W. Kennard's Dry Goods and General Confusion. He lifted his head to leer at Krysty and Mildred as they passed without missing a beat with his broom.

"For a fact," Doc observed, "the people of the ville do not seem intimidated by the presence of visibly armed strangers."

"Mebbe that's because a lot of them are packing heat themselves," J.B. observed.

Ryan had already taken that in.

A sturdily built, handsome woman with short red hair appeared in the door of the general store, scrubbing her hands on a rag.

"Wilson," she commanded the sweeper, "stop pestering the pretty ladies and get your butt inside. You've got serious work to be done."

"Sure, Kris. Anything you say."

His apparent wife lingered a moment in the doorway, giving Ryan a far from disinterested look. He nodded politely and walked on. She laughed and vanished inside.

"They go to pains to not show it," Ryan remarked, "but this seems like a pretty flush place."

"Peculiar," Doc said. "Inasmuch as this is not precisely prime farming land. Nor is there any other visible source of wealth, beyond the Library Lounge. The ville is not even situated on a river."

"I think the people probably grow gardens in their back lots," Krysty said. She smiled at the old man. "As for where their water comes from, I suspect the name 'Amity Springs' may hold a clue."

Doc laughed. "Indeed, you are most perceptive, as usual."

"Still doesn't explain where they get the jack to afford pretty decent sidearms," Mildred said.

The ville ended abruptly, though a busy wag yard sprawled just beyond its west end. It gave way to what the locals termed Newcombe Flats, which occupied most of the Santana Basin: land as level as advertised, furred with still-brown grass and dotted with rabbit brush, saltbush and true sagebrush scrub as far as the eye could see. A dirt road led straight on, meeting up in a mile or so, they were told, with the Río Piojo, the largish stream that ran from east to west across the basin and provided most of its water.

They followed that for about half the distance, Jak walking point, then Ryan with Krysty by his side, and then Doc and Mildred, with Ricky and J.B. bringing up the rear deep in conversation. They passed various wags, mostly horse-drawn, headed toward the ville. The occupants watched them warily but without undue alarm as they passed.

"Looks like they don't get too much trouble hereabouts," J.B. called.

"Not before we got here," Ricky said, and then laughed too enthusiastically to show it was a joke.

"Yeah, well, be glad nobody's going to take us for Crazy Dogs," Mildred said. "These people look like they're ready for trouble when it does hit."

"Suggesting that, while they have little to fear from day to day, trouble nonetheless does find its way here occasionally," Doc commented.

"Isn't that why they try to conceal their prosperity?" Krysty asked. "To avoid attracting that kind of attention?"

"Yeah," Ryan said. "But that kind of attention has a way of sniffing out ace targets. It's likely why the Crazy Dogs have started sniffing around."

They came to what looked like nothing but a pair of wheel ruts that ran off the main drag a bit to the north of northwest. A few low lumps of hills and longer yellow bars of ridge were visible off that way. Instructed by Mikey-Bob before they'd left the gaudy, they turned onto the track.

A short while later the track veered right to run up a stream that seemed to be flowing from the ridges to meet the Río Piojo. "This must be Arroyo de Bromista," Krysty said.

"Why would they call it Joker Creek?" Ricky asked.

"Anybody's guess," Ryan said. "Odds are nobody even remembers why now."

They began to pass through cultivated lands. Houses grew among the early sprouting crops, mostly low one- or two-room blocks with adobe walls. People were working erecting frames of sticks for beans and vine crops to climb. Others turned compost heaps with shovels and pitchforks, or tended already-sprouting plants in neat raised beds with sides made of stone or scavvy.

As they worked, they chatted and laughed among themselves. They did stop talking and working to stare at the intruders when they became aware of them, then they resumed work and the conversation began to flow again. More guardedly, Ryan thought, as if the farmers were keeping an eye on the party as it walked upstream.

"They don't seem oppressed," Mildred said. "I hope that's a good sign."

Ryan took her meaning. They were about to approach a baron who had paid to have some valuable object stolen—to demand that the baron give it *back*. Even an average baron—meaning no crazier nor cruel than most—would tend to react unfavorably to such a request.

"That's a pretty imposing house," Mildred said, nodding ahead, where the road ended on a slight slow rise.

"Yeah," Ryan said.

The baron's residence was just a single story that sprawled considerably. Though "sprawl" didn't seem quite right for a building so imposing. It was built in the style of the old Colonial buildings a person might see farther south, down along the Río Grande Valley and points west: blocky, flat-roofed, doubtless with a parapet, and thick sawed-off beam ends protruding from the rafters that held up the roofs.

The walls, he didn't doubt, were also of that style: a good three feet thick and made of adobe. Which would stop a round from his .308 rifle stone cold, and give a direct hit from a howitzer or a wag-chiller missile a run for its money.

"I'm guessing a direct assault is right out?" Mildred asked.

"That's good, Mildred," Ryan said. "One of these days you might actually learn a tactic."

"Thank you so much. Somebody remind me, what does 'Casa de Broma' mean? My pitiful Spanish isn't up to the task."

"'Funhouse,' basically," Ricky answered. He sounded pleased, as he always did when he got to show that he knew something. He didn't do it enough to be a pain. Usually. "Or playhouse."

"*That* could go either way," Mildred said.

"I know which way I'm going to expect it to go," Ryan said, meaning due south.

"Well, the building's defensible," J.B. said, "but I can't say as much for the location. Not that close to the heights."

"Yeah," Ryan said.

The ridges, which looked to be some kind of yellow sandstone cliffs, rose steeply a couple hundred yards beyond the big house and its gaggle of wood and adobe outbuildings. Including, Ryan noted, a pole barn and a large

windowless structure with adobe walls and a lean-to style
roof that looked to be a mix of sheet metal, planks and as-
phalt tiles that lay behind the playhouse. The creek ran
down an arroyo that split the cliffs. A narrow, somewhat
steep dirt road ran alongside it.

"Those cliffs aren't close enough for people to jump on
the roof or throw stuff down on it," Ryan said. "But sharp-
shooters up there could lay waste to anybody trying to defend from the roof. Plus shoot down through it at an angle
that could lay some serious hurt on people inside."

"At least there aren't any guards," Ricky said.

He'd pushed it too far in his eagerness to show off. Jak,
cruising a bit ahead of the rest, yipped a laugh like an
amused coyote. Then Ricky uttered a surprised yip of his
own.

"Ow!"

Ryan looked back. Ricky had ducked his head into the
collar of his shirt. J.B. had his left hand up behind the boy's
head, which he had obviously just thwacked with his two
upraised fingers.

"What?" Ricky asked.

"No guards that you *see,* boy," J.B. said. "Keep mixing
that up with there not *being* any guards, you'll wind up with
dirt hitting you in the eyes before you know what's what."

"Oh."

"Well, Jak," Ryan called, "you had your laugh. Are there
guards?"

"No. Ricky assumed. Made ass."

"Oh, for heaven's sake," Mildred said. "The expression
is, 'when you assume, you make an *ass* out of *u* and *me.*'
But that'd require Bayou Boy to use actual prepositions."

There were plenty of windows, Ryan noted. They looked
to be made out of good glass, clear and not too wavy. That
made them triple expensive, whether they were scavvy or

modern manufacture. Pale curtains hung on the insides—
and as they approached the pink-painted wooden door, he
could see they were hanging at least three feet in.

Fortress, all right.

"So, do we just walk up and knock?" asked Krysty.

Jak walked up almost to the door, then along the front
of the house to the right, where he stopped and peered suspiciously around the corner. From the direction of the pole
barn, now out of sight behind the house, a horse or two
nickered at the approach of strangers.

Jak leaned back and shook his head. Nobody in sight.
He tipped his head slightly to his left. Ryan knew the albino was asking if he should cruise around and check out
the back. He shook his head.

"I notice none of the happy peasants came running to
alert the big boss man that there were armed and presumed
dangerous strangers headed up to his doorstep," Mildred
said. "Maybe the peasants aren't all that happy with the
existing social order, after all."

"Just because we don't see any guards, doesn't mean
there weren't lookouts," Krysty said. "Also, there's a reason
they call these 'flats.' They could have seen us coming a
quarter mile away. We don't know if the peasants didn't see
us and sent word. In fact, I'd be surprised if they didn't send
a kid or two running to tell the baron. Meaning the baron
decided we weren't threatening enough to merit breaking
up the workday to go into defensive mode."

His companions gathered, Ryan stepped up to the door.
Its carved wood projected solidity. He reached up to give
it an authoritative rap.

The door opened.

Inside stood, or slouched, a slender young man. He wore
a loose and dirty off-white smock over dark pants. His
brown feet were bare.

He blinked big black eyes at Ryan. His face was a narrow oval, with a hint of puff to the jawline and below the eyes. A dark beard and mustache framed his pouty lips, just past the stubble point.

"What took you so long?" he asked with languid insolence.

Chapter Nine

"We keep our own schedule," Ryan said. "We're here to see Baron Sand."

"Of course you are." The young man yawned. "Everyone wants to see Baron Sand. And what is that to me?"

Ryan opened his mouth to tell him it was a matter of whether Ryan went past him or through him.

"Oh, knock off the posturing and invite our guests in, Mystery," a contralto voice said from the dimness beyond. A waft of jasmine and incense hit Ryan in the face.

Mystery scowled rebelliously and jutted his jaw. But he stepped back from the doorway with a dancer's grace. With a wordless flourish he invited Ryan inside.

The one-eyed man crossed the threshold and took a quick step right. That was to get away as fast as possible from being silhouetted against the brilliant daylight outside—an ideal target. Also, it was to spoil the targeting solutions for any lower-energy attacks that might be heading his way, like a bat to the brainpan.

He ended up bumping into a table with his upper thigh. It promptly tipped over.

"Fireblast," he said. He bent his knees and grabbed, catching it and righting it before it fell over.

"You are a bit on the clumsy side," the butter-smooth voice said, "but you have a panther's grace and reflexes."

"Not so fast," a man said, stepping forward. He was a bulldog; not tall, but wide in the shoulders, chest and gut.

"No blasters or weapons of any kind allowed. I'm going to have to pat you down."

"Not with any hands you got an interest in keeping," Ryan growled. He badly wanted to talk to the baron, and preferred to defer trouble as long as possible, if not avoid it altogether. But once you let somebody like that get away with something, they wouldn't ever stop until they were grinding your face in the dirt. Ryan reckoned he had to shut this evident sec boss down and fast, whatever that took.

"Oh, put it back in your pants, Trumbo," the contralto said. "They can stack their longblasters inside the door. I have my standards. But I'm not so timid as to get the vapors from the sight of a few holstered weapons."

The man turned back. "It isn't safe, Baron."

"What is that's any fun?" the baron said. "Are you saying you don't trust you and your men to stop them if they try anything?"

Trumbo growled low in his thick throat and backed away. He had a round, jowly face and thick black eyebrows. It was a face made for scowling, and he made the most of it.

"I'm Baron Sand, for the benefit of those crowding around the doorway outside. You might as well come in, dears. We'll make room."

For a fact, though the hacienda's front room was spacious beneath the heavy exposed roof beams known as *vigas,* it looked a bit crowded. As much by the swathes of fabric, mostly black and purple, hung along the walls as by a handful of what Ryan guessed were the baron's favored lackeys—who were young and pretty, like Mystery, and seemed to be both male and female. The hangings made the place look as if it was the lair of a large and somewhat psychedelic spider.

Ryan suspected that was more or less the case.

Doffing his hat politely, J.B. nodded at the far wall. "Nice," he said.

Ryan followed his gaze. On a bare spot on the white-stuccoed adobe hung a large painting of Elvis on black velvet in an ostentatious gold-painted frame. Despite himself, Ryan grinned.

"Now you know who I am," the baron said, puffing on a cheroot. "The polite thing would be for you to introduce yourselves. I know who you are, of course, but I like to hear it just the same. I'm terribly old-fashioned that way."

Ryan frowned. "How do you know our names?"

"Spies in the ville, of course. Certainly you already figured out I had them. After all, I knew precisely where to send my dear friend Madame Z's delightful wall-climbing kiddies, as well as what to look for.

"I won't insult your intelligence, Mr. Ryan Cawdor, without due provocation. I ask you to return the favor. Especially since you are my guests, in my pirate stronghold."

"You're really a pirate?' asked Ricky, coming in last after everybody else had stepped inside and shifted to put their backs to the front wall. He sounded both eager and afraid.

"As far as you know," Sand murmured. Her lids were at half mast over green eyes set in a sort of plump-cheeked moon face. Her hair was short and blond. "Robber Baron might be a more…current term. And you must be the Morales boy."

Ricky lowered his eyes, blushed, nodded. "Yes, ma'am. Sir?"

"Either," Sand said.

The others introduced themselves.

Meanwhile Ryan was sidelong eyeing a huge, silent figure, with brawny arms crossed over a gigantic chest, standing by a side wall next to a door to another room. Between the man's statue-like silent immobility and the random sweeps of gauzy fabric, it had actually taken him a moment to spot him.

Burly though Trumbo was, Baron Sand's sec boss was short. A man like that would tend to employ sec men subordinates who needed pretty constant real-time intimidation to keep from challenging their boss at every other breath. That meant he had a shadow. Or something a bit more substantial: a right-hand man of unquestioned personal loyalty who was big enough to discourage that sort of dominance play from the subordinates.

And Ryan had duly located him. Apache, he guessed, from the long black hair, deep-set obsidian eyes and wide powerful cheekbones. From the man's height, Ryan guessed he had more than a little of one the Plains nations in him, too: Lakota, probably, or mebbe Cheyenne. Apaches tended to be wiry, smart as they were tough and mean, and tough and mean as a diamondback.

The two of them were as out of place as sledgehammers in a vase of lilies. Ryan wondered about the dynamic inside this place. It could be important.

"You know what we came for, Baron," Ryan said. "The only question is, then, how you want to play it."

"You are so delightfully macho, Mr. Cawdor," Sand purred, "without the tedious accompanying overcompensation we call machismo. Are you paying attention, Trumbo? You could learn a thing. Or two. But I try not to be overoptimistic."

The sec boss growled low in his bull throat.

"I stole the Great Whatsit fair and square," Baron Sand said. "I'm not giving it back."

"What is it, anyway?" Ricky blurted. His obsession with gadgets had overpowered his common sense. Again.

"Valuable," the baron said. "For what it's worth, I have no more idea what its function is than you would if I let you have a look at it, which I won't. It's locked away somewhere safe and will so remain."

Mystery came and sat on the arm of her chair. "This is boring, Baron," he whined. "Make them go away."

She reached up absently to caress his softly bearded cheek. "I find them stimulating, Mystery," she said. "If you need more diversion I suggest you go in the back and find some of your…toys."

He pouted but said nothing more. Instead he slouched into an attitude of sullen defiance directed at the companions.

"We could just take what we came for," J.B. said.

"You could try," Trumbo snarled.

Sand laughed. "For once I'm inclined to agree with my sec chief."

She leaned back in her lounger and crossed her legs. She was visibly overweight, but even reclining she gave off an aura of grace—and several kinds of strength.

She was definitely weird. Mebbe not for a baron, Ryan acknowledged. The fact was, the average baron that Ryan encountered tended to show a bit more overt craziness. But Sand was a different *kind* of weird.

"I puzzle you. I know that. I puzzle everyone, including myself. I am a thief. I am a shameless hedonist. I have dark secrets. I am no more scrupulous than I need to be.

"But I am *not,* as some would have it—like a certain party in Amity Springs who swaddles herself in black and acts as if she has a pool cue up her pretty little butt—amoral. I consider myself Lord of the Manor and—surprise!—I am. I prefer to identify myself as baron, because that's my whim. I take my pleasures seriously. I also take the welfare of my people seriously. And I did not get to where I lounge right now, in the lap of luxury remarkable in our time surrounded by beautiful boys and girls—and the occasional but necessary sore thumb—by being either weak or foolish.

"So, my friends. Should you care to abuse my freely offered hospitality by attacking me, or attempting to take some of my people hostage, why, then, feel free to try your hand. You might surprise me. And I'm certain it would prove most diverting. Although one of us would find it a great deal more fun than the other."

"I think what Mr. Dix was trying to do was make sure everyone understood what was at stake here," Krysty said.

Sand laughed. "You are diverting. For a random pack of desert wanderers, I find you quite unusual."

"We mean to take the object back to Dark Lady," Ryan said. "One way or another, we will. What we're here to find out is if there's an easy way."

"No," Sand said.

"Then I guess we're done here," Ryan stated.

"A pity. We could put business aside and get to know each other better as friends. No? Well, I would offer you refreshments, but I suspect you would fear they had been tampered with. And that would wound my sensitive nature. And believe me, none of us wants that."

Ryan started to gesture his companions to the door. He'd be last out. He'd known this place was a potential death trap long before Sand had obliquely pointed it out. And he didn't trust the baron as far as he could throw her—and given that the woman looked to be nearly as tall as he was, as well as hefty, that wouldn't be far at all.

"There is one thing that might…ameliorate our situation," the baron said. "I have a counter-proposal."

"If it doesn't involve our taking the item back to our employer," Ryan said, "you may as well just save your breath and our time. We're done."

"Perhaps not. I will give you something to take back

to Little Miss Self-Righteous Whore-Mistress—not that that's a *bad* thing—back in her Library Lounge. But it is not your precious object, nor anything material. But rather, a reminder of my offer."

"And what offer might that be, Baron?" Doc asked.

She raised a narrow-plucked eyebrow at him.

"At last you speak, Dr. Tanner. Your manner is…unusual in this barbarous age of ours. I look forward to the opportunity to expand our acquaintance on more amicable terms."

He made a courtly bow. "May it be so, Baron," he said. "I do, however, urge you not to underestimate the resolution of my friend and associate Ryan Cawdor."

"Oh, I don't, believe me. But I know there are more twists and turns in the situation than any of you are aware of, or can even guess at. So in our present case the future is even harder to predict than usual."

She fixed Ryan with a gaze as cool as glass and just as soft.

"When you report back, please remind Dark Lady that my offer still stands."

"Like the man said…" Ryan said. "What offer?"

Her laugh was gusty, like a man's laugh. It wasn't the laugh of a person who was afraid of much. Even Ryan Cawdor and his hard-bitten band.

He felt a strong inclination to like this baron. Not that it would slow his hand if the need arose to chill her, of course. Ryan had long ago learned the sad necessity of sometimes putting considerations like that aside.

She wasn't one of his people, so she was expendable. As he knew he and his companions would be to her.

"My offer to buy the ville of Amity Springs, of course," she said.

Chapter Ten

"You want to buy the ville?" J.B. asked.

"Of course," Baron Sand said. "Did I stutter, perchance?"

"You can *afford* to buy the ville?" Mildred asked in amazement.

"I have resources, Ms. Wyeth." She gestured around the bizarrely appointed room. "Obviously, I believe I can meet any reasonable terms."

"Why would you want to buy a whole ville?" Ryan asked. "Looks to me like you got yourself a sweet thing going here."

"Oh, I do. I do. But a girl is always looking to upgrade. As for why I might want to buy a ville, and Amity Springs in particular, I suggest you ask your employer. I'm eager to learn what the poor girl has to say."

The door opened.

Everyone froze. Ryan, having carefully positioned himself out of line with the doorway at the outset, was confident that if it was trouble coming in, the trouble would be more surprised than he was.

After an instant both Ricky and Mildred started going for their handblasters. They had arranged themselves to the left and right of J.B. Without his calm expression flickering, the Armorer reached out to touch them both on the arm.

Both had presence of mind to know what that meant, and stopped.

Scowling, Trumbo dropped his hand to the butt of the

blaster in its holster hung from the web belt half hidden by his overhanging gut. There was no mistaking the piece; it was a Desert Eagle, of what caliber Ryan had no way of knowing.

The Eagle was a well-made weapon, he knew, designed to fire a powerful cartridge and hold up under the punishing recoil—even of a .50-caliber handblaster round. It was also high-maintenance, and mostly a big old unwieldy boat anchor, heavier than most seasoned blasters cared to weigh themselves down with.

So it was either a specialist's tool, or another mark of a man with something to prove. Ryan already had calculated which he thought Sand's sec boss was.

"Leave it, Trumbo," Sand said sweetly. "It's just another one of our guests. Come on in, kid."

Trumbo's face went red to his dark receding hairline. Not for the first time Ryan thought that was perhaps not the smartest way to treat your sec boss, but it was far from his place to say so.

The door opened the rest of the way, admitting a spill of sunlight that was almost dazzling after the pervasive dimness of the room. Jak Lauren stepped inside.

"Not 'kid,'" he said, annoyance in his tone.

"Fair enough. But you are a sufficiently pretty young man to invite comparison, all the same."

Jak gave her a narrow look of his ruby eyes.

Ryan reckoned it was more in suspicion, and likely befuddlement, than taking further offense. For one thing, if you got seriously crosswise of the albino, he tended to let you know about it right away.

He shifted his blood-red gaze to Ryan. "Trouble," he said.

Mildred scowled thunderously. "If this is some kind of tr—"

Sand gave her head a quick shake. "It has nothing to do with my people," she said.

"No," Jak said. "Coldhearts."

"Ah, yes," Baron Sand said, easing away from the window in the back bedroom of the playhouse and lowering the brass telescope from her eye. "Our dear little friends and would-be masters, the Crazy Dogs."

"You recognize them at this range?" J.B. asked.

"It's more a matter of who else would it be?" the baron said. "While they haven't yet managed to secure a toehold in Newcombe Flats, they certainly have been circling like wolves around a campfire. And so provide us the unintended benefit of keeping other vermin at bay."

She turned to Jak, who stood well away from the window. At J.B.'s quiet suggestion, the baron had hunkered down well back from the window, propping her elbows on the bed, in the shadows of the room where even the presumed enemy watching from the ridge top through binoculars couldn't make her out.

"Careless," Jak said. "Reflection."

Krysty glanced at Ryan, who stood with his back to the unadorned wall by the door. He now had his Steyr Scout slung. Ricky and J.B. had likewise recovered their longblasters from the door before trooping back to see for themselves what was happening—though Ricky, with Mildred and Doc, was forced to remain in the hall. Trumbo had started to object, but the baron had quelled him with a look and a shake of her head.

Krysty could tell instantly that Ryan understood as well as she did.

The spy had taken up position lying on the top of a ridge slightly to the east as well as north of the funhouse. Though he was reasonably well hidden by some rabbit brush, he had made an amateur's mistake: not counted on the sun rolling down the western half of the sky as the day wore on to afternoon—and, with the season, still fairly well to the south.

Jak, while prowling outside on the lookout for trouble, had caught a glint of sunlight off the big objective lens of the spy's binocs. Krysty knew without needing to be told he had showed no sign of reacting. Because the stalking of prey was a game he knew triple well from both sides. Instead he'd gone on as if concerned with nothing beyond the stables and the big windowless structure, and then vanished around the side of the house and come straight in to report.

"At least there's only one," Sand said.

"That you know of," Ryan said.

Her brow furrowed and her pale-green eyes narrowed at him. Then she smiled a wide smile.

"Point to you." Her expression changed to thoughtfulness.

"Want me to take care of him, Baron?" Trumbo asked. He stood on the other side of the door from Ryan.

"No. I want you and your men staying here and guarding my house and my people, the way I pay you to."

She sat back on her well-padded, velvet-clad haunches and regarded Ryan.

"I have a proposition for you, sport," she said.

"We've got a job," Ryan replied.

"What?" Trumbo barked. "You mean you won't sell out to the highest bidder?"

"Not good practice," J.B. said. "We don't get a lot of repeat custom in our line of work, but we like to leave our options open."

Sand shook her head. "Nothing to cause you conflict of interest, my dear curly wolf," she said to Ryan. "Indeed, I hardly think even Dark Lady could find fault with it. These

Crazy Dogs are starting to cause problems for everyone in the Basin, but mostly for me and mine. Their unwholesome activities have led to my recently increasing the size of my sec force several-fold, which you might imagine I find distasteful, not to mention expensive. If you can help me with that little issue, I will reward you well for it, regardless of anything else that transpires between us."

"Can you trust her, Ryan?" Mildred asked from the hall.

"No less than I do anyone," he said. "She's just offered to pay us for chilling work. Do you really think she's stupe enough to risk trying to hold back her side on a deal like that?"

Of course plenty had tried to do just that to Ryan Cawdor and his companions. Krysty smiled. In his own cunning way her man had just reminded Sand of the folly of trying to play such a trick on his kind.

Sand laughed and stood. "Last thing I want to do is to give you more motivation to come after me. Though I really want you to reserve judgment until you've heard and seen Dark Lady's response to my offer. Anyway, you sort of have to at this point. And to sweeten the pot, if you take care of this sneaky little bastard, I'll pay you on the spot. And after that—what happens, happens."

"Right," Ryan said with a nod.

Trumbo sidled up to Sand and put a hand on her arm. "I can take care of you," he said in a husky voice. The tone made Krysty's ears want to prick up like a hunting fox's.

Sand shook him off. "Hands off the merchandise," she said. "As far as you're concerned, I'm a lesbian."

She winked at Krysty. "You can feel free to make that assumption, too, Red."

Krysty laughed. She was neither interested nor offended. But she traded quick glances with her mate.

He wasn't the sort to take offense at that, either. But

the slight furrowing of his brow told her that, like her, he thought that was a triple-stupe way to treat your own sec boss.

It wasn't their problem, she knew. Clearly, the baron had at least been telling truth when she'd said there were undercurrents and implications in the situation that the outlanders couldn't even guess at. Not that there weren't always. She still wondered if Sand wasn't showing a chink in her otherwise sound-looking armor.

"How do you intend to play it?" Sand asked. "It'll take you a while to get up those heights and sneak up on him."

"No need," Ryan said.

"We'll need a diversion," J.B. added.

Krysty smiled. "Gentlemen," she said, "leave that to me."

RICKY MORALES CROUCHED by the front window of the playhouse, peering out. The frilly curtains had been pushed to the sides and tied with ribbons. He was trying hard not to be too conscious of the elbow digging into his left ear or the smells—mostly perfumes, but not all—of the warm bodies pressed against him, sides and back.

Most of all, he was desperately trying not to pop wood.

Alone, Krysty walked from the front door of the building. She followed a neatly raked path that led toward where the stream ran by to the west of the huge house. She seemed to be swinging her jeans-clad hips more emphatically than usual.

Ricky swallowed.

He was acutely aware of Mildred watching over his shoulder. She had told him if he watched he'd be struck blind, possibly by her. Krysty had only laughed and said the point was to be seen....

Some of the people working near the big house glanced

up as Krysty approached the stream. She was an outlander, so naturally they were curious. Also she was tall, with that vivid red hair looking almost metallic in the sunlight, and breathtakingly beautiful. Naturally she'd attract eyes.

And, as she'd said, that was the point of her little show.

As she neared the stream, he could tell by the way her elbows started moving around by her sides that she was unbuttoning her blue shirt. As she approached the water, she pulled the hem out of her waistband.

She crouched to test the water with a finger. When she stood again, she shucked off the shirt and let it fall on the grassy bank by her feet. The only thing she wore on the upper half of her body now was a gray sports bra supporting her generous breasts.

More and more faces were starting to rise from shovels and hoes and other tasks. Many expressions were shaded by wide hat brims and hard to read by way of distance. But the way their faces were turned made it obvious where they were looking.

Kneeling at Ricky's side, Jak moistened his lips. This wasn't where he wanted to be right now—he claimed. But it was where Ryan had told him to stay. For once he'd obeyed without much fuss.

Standing first on one leg, then the other, Krysty pulled off her blue cowboy boots. She showed a balance that surprised Ricky, and he'd spent pretty much every day of the past few months in her presence. The well-worn socks joined her shirt.

To Ricky's right, by the window on the other side of the front door, someone tittered. He heard a thwack, followed by a muted, "Owww!"

There had to have been a dozen people crowded into the front room of the hacienda alone, craning and jostling for a view through the narrow windows. Ricky had the impression the other front-facing windows had drawn crowds, as well. Aside from Ricky, Jak, Mildred and Doc, everybody in the front room belonged to the hacienda. Baron Sand herself stood by the other window, leaning forward with keen interest on her oddly handsome moon face, taking advantage of her height—augmented by the ankle boots she wore—to see over her retainers.

She had issued stern warnings against making the least bit of noise no matter what happened. Apparently she had given the violator a thump on the head to punish his breach.

Or hers. In some cases, Ricky wasn't triple sure.

Krysty bent over, skinning the jeans down her legs. Her skin was so white in the bright afternoon that it was startling. As was the tapered perfection of those legs, so leanly muscled. Ricky might have moaned, but he wasn't the only one.

She was now dressed only in the sports bra and some faded lavender panties. She turned profile to the house as she skinned the bra off over her head. Her breasts popped free in their full glory.

"Ooh," said several voices at once. Sand didn't even shush them. Ricky suspected hers might have been among them.

He bit his lip so hard he would've been afraid he'd make it bleed had he any consciousness left over for such things. Pretty much since the moment he'd met Ryan and his bizarre crew Ricky had been in love with Krysty. He was a healthy, if sheltered and naïve, adolescent boy. She was clearly the most beautiful woman in the world.

He had tried to hide it, with what his new companions had made clear, not always gently but usually humorously, were the usual results.

His lust for the statuesque redhead caused him more than

moral qualms. If Krysty was the most beautiful woman in the world, her mate was the deadliest man.

Taking too keen an interest in the mate of a man like Ryan Cawdor was a triple-good way to wind up humiliated. Or dead. Fortunately neither Ryan nor Krysty showed much outward sign of jealousy as such. They were just so absolutely confident both in themselves and their love for each other that nothing could challenge them. Especially not the blushing half-hidden attentions of an awkward teenage kid.

He'd seen glimpses of Krysty nude. There was no way to help it, the way they lived. But he had never seen anything like this from her—this deliberately provocative display.

He had never seen anything like this, period.

Pretty much all the workers in eyeshot had dropped whatever they were doing and stood to stare. Ricky vaguely gathered that, because he had a pretty strong case of tunnel vision himself.

Krysty turned back toward the water. She put her hands up behind her neck and fluffed her glorious hair. Suddenly it seemed to expand into an incredible mane of fire. Ricky knew that was because her hair actually moved of its own accord, though fortunately there was no way the watchers could know that.

She put her hands behind her back and hooked her thumbs in the often-shortened elastic of the waistband. She paused a moment that way, as if contemplating.

"Oh my God," somebody whispered. "She's really gonna do it—"

Then everybody in the room except Jak yelped and screamed as a sound like thunder broke the air.

Chapter Eleven

In the corner of the baron's barn, Ryan threw the bolt of his Steyr Scout Tactical longblaster as recoil made the weapon kick his shoulder hard and rise inevitably upward. Behind him horses neighed and stamped in alarm and annoyance at the sudden noise that had agonized their sensitive ears.

As the carbine settled back into line with his eye again, he felt it scrape against one of the wooden corner panels of Sand's pole barn. He'd poked it out between them when he shouldered the longblaster to take the shot. Then he was looking once more through the longeye-relief Leupold telescopic sight at the Crazy Dogs' spotter's position, up on the ridge behind the hacienda, 150 yards off. He saw nothing.

Nothing was just what he'd expected. Even as the recoil from the powerful 7.62 mm cartridge pushed up the short-barreled longblaster, he had seen pink mist spray from behind the head and the binoculars that obscured most of the spy's face.

The binoculars had been fixed on Krysty as she'd disrobed by the stream.

Just as it had all been planned.

He held on target a moment more, breathing regularly. Aside from a sense of satisfaction at a job well done, he felt nothing in particular. His heart rate wasn't elevated. For him, this was business as usual.

"Get him?" J.B. called from the barn's front door. The horses were stamping and swishing their tails, but settling down. Now they seemed mostly annoyed at the strange intruding monkeys and their noise.

"Yeah," said Ryan. "How's Krysty?"

"Almost naked."

"Enjoy the show?"

"Nothing we all haven't seen before a time or two. Except mebbe Ricky."

Ryan laughed. "I guess you're right."

They'd needed a cunning stratagem. And Krysty had come up with it.

There was a problem shooting a dude who was already scoping your position through binocs. The usual trick, a variation of which they'd taught Sand to spy the guy in the first place—of positioning yourself far enough back from a window your enemy couldn't make you out in the shadows of a room—would not work here. The playhouse walls were so triple thick that the large blond woman had barely been able to lay glass on the spy without the risk of being seen. The angles were just wrong from the side windows as well as the rear ones. Unless he cared to try a snapshot, which he did not, that wouldn't work.

Jak's recon and a quick question to Sand had confirmed that the pole barn would give him a better angle to shoot from. The problem remained that, while he could safely watch the target from concealment with his own binoculars, if he presented the rifle long enough to catch a good sight picture it still gave the presumed Crazy Dog too much of a chance to see him.

Ryan didn't *know* the spy had a scoped rifle of his own. Then again, he didn't know he didn't. Nor even that the dude might have been spotting for a sniper himself, who was waiting out of sight from below until the time came to take a shot. But Ryan had also not lived the kind of life he had as long as he had by failing to take even slim chances into account. At least when he had luxury to work the odds.

And anyway, if the spy had noticed Ryan drawing a bead on him, all he'd had to do was to duck and it was game over. Then Ryan wouldn't get paid. And that would be too bad.

"I'M IMPRESSED," Baron Sand said.

She, Ryan's friends and a gaggle of her followers all waited for Ryan in front of the big house. An unsmiling Trumbo stood to one side with brawny arms crossed over his chest. His big bruiser lieutenant stood to his right, a lean little Mex-looking man with a more successful stubble than Mystery to his left.

"My pleasure," Ryan said as he walked out of the barn with his longblaster tipped back over his shoulder and his binoculars hanging around his neck from the strap. J.B. stepped out after him.

"I was talking about Krysty's striptease," Baron Sand said, "which was definitely *my* pleasure. But you did a pretty decent job, too."

Ryan nodded.

"I was wondering why you took so long to take the shot," Doc said. "I was afraid all of these fine people would see Krysty in her birthday suit!"

Putting his arm around her shoulders, Ryan turned to the others.

"I wanted to make sure the scout's full attention was focused away from *me*. Watching through my binocs, I saw him visibly react. I figure it was the time she was about to shuck out of her skivvies. That told me his attention was riveted enough to take the shot."

"It was a kindness, of sorts," Doc said, "to send the poor devil to the Beyond with a vision of Heaven in his eyes."

Krysty laughed. "Thank you, Doc. You're always so courtly."

"I'm not triple sure that wasn't a final bait and switch on the bastard." The baron mimed twirling a nonexistent mustache. "But from where I stood the vision was pretty heavenly. You folks sure you don't want to stay a spell? We'll be happy to show you why I call this place the playhouse."

"Thanks," Ryan said, "but we need to be getting back to Amity Springs. Time to settle up."

"Hold on just a rad-blasted minute," Trumbo said. "Aren't we getting way out ahead of ourselves here? Talking about paying a bounty when we don't even know there's a chill?"

"There's a chill, all right," Sand said. "Once he started out front I slipped back into the bedroom and watched through my own spy glass. Just in time to see the shot hit. If the dude's not dead, he has a different central nervous system than you or me—one that can run without a brain."

She put her hands on her wide hips and looked askance at him. "Well, different from *me*."

Trumbo growled.

"But I tell you what," the baron said. "Why don't you send a couple of your boys up to check for a body, see if there's something useful they can bring back. Information. Scavvy. Weps. It's time they earned their three hots and a cot, the way they eat."

Trumbo nodded and muttered instructions to the lean dark guy. Shooting a dagger-pointed look at Ryan, he sidled off.

Sand stuck out her hand. Mystery counted the requisite amount of jack used in that area of Deathlands into her palm from a purse he produced from somewhere. She held it out. Ryan stepped up and accepted it, gave it a quick count, then nodded and took a step back.

Sand draped one arm around Mystery's narrow shoulders and the other around the bare shoulder of a plump dark-haired girl with a pretty face and pink complexion.

"Remember," she said, "there's more where that came from. And just a helpful hint—forget about Dark Lady's missing trinket. You and we'd be far prettier friends than enemies."

Ryan said nothing. He just looked at her steadily.

The baron shrugged and laughed. "At least remember to tell Dark Lady my offer still stands to buy her ville. She'll thank me in the long run."

"So we seem to be running into plenty of folks who are uncommonly accepting of muties," Mildred said as they walked across the flats toward Amity Springs.

"You noticed that, did you?" Ryan asked.

He was carrying his Steyr in both hands and on triple alert. He owed the Crazy Dogs two blood debts, and they wouldn't wait forever to try to collect.

Nonetheless there was at least a chance there had been just the one spy, and no one to carry back word of his demise. Or at least who caused it.

Mildred snorted. "Did you think I went blind gazing at Krysty's pretty white backside? A little hard to miss a couple of them. Like the one with the extra eye in his cheek. Or the one with the oozing hole where his nose should be, and those little pink cilia around it."

"I still don't know what the big deal is," Ricky said, shaking his head.

"You been with us long enough to know most people don't take kindly to muties," Ryan said. "Not like the place you come from, where you might see a scabbie walking down the street and not think anything of it. To say nothing of running across a whole ville full of friendly stickies."

"Well, it's not like they bothered me," Mildred said. "Not like some of the baron's playmates. They gave me the creeps, big time."

"Compared to some of the barons I have encountered," Doc said, "Baron Sand's diversions appeared quite…sedate."

"Look!" Ricky exclaimed suddenly. "Over there!"

Everybody turned back. He was bringing up the rear, visibly feeling proud of himself because Ryan didn't tell one of the grown-ups to hang back and keep an eye on him. The fact was, Ryan knew the youth was keen-eyed and so eager to please he'd be endlessly alert.

He was pointing at something south of their track. Ryan saw a rustle of motion in some taller-than-average grass. He had his Steyr halfway to his shoulder before he saw what had caused it.

"Dark night!" J.B. exclaimed. "Haven't you ever seen an armored coyote before, Ricky?"

"Well…no," Ricky said.

Ryan lowered the blaster. The creature was the size and general shape of a middling dog, like any coyote. And not looking any better groomed nor fed than most. The only thing that set it off from the usual run was the flexible gray-scaled carapace like an armadillo's protecting its back and sides.

It had its head up and ears pricked. It watched them from about forty yards off. It kept standing there for a good five, ten seconds after it was perfectly aware they'd seen it.

From the corner of his eye Ryan saw Ricky, over-excited, fumbling as he tried to raise his silenced DeLisle for a shot.

"Hey!" Ryan barked. "Stop that!"

Ricky froze. He turned a wide-eyed look at Ryan.

The coyote turned and vanished as quickly and completely as if it had teleported to another world.

"What's the matter with you?" Ryan said. "You were going to waste a cartridge on that mangy thing? When it and its whole tribe couldn't threaten a one of us, armor or no, unless we were blind drunk and stuck in a hole?"

"Well, but, it was—" He tightened his mouth in a look of chagrined confusion. "It was scary."

"You're the one hails from a place they call Monster Island," J.B. said. "Anyway, remember what Trader always said—no chilling for chilling's sake."

Ricky jutted his underlip and hung his head.

"I didn't know Trader," he said sullenly. "I'm not, like, old."

"Mebbe just as well for you, you didn't," J.B. said. Then he looked at Ryan.

"You hear that? The boy talked back." He sounded proud. He grinned briefly.

"Yeah," Ryan said. "Good for you, kid. Just don't let it get too stiff, or it'll snap all to dreck next time one of us has call to kick your ass."

"Yes, sir," Ricky muttered.

Chuckling, Ryan led them onward. They were bleeding daylight. The sun had fallen well down the sky and their shadows were gaining an ever-greater lead toward their destination.

"So you gave the place a once-over, Jak," Ryan called to their point man.

He waited a minute but the albino didn't answer. Apparently he reckoned Ryan had already worked that out for himself. No need to waste a precious syllable acknowledging it.

"So what did you see?"

"Back door. Goes to kitchen. Separate building out back, same triple-thick walls. Sec men barracks."

"I'm impressed," Mildred said. "It's like he exhausted his whole allotment of vocabulary for the month."

"I don't recall seeing any more sec men but Trumbo, his big goon and that skinny Mex-looking guy," J.B. said to Ryan. "You?"

Ryan shook his head. "Me neither."

"I did," Krysty said. "At least half a dozen of them came out of the barracks to watch my little show. Sorry I didn't mention it earlier."

"No call to earlier," Ryan said.

"Think that's all of them?" Mildred asked.

"How about it, Jak? How many do you reckon could live in that other building?"

"Dozen."

"Where were they?" Krysty wondered. "Unless the extras are straight women or gay men?"

"Mebbe out doing stuff for the baron," J.B. said.

"Why would Baron Sand require so many sec men?" Doc asked. "She appears most cultured."

"We've known more than a few cultured coldhearts and crazies who were barons, Doc," Krysty said.

"True. But her people seemed notably carefree. Nor did they seem to require an overseer with a whip to keep them at their tasks."

"Yeah," Ryan said. "Whatever's happening there, heavy-handed domestic repression isn't a major part of Sand's game. The impression I got is that most of the people there love her. Mebbe die for her."

"Especially that sec man," Mildred said. "He had a bad case, didn't he?"

"Yeah," Ryan said. "Well. Can't say I thought much of the way she rode his ass."

J.B chuckled. "First time I ever knew you to have a soft spot in your heart for a sec boss."

"It just didn't strike me as a smart way to treat somebody in charge of keeping you safe."

"I have to admit," Ryan continued, "that Sand doesn't strike me as being very stable. Although she's certainly crazy in a different way from your average baron, which leads us back to the question of why she'd pay and feed so many blaster men, since she doesn't need them to keep her subjects from nailing her to the barn and peeling the hide off her carcass."

"Well, there are the Crazy Dogs," Ricky said.

"Then why'd she hire us to take care of them?" J.B. asked.

"Mebbe she wants to preserve her sec men," Ryan said, "which still leaves the question of what for. Then again, she is there at the border of the Basin, and borders are triple-dicey places. Crazy Dogs probably aren't the first problem she's had of the sort. Though mebbe the most persistent."

"She might be trying to get under Trumbo's skin," Krysty said.

"It's working," Mildred stated.

"So, Jak," Ryan called, "see an easy way in?"

Jak yipped a laugh, not unlike a coyote himself. "No way!"

"That's what I reckoned."

"We did get to see the back room," Mildred said.

"Eager to try climbing through one of those windows?"

"Not me."

"I'm not even considering frontal assault," Ryan said, "since those are for when you let yourself get triple-screwed out of any other option, or got loads more warm bodies and blasters than tactical sense. Not to mention it'd take an armored wag's main gun to poke through those walls, mud or not."

"So are you still willing to go for it?" Mildred asked. "Getting Dark Lady's thingamajig, I mean?"

"You size her up for the sort who'll pay us for a job that produces no results?"

"Hell no!"

"Then absolutely."

"How?"

"I'm working on it," he said.

THE SUN WAS near to setting and the street in front of the gaudy house was unusually vacant. The gaudy was all lit up per usual, though.

Nobody was outside. When Ryan stepped up to the door, he couldn't hear the usual music and merriment.

Instead he heard voices raised in anger.

Chapter Twelve

"Allow me to remind you," Dark Lady was saying in a whip-taut voice when Ryan pushed open the door, "you are guests in this establishment."

There was a good crowd in the gaudy for late afternoon. Most of the tables were occupied, and at least half a dozen of Dark Lady's "entertainers" were standing or sitting in conversations with guests that might turn into business transactions. The gaudy's star performer, the lovely blond Lucy, had drawn a crowd all her own.

Ryan took that all in in a flash as he entered, followed by his friends, except for Ricky, who had to have his sleeve grabbed by Jak and be towed out of the doorway to stand in front of an unoccupied table.

Some of the customers glanced at the newcomers when they came in and their eyes got wide. Some visibly began to think even harder about bolting out those self-same doors.

The "guests" Dark Lady was addressing in a not-double-friendly voice never bothered to glance around.

"We're not guests," said a tall guy with a sharp knife-scarred face and a shock of sandy-blond hair. He was tall and wore some kind of yellow pelt draped on the shoulders of his black leather jacket. He had a sawed-off lever-action longblaster holstered to his right thigh. "We go where the fuck we please."

"Please do not ever address me that way again," Dark

Lady said. Her tone of voice suggested the "please" was mere formality. She wasn't making a *suggestion*.

The tall, rangy blond man in the fur had a pair of back-ups, shorter but no less mean-looking. One was a woman with stubble starting out on a skull shaved up to a Mohawk so ludicrously tall it might as well have been shellacked that electric shade of blue to make it stand up. She wore black leather with studs and spikes, and her face might not have been unattractive without the sneer and the black paint on her lips. She had a couple big knives sheathed at her chain belt.

The other person was a man even shorter, even aside from the hair, than she was, and heftier built than his partners. He had greased-back hair that was probably a shade of brown, and a seamed, jowly, stubble-cheeked face. His back was turned to the door; if he carried a visible weapon Ryan didn't see it. Nonetheless he took one's presence for granted.

"Crazy Dogs?" J.B. murmured from Ryan's left elbow.

"Reckon so."

"Listen up," the blond man said. "Listen close. You're the closest thing to a baron this shithouse ville has, so you have to answer. And if you care about the people, or anything but your pussy-selling profits and your own pretty little pale ass, you'll think twice before you *do* answer. Unless mebbe it's time to set up a proper baron here, and cut through the bullshit?"

Dark Lady's face was whiter and tighter than usual. She obviously deemed that a rhetorical question, and not requiring an answer. She showed no sign of backing down, even to a much larger, deliberately brutal man and his two cold-heart pals. Indeed she looked even less intimidated than she had when they had first seen her, having a rude patron pitched into the street by her two-headed giant.

That patron was standing behind the bar right now, rubbing it with a rag and not looking directly at the intruders.

"You hired yourself a bunch of no-account mercies from the outlands to run some errands for you," the blond man said, leaning closer. "Well, they shit the bed. They're all out of Newcombe Flats' privileges. Nukefire, they're out of life privileges. So you want to give them up nice and sweet."

As he reached out to take her chin, she reached a black-lace-gauntleted hand up and steered his away.

"So that's the way you like it? Playing rough?" He laughed. "Listen, sweet cheeks, it doesn't have to be that way. Diego can be generous too. But if you cross him, you are seriously screwed."

Diego. That was the name of the Crazy Dogs' boss, all right. Ryan flicked a gesture to his companions to get ready to rock and roll. He eased open his coat to free up the SIG-Sauer and his panga. The companions had left their packs cached outside the ville, but he, J.B. and Ricky still carried their longblasters slung.

Mikey, the better-looking head, lifted his down-turned face just enough to catch Ryan's eye. He gave his head a single shake. His twin kept staring down and polishing the bar as if he meant to wear a hole in it.

Interesting, Ryan thought. That was the impulsive member of the team. If *he* was telling Ryan to hold off…

With a slight raise of the two front fingers of his left hand, Ryan passed the signal for his companions to stay out of it. *For now,* he didn't need to tell them.

"Tell Diego," Dark Lady said in a surprisingly business-like tone, "that it is you and he who have worn out their privileges in Newcombe Flats. And especially in this ville. Now leave and never return. Unless you mean to stay forever."

This time Pelt Boy put back his head and laughed uproariously. "Then it's gonna be forever," he said, clearly missing the import of her words.

"And now—"

He moved with sidewinder speed, grabbing the wrist of the right hand she'd used to deflect his, stepping past her to put his back to the bar and spinning her into an armlock.

"I'm gonna knock some sense into you right here in your own bar," he said, and suddenly he was holding a huge Bowie blade-first against her slender white throat and grinding his crotch into her rump. "Then mebbe I'll have a taste of your own sweet self before I turn you over for free to anybody who wants to try you out. I hear you're too high and mighty to peddle your own sweet thing. And after that, if you see reason, mebbe I'll settle for cutting your pretty face some, and not your throat."

Ryan saw Dark Lady's left hand push behind her back as if to join its captive mate.

Yellow-white light flashed to either side of her wide skirts at hip height. A muffled *bang* sounded.

The blond Crazy Dog's blue eyes stood out of his head. The knife fell from his fingers. He bent over as Dark Lady tore herself out of his grasp.

Even through a dense coating of various filth and stains, Ryan could see the crotch of his jeans was spreading with a stain as if he were pissing himself. Except Ryan knew that wasn't piss, and the grimy fabric was smoldering. He smelled burned propellant.

"I told you not to call me that," Dark Lady said, raising the hidie blaster in her left hand. Smoke trailed from its upper barrel from the shot that had smashed his cock and balls.

His eyes went wide as he stared down the lower barrel of the 2-shot derringer. She let him get a good look into it, then she fired.

The bullet exploded his right eye in a spray of blood and nastiness. Whatever she had chambered didn't exit the back of his head. Instead it evidently ricocheted inside his skull and turned his brain to jelly to match his balls.

The back of his head slammed against the bar top as he toppled backward, stone chilled.

Dark Lady's action had astonished his two backups at least as completely as it had him. If not as painfully. Or fatally. Yet.

The greasy-haired guy's right hand came out of his jacket holding a pitted 1911 blaster. As he turned it toward Dark Lady something flickered from Ryan's left, where he had no peripheral vision.

One of Jak's throwing knives, which he had no doubt palmed the instant he'd seen the Crazy Dogs, punched through the back of the coldheart's blaster hand. The man shrieked like a wounded horse.

Mikey-Bob reached a plate-size hand across the bar and wrapped it over the top of the Crazy Dog's head. Then he slammed it against the edge of the two-inch-thick hard-wood slab he'd spent the past few minutes polishing so assiduously.

The bar was better built than a coldheart's skull. Ryan learned that beyond any doubt when he saw the side of the Crazy Dog's head flatten and heard a loud crunch with a back of wet squishing that gave even his vanadium-steel stomach a twinge. The man slumped as lifeless as the boss he'd failed to protect.

The Mohawk girl was more decisive. She had her big blades out and whirling as she closed on Dark Lady, hissing like an angry wildcat and just as fast. Ryan had his own handblaster out but couldn't shoot for fear of hitting the gaudy owner.

But she didn't stand there meek and mild to be sliced to

ribbons. Rather she sprang to meet the taller woman. She turned counterclockwise as she did, slapping the Crazy Dog's right wrist with her left hand, pushing the forearm with her right. That created an opening for her to turn her hip hard into the woman's flat belly, inside the arc of the left-hand blade.

Cupping right fist over left, Dark Lady drove her left elbow into the coldheart's solar plexus. The Crazy Dog doubled over with all her air blasting out her narrow nose and wide-open mouth.

Dark Lady stood her up again with a right-hand palm-heel strike that flattened the nose all over her hard-bitten face with a crunch of smashing bone and cartilage. That wasn't a kill-shot, no matter how many stupes still thought it was.

But breaking her nose did disorient the coldheart. Dark Lady grabbed her left arm and spun out again, straightening it. Holding the wrist with her left hand, she gave a right-forearm shiver to the coldheart's locked-out elbow, putting a lot of hip into. The joint snapped with a noise like a handblaster shot.

The Crazy Dog screamed just as loud. Dropping the knife from her right hand she went to her knees, clutching her destroyed elbow and wailing.

Dark Lady looked past her at Ryan. Her black eyes were wide and wild, her little jaw set. But it was not *fearful* wild. It was the sort of look Ryan knew well from the inside.

She simply nodded once. Then she looked down at the whimpering coldheart.

"Now it's your turn to listen," she said.

She grabbed a fistful of the woman's hair and yanked her head up and around to look at her. Tears sheened her thin cheeks. A glistening false beard of blood and snot covered her mouth and chin.

"Tell Diego to leave this Basin and this ville alone. I am not the baron of Amity Springs, but this ville and its people are under my protection. Anyone who threatens them will die. Nod if you understand."

The Mohawked woman shook her head and gobbled something incomprehensible.

"If you don't understand my message to take back to your leader," Dark Lady said, "I have no reason to leave you alive. If you want to live, tell me you understand clearly and now."

Her voice was now eerily calm, almost conversational. Ryan didn't know if the fact was getting through to the coldheart she'd beaten so efficiently and comprehensively, but *he* reckoned it was more chilling than even a cold, hard voice would have been.

"Yuh—yuh—yes!" the coldheart sobbed. "Please don't chill me."

Dark Lady flung her forward onto the floor. She didn't look *that* strong. But then again, the coldheart wasn't exactly resisting at this point.

"Then go," she told the sobbing puddle of wretchedness. "Give Diego my message. And tell him not to bother coming to collect these two. They will feed the armored coyotes."

The Crazy Dog picked herself up off the floor. She left behind a blot of blood-soaked sawdust. Ryan was surprised she could navigate on her own, but she lurched toward the door on rubbery legs.

J.B. held it open for her. She vanished into the indigo dusk.

"Always a gentleman, John," Mildred said.

Ryan looked around at his crew as J.B. let the door fall shut. Somewhat to his surprise, Krysty and Mildred were grinning all over their faces.

The men, even Jak, still had big eyes. No doubt they were still feeling that nut-shot. Ryan knew he was.

Not that it could've happened to a nicer guy.

Dark Lady turned toward the bar—and reeled. Mikey-Bob started to reach a huge hand to steady her. But she caught herself with one hand and forced herself to stand upright.

She cleared her somewhat disordered black bangs from her face with a defiant headshake. Her cheeks had actually started to go pink as blood returned to her face. Ryan hadn't noticed it at the time, there being other matters more urgently claiming his attention, but he knew that blood had drained away with the adrenaline dump preceding her move on the coldheart with the blond hair and the informal castration.

"I need a drink, Mikey-Bob," she said. "Pour me a double. Then a round for all on the house."

"Yes, ma'am!"

She turned and flung an arm out to point at Ryan and the companions.

"You," she said, "come with me. Upstairs. Now."

"Yes, ma'am," Ryan said.

Chapter Thirteen

In her office Dark Lady practically collapsed in her chair. She slumped so completely that Ricky feared she would break down crying, if not actually deflate.

"You handle yourself double well, ma'am," J.B. said mildly.

"I have spent the past five years building up this establishment and this ville," she said. "I could not have done so, or even survived, without learning how to take care of myself."

"Well, great job," Mildred said fervently. She had forgotten her distaste for the woman's profession, at least for the moment. Instead she gave her a toothy grin and a thumb's-up.

"Thank you."

For a moment she sat with her pointed chin sunk to her clavicle. Then she lifted her head and looked at each of them in turn.

"I take it you have yet to recover my item."

"You take correctly," Ryan said. As before, he had seated himself across from her. Krysty stood behind him with hands on his shoulders. The rest, including Jak this time, were stuffed into the office among the bookshelves and the knickknacks as best they could get.

She sighed. "Nothing is ever simple," she said, steepling her fingers in front of her chest.

"Tell me what happened."

Ryan did, in his usual brisk, efficient, matter-of-fact way. As he was getting to the point where Sand asked him to take a message to Dark Lady, Ricky jumped at a sound from the door like somebody beating on it with a ham.

"Come in," Dark Lady called. The door opened to reveal her enormous chief assistant and bodyguard. He bent down and poked both heads into the room.

"Got everything straightened up downstairs," Bob said. "And talked some of the entertainers down off the ledge. Customers took the whole thing pretty calm, though. Lani's holding down the bar."

"Excellent," Dark Lady said. "Thank you."

Mikey-Bob withdrew his heads. He stayed standing in the open door. After a moment Dark Lady gave him a raised eyebrow.

Mikey-Bob crossed his arms over his wag-wide chest.

Dark Lady sighed and looked at Ryan. "Continue."

He did.

Dark Lady didn't seem put out by Sand's bland refusal to surrender the item, nor Ryan's—temporary—acceptance of same. Her brows furrowed slightly at the mention of the baron's offer to buy the ville. But then came the part about Jak spotting the Crazy Dogs' spy.

Dark Lady's eyes narrowed when Ryan described agreeing to take out the observer for Sand. Ricky couldn't see Mikey-Bob's face—faces—but heard a rumble like distant thunder that he guessed came from his chest. Ricky did think Dark Lady perked up a bit when Ryan let Krysty describe her own part in causing a diversion.

"So then," Ryan said, "Sand offered to pay us if we'd help take care of the Crazy Dog situation for her."

"Of course you told her no," Dark Lady said.

"Told her yes."

"What?" both Mikey and Bob blurted at once. "What

the nuke? You're seriously talking about going over to the enemy? D.L., I told you not to do this! They sold you out!"

Ricky couldn't make out which head was saying what. It got worse when they basically started talking over each other and trying to outshout one another. He couldn't make anything out of what they said after that, only their shared terrifying behemoth anger.

But he found himself caught up watching the reactions play out on Dark Lady's thin, pretty, intense face. First her eyes got really big and round. Then she pulled her head down between her bare shoulders. Then her mouth started working and her forehead rumpled. He thought she might be trying to battle back tears.

Mikey-Bob put his hands on the sides of the doorframe and started to thrust himself into the room. Dark Lady held up a palm. He stopped.

There followed a moment of silence.

Dark Lady took a number of deep, almost gasping breaths. She kept holding her hand up. Eventually, with a final subterranean rumble, Mikey-Bob backed out of the door.

"All right," she said finally. "I presume you have an explanation for this."

"The way I saw it," Ryan said, "this doesn't pertain to the work we're doing for you."

"You don't think working for the person who stole from me, while at the same time working to get back from her what she stole from me, constitutes a conflict of interest?"

"No."

She frowned, looking as if she were getting angry.

"Please," Krysty said, "hear him out. It sounds crazy, but I think he's right."

"Stop helping," Ryan said darkly. "But think about it. The deal we cut with Sand—I cut with Sand—has nothing to do with this...*thing* of yours. It has to do with the Crazy Dogs."

She was nodding now, although it was as if she were forcing herself to do so against a hand trying to hold back her forehead.

"I begin to see," she said. Then she turned her head slightly away and eyed him sideways. "I also begin to see why the Crazy Dogs were so insistent I turn you over to them this afternoon. At first I wasn't even sure they were *talking* about you. I had no idea what they were on about, frankly."

"Today was not our first encounter with that particular band of blackguards," Doc said.

"We had a bit of a dust-up with them when we first hit the Basin," Ryan said. "The Dogs had a wag with three Mormons down from the Deadfalls in it, trying to persuade them they were a customs checkpoint or some such crap. We started to walk by. The coldhearts thought they had a right to stop us. We thought differently."

He shrugged. "And we're here. So you can reckon how that turned out."

"They're getting bold," she said, shaking her head. "The mountain folk are really not to be trifled with."

"These acted pretty meek and mild, ma'am," J.B. pointed out.

"They were out of their element. They don't actually like to leave their high valleys and their flocks. They're decent folk, although their ways aren't mine."

She smiled slightly. "And I'm *well* aware that my ways aren't theirs. But they know better than to try to impose their values on others hereabouts. Nobody's much interested in their proselytizing here in Newcombe Flats. For the most part they're content to live their lives in their mountain meadows and let the rest of the world continue its well-advanced journey to Hell in its own way."

"They got hit hard by the plagues after the Big Nuke and skydark," said Bob. Mikey was still looking sullen and rebellious. His calmer twin seemed to be trying to smooth things over. "Especially among their women. So polyandry became the rule."

"Hmm," both Krysty and Mildred said. They looked at each other, then burst out laughing.

Ryan made a growling sound deep in his throat.

"Don't get too excited," Mikey grumbled, as if reluctantly drawn to play along. "If it sounds like fun, they're against it."

"Word has it they're prone to sectarianism and doctrinal disputes that sometimes turn violent," Dark Lady said. "But should anyone try to come into their land and impose on them, they pull together instantly and go after them like stickies on jolt."

"So these hill saints are rather like the ancient Swiss," Mildred commented.

"Yes," Dark Lady said. "They may even deliberately model themselves on the ancient Cantons to some degree."

"I'm amazed you know that! It's ancient history now. And this is by no means a time that venerates history— when it has so much in the past to fear."

She laughed and waved a hand around at the book-crowded shelves. "These aren't merely for decoration, Ms. Wyeth. The Library Lounge is both things. We provide a wide spectrum of services here."

"So," Ryan said. "Like I say, a separate gig. At worst I figured a little goodwill wouldn't hurt with negotiations. And you didn't seem on any better terms with the Crazy Dogs than Sand, even before this evening's fandango."

"No negotiations," Dark Lady said crisply. "I want my property returned. And that's that."

"We're working on that," Ryan said. "Speaking of negotiations, there is one more thing. I can't rightly claim to understand it, but Sand asked us a couple times to remind you that her offer to buy the ville still stands."

"Absolutely not," Dark Lady said with a firm shake of her head that made the ends of her hair swish around her narrow chin. "I've told her that will never happen."

"Wait," Mildred said. "You did say no, right. But you also acted as if that whole thing makes sense."

"Oh, she's offered to buy Amity Springs before."

"But why would anyone buy a *ville?*" Mildred asked.

Dark Lady smiled. "Our trash."

She stood, then laughed at their expressions.

"Come with me," she said. "I've got something to show you."

Chapter Fourteen

At first Ryan's eye refused to make sense of what it was seeing by the light of several bull's-eye lanterns.

"Okay," Mildred said. "It's a wall of crap."

Dark Lady smiled. "It is our treasure," she said. "The lifeblood of our ville."

"Beyond the trash?" Mildred asked.

DARK LADY HAD led her guests down the stairs and into a back room, trailed by Mikey-Bob like a rolling mountain on a leash. There she produced several lanterns with reflectors and lenses to focus the light, which she lit with her huge assistant's help. Keeping one and handing another to Mikey-Bob, she'd passed the others to Ryan and J.B.

From there she'd led them into a cool cellar, smelling of slightly humid earth and walled in what Ryan took for stabilized adobe brick. There were big wooden casks down there, which Doc eyed hopefully and Ryan and J.B. appreciatively. But neither the heady house brew nor the various wines in cool storage were the objects of the expedition.

Instead Dark Lady led them to a large double-valved trapdoor by a rear wall. Deftly sweeping back her skirts with her hands, she knelt and opened a heavy padlock with keys from the ring she carried at her narrow waist.

"From the looks of it that thing's more to keep something down there from getting up here, than people up here from getting down there."

"Both," the dark-haired woman said, standing and gesturing imperiously for Mikey-Bob to open the doors. He complied without so much as a rebellious glance from Mikey.

Mildred was starting to look concerned. She didn't look relieved when the cool air that gushed up from below smelled of staleness, mildew and general decomposition. Not rotting flesh, anyway—as even Ryan was relieved to note. But there may have been a hint or two that something had died down there.

"What exactly are you afraid might get out?" she asked, her eyes widening as she stared at the yawning pit of blackness.

"Who knows?" Mikey asked.

"We don't want to take anything for granted," Dark Lady said seriously. "We know how the world is."

"Straight up," Ryan said, "is there anything likely to be down there you *know* to be afraid of?"

"Afraid?" Mikey hooted.

"No," Dark Lady said. "I assume that you people have the sense to keep your wits about you at all times in unfamiliar surroundings."

"If only we had the wits not to keep putting ourselves in those kinds of surroundings," Mildred said.

Without ceremony Dark Lady led the way down the ladder, holding the lantern high in her right hand.

Ryan wasn't sure she wasn't engaging in a bit of bravado, here, but he was also rad-scoured if he was going to let this skinny pale woman show him up. He went down right after her.

The weird musty decay smell was much stronger here.

There was cool hard-packed dirt beneath his boots. The walls were reinforced here and there with fieldstone and more adobe blocks, and the roof was braced by beams that had to have been brought down from the mountain pine and spruce forests.

They were at the center of a circular chamber about thirty feet across, with tunnels about ten feet around radiating in four directions.

"This took some digging," J.B. said thoughtfully.

"Not as much as you might think," Bob said. "Soil's clay and pretty stable. Moisture from the underground stream keeps it from getting too hard or crumbly. This far below the surface it's not double hard to work."

"Underground stream?" Krysty asked.

"What do you think feeds the springs?" Mikey countered. "Or did you think the ville was named by the tourist bureau?"

"It's not close," Krysty said.

"Not here," Dark Lady replied. "It's not what I've brought you down here for. Follow me."

SHE LED THEM fifty feet down a tunnel before it ended in a wall of trash. Unmistakable trash: soda cans, brittle plastic drink cups, random metal nuts and chunks stuck tight together in a matrix of compressed, damp, decomposing paper.

The gaudy owner turned to the skeptical Mildred. "I told you. This is the secret to the wealth of Amity Springs. This is why Baron Sand wants to buy it."

"I heard it," Mildred said. "I see. But I don't exactly believe it. Or *understand* it, anyway."

"Are you calling Dark Lady a liar?" Mikey asked, his broad-jawed face darkening.

Ryan pushed in between the behemoth and Mildred. "Easy now, big fella. We're new here, remember? And kind of in the dark. So mebbe you could help us understand."

Bob laughed. "For a guy who looks like a stone cold-heart, you do have a silver tongue in your head."

"So I'm told," Ryan said.

He turned to Dark Lady. "What about it?"

"Your silver tongue? I admit, now I'm intrigued."

"What?"

"This is what we call the 'trash face,'" she said as if she'd never made the previous comment at all. "Our most recent excavation. We're still digging into this deposit, old-days landfill. We haven't yet found anything too valuable. But we're hopeful."

Holding her lantern in front of her, she walked back the way she'd come. Ryan and company stood aside to let her pass. Then, after exchanging bemused glances, they followed her once again.

This time she turned right. Within twenty yards the tunnel suddenly widened—farther than the lantern shine initially carried.

Dark Lady halted them on what turned out to be a ten-foot ledge running halfway around a pit thirty or forty feet across. Its surface was about five feet below the ledge. It was lumpy and blocky.

Running his beam over it, Ryan saw that it was more trash. But a different kind: a lot of it looked like pieces of furniture and equipment—metal boxes, cabinets, an up-ended set of metal shelves, a console with half the panels and long lightless blinky lights bashed in, all partially buried in dirt and crud.

"This is one of our most productive digs," Dark Lady said brightly. "We've got a lot of prime scavvy out of here."

"Who digs all this?" Mildred asked, running her fingers in awe along the raw clay walls of the chamber.

"Gaudy employees," Bob said. "Townsfolk. Often as not, me."

"Sometimes even herself," Mikey said. "Depends on what else is going on at any given moment."

"Even the…entertainers?" Mildred asked.

"Of course," Dark Lady said. "If they wish to earn extra pay. Also they get rewarded for coming up with good scavvy."

"What do you find down here?" Ricky asked. His eyes were bright with the prospect of unearthing predark gadgets.

"All manner of refuse, as you can tell," Dark Lady said. "But what we're really looking for is predark technology."

He turned huge dark eyes to her. "You mean…?"

She nodded. "Old-days gadgets."

"Why would there be any of that down here, more than the occasional odd or end?" J.B. asked, tipping his hat back on his head. "I mean, why here in particular?"

"Because this was the trash dump for a top-secret military research facility," Dark Lady said.

"All this paper and plastic junk came from some kind of whitecoat lab?" Ryan asked.

"It was quite sizable," Dark Lady admitted. "A substantial residential community grew up here in connection with it, according to what we've found. It's not just here beneath the Library Lounge, of course. Although these particular deposits are why I chose to build my establishment on this site."

"People are always digging up stuff, all over the ville, out on the outskirts," Bob said. "Tools, measuring equipment, components—you name it."

"And the piece you have hired us to recover from Baron Sand?" Doc asked.

"That would be classified as 'you name it,'" Dark Lady answered with a cool smile.

"I don't understand," Krysty said. "Amity Springs

certainly doesn't look as if it was built out of any predark complex I've ever seen."

"Oh, it wasn't," Dark Lady said. "There was very little of it left after the war."

"Why?" Ryan asked.

"Got nuked flat," Bob said.

Mikey sniggered. "Why do you think they call this Basin 'Nukem Flats'?"

Ryan and the others stared at him for a moment, until even the saturnine Bob head grinned a snaggle-toothed grin.

"You mean," Doc said with exaggerated delicacy, "it is not spelled N-e-w-c-o-m-b-e?"

"That's what I reckoned, too," Ryan said.

"Nope," Mikey said. "N-u-k-e-m. As in, well…"

"The first survivors to return to Santana Basin didn't exactly have sophisticated senses of humor," Bob said.

Krysty was looking at her man in wide-eyed horror.

"Ryan," she said. "The *radiation!*"

By reflex he glanced at the minute radiation counter attached to the lapel of his coat. "I checked it when we came into the Basin, and off and on since," he said. "Same as usual. High background, but no more than you find a hundred other places. Not a real hotspot by any stretch."

"Of course not," Dark Lady said. "Otherwise why would we choose to live here in the midst of it, however much wealth we could extract?"

"I've known plenty of people who'd do a lot more stupe things than that, if the payoff was big enough," Ryan said. "But I take your point."

"In my collection I have journals kept by some of the first to resettle the Basin after skydark," Dark Lady said. "They estimate a 150-kiloton warhead was air-detonated approximately 1800 feet above the middle of the actual facility, which lay about a quarter mile south of here—well outside the current limits of the ville. There is a hotspot there, at the hypocenter, although it's small. Most of the unconsumed fissionables and the reaction by-products were carried away by the wind. Where—" she shrugged her bare white shoulders "—they became someone else's problem."

"So you built your ville deliberately..." Mildred began.

"On top of the dump. Yes."

"What about your fresh water supply?" Krysty asked. "Weren't the people who built the place concerned about contamination?"

"Like they cared about that stuff in the old days," Mikey said. For once his twin nodded grumpy agreement.

"Actually, they seem to have been careful to isolate their landfill pits from the aquifer," Dark Lady said. "They needed fresh water, too. Lots of it."

"So who buys the high-tech scavvy you recover?" J.B. asked. Ryan thought the shine in his eye didn't look double different from the one in Ricky's.

"The highest bidder," Dark Lady said. "Shall we adjourn back to my office?"

Chapter Fifteen

"Cognac, anyone?" Dark Lady asked. She held up a cut-crystal decanter half full of amber liquid taken from a cabinet behind her. "Well, not technically cognac, I suppose. But it amounts to the same, even if it's not imported from what used to be France."

"Still must be some primo scavvy," Mildred said as Dark Lady began to pour the fluid into a number of shot glasses on a maroon pottery tray painted with Day of the Dead figures an uncharacteristically silent Mikey-Bob had set on the desk in front of his mistress.

Dark Lady looked at her from under abruptly upraised brows.

"It isn't scavvy at all," she said with some asperity as she continued to pour a couple of fingers into each glass. "It's made by monks downstream in the valley to the west of the Basin, in fact. They have a fortified monastery and their own vineyards, and they do quite well, thank you very much."

"I'm sorry. I should have considered that possibility."

Dark Lady finished pouring and set the near-empty decanter on her desk.

"You will forgive me if I overreact," she said, still pretty briskly, as she straightened with a tumbler in hand. "You touched a sore spot. I am not a fabricator myself. That's not my training nor inclination. But I appreciate the making of things, and its necessity."

She raised the glass to her black-painted lips. For a moment she looked as if she was going to throw back the brandy. Then she took in a deep breath through her nose and visibly reasserted control.

She took a tiny sip. "It frustrates and infuriates me how many people in our current age seem willing to accept their fate, to live in a world constantly devolving, constantly descending into some…some pit of apathy and misery. Yes, a terrible thing happened to the world. Terrible things happen today. And terrible things have always happened."

She took a bigger drink.

"Fatalism may have its uses," she said. "But dwelling in it makes you a willing victim. Makes you an accomplice in your own slow destruction. That is what I am sworn to counteract. That's what I do."

"What *do* you do, Dark Lady?" Krysty asked.

She shot a warning green glance at Mildred, who just might've made an incendiary comment about Dark Lady's trade.

"Aside from the obvious, I mean." Krysty took her own glass in one hand as the other gestured around at the bookshelves in the neat office, and by extension, the entire gaudy.

Dark Lady was sitting back clinging to her glass with both hands and gazing down into it as if it comforted her and she was hoping it would counsel her.

"Rebuild," she said. "With books. Knowledge. A spirit of doing, of *making,* not blankly accepting. Or just taking. And yes, our trash."

"So if you aren't baron, who is?" asked Ricky, who looked only briefly sulky when J.B. waved the brandy tray away from the youth.

"Nobody," Bob said.

He set the mostly empty tray on the desk and looked a question at his employer.

"Of course," she said. "I poured for you, as well."

Both hands came out and picked up the two remaining shot glasses of brandy. They raised them, then the heads turned toward each other.

"Here's looking at you," Bob said.

"Here's mud in your eye," said his brother. They clinked glasses and drank.

"Why has not a power vacuum arisen, then, in the absence of a strong central figure?" Doc asked.

"What the nuke do you think Dark Lady is?" Mikey asked. He belched, set the glass down and wiped his mouth with the back of his hand. The right one.

"Excuse you," Bob said.

"Whatever."

"The residents of Amity Springs seem to find their own autonomy, as individuals and family groups, sufficient."

"She's way too modest," Bob said. "She pretty much runs the show. She lets everybody make up their own mind. Then they usually do it her way."

"Not always," she said.

"They wouldn't if you were an iron-fisted baron, either," Ryan stated.

She finished her glass and glanced at the decanter. With something that struck Ryan as a lot like regret she leaned forward and precisely set the empty tumbler on the tray.

"I negotiate on behalf of the ville," she said. "And regardless of the impression the boys might give you, I do consult the others. I have no authority here."

"She's just always right," Mikey said, then to his twin, "What? It's true."

"That's why Baron Sand asked you to remind me of her offer," Dark Lady said. "And why I felt able to refuse it without consultation. Again. As I have when the white-coat representatives have made similar offers."

"Whitecoat representatives?" Ryan asked.

"Who do you think buys the hot-stuff scavvy?" Mikey asked.

"Oh, way to go, asshole," Bob said. "Loose lips sink shit."

"It's 'ships,'" Mildred said before she could catch herself. Then because she reckoned it was too late to stuff that bullet back in the blaster, and also because she was Mildred, drove right on. "It was a saying from—"

"The Second World War," Mikey finished smugly. "Yeah. I know. I actually read. You wouldn't think I'd need to, with these good looks. But the boss kinda insists."

"My brother especially likes books about war," Bob said. "Go figure."

"I see no great harm in revealing that fact," Dark Lady said. "After all, our guests aren't stupid. If they were, I wouldn't continue to repose faith in them recovering my stolen property. The ville's stolen property, to be exact, although I own a share."

"You said 'whitecoat representatives'?" J.B. asked.

"Yes," she replied. "From a facility somewhere outside the Basin, is all I know for sure. They take some pains to disguise where they come from. For obvious reasons."

She shrugged. "I suspect they disguise themselves, too, and that instead of hirelings negotiating on behalf of this group of whitecoats, they're members—whitecoats themselves. But of course the prejudice against whitecoats still runs hot and wide."

"Not without reason," Krysty pointed out.

"Perhaps not. Still, they would risk humiliation, harm, or even outright lynching should it become widely known they are whitecoats. For my part, I'm willing to accept them so long as they follow the same rules of decent behavior I expect everyone else to. At the very least, the whitecoats who were responsible for destroying the world are long dead."

"For the most part," Mildred murmured.

"Amity Springs has a reputation for unusual tolerance," Krysty said. "Of muties especially. Both Madame Zaroza and Sand mentioned it."

"And Sand seems to have a soft spot for muties," Mildred said, "not to mention other kinds of freaks."

"Among Sand's many vices and crimes," Dark Lady said, "no one could truthfully accuse her of intolerance. Except perhaps for behavioral norms. Especially rules concerning other people's goods.

"But as for Amity Springs, yes. While no muties live openly among us, at least overt discrimination against them is rare. For what it's worth, and as Madame Zaroza may have told you, it's her preference that her caravan camps well outside the limits of villes her traveling show plays. I cannot say her people would be accepted with open arms in this community. But they would be safe."

"What about Mikey-Bob?" Ricky said. "Uh, sorry."

"We told you, we're not muties," Mikey said. "We're conjoined twins. Dumb-ass kid."

"Sorry! Sorry!"

"Don't worry about it," Bob said. "It's a good point. Easy enough mistake to make, even a dolt like you's gotta admit."

"It's hard to imagine anybody discriminating too actively against you, Mikey-Bob," Krysty said.

"Not twice," both heads said in unison. They smiled.

Ryan thought they looked as if they might be reminiscing a bit.

"Is that your influence, Dark Lady?" Krysty asked.

"I do what I can. Let me emphasize that you use the right word—influence."

"So, is there anything else you need to talk to us about?" Ryan asked. "We all had a long day."

She looked at him with challenge in her dark, black-painted eyes.

"Can you recover my stolen artifact?" she said. "Please answer honestly."

"I have no idea," he said. "Honestly. She may not still even have it. I reckon you're not the only one who can have dealings with these whitecoat reps or whatever they are."

She nodded.

"Also, her place looks like a tough nut to crack. Even sneaking in for another crack won't be triple easy. Her peasants or subjects or whatever the fireblast they are seem to like her fine. If they or their dogs find out strangers are creepy-crawling the area, they'll run right and tell her."

He frowned and scratched his jaw.

"One thing in line with that—I won't tell you exactly how we are gonna play getting your doodad back. Because you got a spy in your house."

Mikey-Bob growled in outrage.

"Are you implying—" Bob began.

"—that we're the spies?" Mikey finished.

Ryan faced them both with a cool stare. He instantly discovered he couldn't look both of them in the eye at once. So he settled on fixing his gaze at a point between their heads, where their ears almost touched.

"I'm only saying there is one."

"I know," Dark Lady said.

"We might assist you in divining the miscreant, my dear lady," Doc said brightly.

"And dealing with him," J.B. said. "Or her."

Sadly, the black-clad woman shook her head.

"It isn't that simple. If I eliminate the current spy, Sand

will merely emplace another. And be aware that I'm on to her."

She gave her head a little shake and produced a wan and wistful smile. "Well, she knows that, too. It's one of these games of 'I know that she knows that I know.' And so on ad infinitum. But at the least it would alert her that something is afoot."

"If I take your meaning correctly," J.B. said, "don't you think she knows that already?"

"Again—it's a matter of degree, Mr. Dix. Heightened awareness on my part would lead immediately to the same on her part. And I should think that would be the last thing you would all want. If you do still intend to carry out my commission. You do, don't you?"

"I said yes," Ryan said. "If it can be gotten back, we'll get it."

She nodded.

Ryan sensed there was something more to her reticence to act against the baron's spy in her house. Was it reluctance to really believe one of her own would betray her, or reluctance to harm one of her own?

"In any event," Dark Lady said, lifting her face and her tone, "neither you nor I need specify further at this present time. I only wanted to make sure that you intended to keep trying. And that you thought there was a possibility you might succeed."

"Oh, there's a possibility," J.B. said. "When you got Ryan Cawdor on the job, there's always a *possibility*."

"So I gather," she said, looking at J.B. and then back at Ryan. The intensity of the way she looked at him was starting to tickle his subconscious. Not enough he was sure what it was trying to tell him, though.

"Before we all retire for our well-earned rest," she said,

"there is one final point I'd like to raise. Baron Sand is right. The Crazy Dogs have become an intolerable nuisance."

"After that scene tonight down in the bar," Ryan said, "it's a safe bet they're about to become more than that."

"Indeed. As a consequence, I would like to extend to you the same offer Baron Sand has. Aid us in solving the Crazy Dogs problem, and I will pay you well. Over and above the agreed-upon price when you recover my property."

"Are you crazy, D.L.?" Bob demanded.

"Crazier than usual?" Mikey said. "You wanna pay 'em for what they're already doing?"

"You trust them?" Bob asked.

"Yes. And yes," Dark Lady said. "I want to ensure they are dealing with more than just the Crazy Dogs that make themselves unpleasant to Sand. And at this stage, frankly, I believe it's in our interests—especially mine—to do what we can to assure ourselves of these people's help."

"It's not like they got your precious jimjam back," Mikey said.

"It's not as if it was an easy task I set them," she replied. "I have little use for excuses. I don't really think they've made them, so far. They have reported factually what happened."

She looked yet again at Ryan. "And this task, at least, is eminently straightforward. And I daresay, more in line with their usual line of work."

Ryan held her gaze a moment more. Then he tossed back the last of his brandy.

THEY WERE STILL climbing the stairs to their rooms when Mildred blurted, "Ryan, what in the name of God's green Earth were you *thinking?*"

"Which time?" he said.

"Well, any of it! But just for argument's sake, let's start

with why the Hell you thought it was a good idea to blurt out every last detail of why you agreed to start working for our employer's mortal enemy."

"Keep it down," Ryan said. "I don't mind having it out. I do mind everybody else in the damn gaudy knowing all about it."

"Don't you remember what Dark Lady said about spies, Millie?" J.B. asked.

"That there was one here," she said, "yeah."

Then in a softer tone, "And so, yeah, I will turn it down. But so what if that Sand has a spy in this cathouse?"

"Don't you reckon Dark Lady has spies of her own?" J.B. asked, as mild as always.

"J.B.'s right," Ryan said, resisting the urge to add, "of course." They'd gotten Mildred quieted down but not yet mollified. "Or at least, I wasn't about to assume she doesn't have a spy in Sand's happy valley. And how do you think she'd feel about us when she found out we'd neglected to mention that one little detail?"

They had come onto the landing and out into the corridor where they roomed.

"Like we'd sold her," Mildred said. "But wasn't there a risk she'd decide that anyway when you told her? Mikey-Bob sure jumped on that conclusion with both his size-eighteen feet."

"Yeah, a risk," Ryan said. "Better than a head shot certainty."

She sighed. "Well—okay."

He turned away. "If there's nothing else."

"There is one thing," she challenged.

"Make it fast."

"What's the *plan* here, Ryan? Don't you think it's time to let us in on it? Or at least, you know, give us a clue?"

"Plan?" He shook his head. "Got no plan. I'm making it up as I go along."

"I don't buy it," Mildred said firmly. "You've *always* got an angle. There's always some devious scheme cranking away in that head of yours. You expect me to believe that isn't happening now?"

"Well, now," he said with a smile, "I didn't say *that*."

Chapter Sixteen

Still groggy and rubbing sleep from her eyes—and remembering, both with amusement and a pang of loss, how hard her ophthalmologist coworkers would have ridden her for that, in an age that was long dead, and so were they—Mildred followed her friends down the stairs to the bar room of the Library Lounge.

It was still early by barfly standards, apparently. Hers, too, the way she felt. The sun had come up, apparently, and a gray light shone through windows bared by thick pulled-back curtains that kept the place sepulchral most hours of the day.

On the bench that ran along the back wall, same as the bar and to the right of it, Ruby, one of the entertainers, sat reading a large open book on a table. She wore a loose dark blue jersey or sweatshirt. Mildred couldn't see what else she might be wearing. She had reading glasses perched on the tip of her pert nose, and seemed very intent.

"Mikey-Bob's in the back, y'all," she said with a wave of her hand as the companions paused on floorboards freshly covered with sweet-smelling sawdust. Mildred wondered where *that* came from. "I'd walk lightly around him if I was you. Both of him's in a growly bear mood this morning."

"You mean sometimes he's not?" J.B. asked.

"You all go ahead," Mildred said, for some reason separating both syllables of *you-all* more carefully than usual, as if she were afraid of being taken for as country as Ruby sounded. "Just get me whatever you manage to wangle out of Mikey-Bob, please."

"Your leg broken, Mildred?" Ryan asked. "You look like you can go fetch for yourself."

"That's all right," J.B. said. "I'll get hers for her."

With Ryan grumbling about J.B. being henpecked, and Krysty looking as if she were fixing to weigh in and have her say, the group went past the bar through the swing doors into the kitchen. When they opened, Mildred heard Mikey's dulcet tones demand to know what the nuke they thought they were doing traipsing into his kitchen without so much as a by-your-leave.

Ricky kind of crab-walked, and then walked backward. He seemed fascinated by Ruby, who admittedly had a striking face, although for her shape she might as well have had two bodies to play counterpoint to Mikey-Bob's two heads, from the bagginess of the garment she was wearing. No doubt he was having no trouble envisioning the full bosom beneath, and the way it had constantly threatened to explode out of her bustier the night before.

He wound up stalled and staring when the doors swung shut on his friends and the loud argument Bob and Mikey were having at the tops of their shared prodigious lungs. The doors opened again. A brown-leather-clad arm reached out, grabbed Ricky by the collar and hauled him bodily inside.

Shaking her head and smiling to herself as the doors swung shut again, Mildred approached the young woman. "Mind if I sit down?"

Ruby glanced up at her. "Oh, no. Not at all. Make yourself at home, Ms. Wyeth."

Mildred sat. "What are you reading?"

"*The History of the Decline and Fall of the Roman Empire* by Edward Gibbon," she said. She closed the book on a finger, picked it up and turned it over to peer at the spine. "Volume, uh, Three."

"You're kidding," Mildred said reflexively. But even as she did she saw the words embossed on the cracked and ancient cover in largely missing gold leaf.

"Why are you reading that?" she asked as Ruby spread the book open in front of her again. She resisted the urge to add, "Of all things?"

"It's interesting," Ruby said.

"Most people these days don't seem any too interested in history. Or in learning to read, come to think about it."

"Well, I didn't think I was, either. But Dark Lady taught me long ago, and suggested I read this one. She says without understanding the past you can't really understand the present. That that's a big problem with the world today—that so many people ignore the past. Or are actively afraid of it."

Mildred frowned. "I thought I heard tell that Dark Lady encouraged everybody to learn some kind of a trade. Mebbe I heard wrong."

"Oh, no," Ruby said. "You heard right. She wants to make sure all of us entertainers find some way of making a living other than... You know, on our backs and knees."

"Well, that's big of her," Mildred said a bit stiffly. "What do you want to learn?"

"Haven't decided yet," Ruby said, her eyes back on her pages of dense archaic text. "Been doing some carpentry kinda stuff. Mr. Coffin's offered to teach me how to make caskets."

"I'll just bet he has."

"It's real kind of him, huh? But lately I've been getting more and more interested in trying to work with metal. You know, make things."

"That'd make Mr. Dix a most happy man to hear,"

Mildred said, thinking, And if he tries to take her on as a student I'll break both his thumbs.

Ruby nodded abstractedly. She was clearly back into the Decline, or Fall.

"So, tell me…" she said. "What's it like, uh, working for Dark Lady."

"Fine," Ruby said. "I like it."

"Really?"

Ruby looked up at her with a hint of a frown. "It's better than being forcibly turned out for muleskinners by the side of the road, for a bottle of whiskey the bunch, Ms. Wyeth."

"Uh. Yeah."

She took a minute to gather her thoughts. That bit of backstory had broken her stride. But she wasn't about to walk away from her principles.

"Don't you feel exploited?" she asked.

"'Exploited'?"

"You know…taken advantage of."

"Yes, ma'am," Ruby said. "I know what the words mean. I just don't know what you mean by them."

That put Mildred back in her chair. "Well, I mean—being compelled to have sex for money. To, uh, make money for somebody else."

Ruby closed her book, looked at Mildred and frowned. "Are you gonna give me some other job?" she asked.

"Well…"

"I told you where I came from. You know what'd happen to me if I started peddling my round little ass just out on the street."

"Well—yes."

"So what else am I gonna do? What would you do in my place? Dark Lady gives me safety and comfort," she said. "People treat us with respect. Or—well, you saw what happens to them."

"Yeah," Mildred said. "Mikey-Bob thumps them and throws them in the gutter."

"See, she cares about us. She cares about everybody. Everybody in the ville. Mebbe in the whole world."

She shook her head. "Crazy, right? But it's a craziness that's giving me a shot at a better life than anything else I was gonna get. Same for everybody here. What do you think would happen to Mikey-Bob, if not for Dark Lady? He'd have been hunted down and butchered as a monster long ago. Or at best had to go off with Madame Zaroza and play a freak in her traveling show. Which, you know, works for some people."

Mildred felt her face tighten into a ball of confusion.

"Talk to anybody you like," Ruby said heatedly. "Here or in Amity Springs. Not everybody likes Dark Lady, sure. Lotta people in the ville butt heads with her regular. But you won't hear anybody say she doesn't care, and doesn't do her best to look out for us all, unless they're a nuking liar!"

Mildred held up her hands. "Okay, okay. You can back off the trigger of the blaster now, hon—"

"You know what? You can even go ask that Baron Sand out to Joker Creek! She'd tell you the same. And she and Dark Lady hate each other like poison. Or love each other like sisters. Or mebbe ex-lovers. Nobody knows for sure. Least of all them, mebbe—"

The kitchen doors opened vigorously to what turned out to be a kick from Ryan. He walked into the room carrying two heavy steaming crockery plates. The others trooped in after him, ignoring Mikey's expostulation about not mishandling the physical plant.

"If you're done browbeating the help, Mildred," he said, plunking down heaping helpings of scrambled eggs, thick bacon slices and stewed pinto beans on the table in front of her, "breakfast is served. And you're rad-blasted welcome."

"How do Dark Lady's employees like her?" asked the woman behind the counter. She was solidly built, with a pretty face, bobbed red hair and a cheerfully matter-of-fact manner. "Why don't you ask them?"

Chagrined by Ruby's words—and her vehemence—but still unwilling to let go of her righteous indignation against Dark Lady and her sex-trafficking ways, Mildred followed her advice. Despite her friends' admonitions to rest up, she'd decided to spend the rest of the day talking to the young woman's coworkers in the gaudy, and then talking to random people in the ville.

Only a couple of the entertainers, another young woman named LaSalle and a young man named Duke, had gotten up and proved willing to talk before Mildred got bored and restless and ventured out into the warm day. They had fairly well corroborated Ruby's account. So Mildred determined to talk to people whose livelihood, not to mention possible safety, did not hinge quite so directly on staying on the gaudy owner's good side.

"Well, I did," Mildred said. "But I admit I'm just a bit uncomfortable with the whole brothel-owner thing."

The woman, Kris, looked genuinely puzzled. "I don't really see why. Sure, some people kind of look askance at the whole thing. But it seems to me like people want the service and she helps her people provide it in a safe, clean way. What's the problem? Anyway, aren't you-all hired blasters?"

"Well, that's not all we do."

The woman laughed. The store was lit only by back-scatter sun through fly-specked windows. It had shelves of various nonperishable items, from bins of nails to bolts of cloth to hand-turned meat grinders to sturdy mechanisms that Mildred had no idea did what.

"Well, we all get along best we can. Reckon it's the same for Dark Lady and her people."

"So how do people in the ville feel about her?"

"What's this about feeling Dark Lady?" asked Wilson, Kris's husband. He was wearing his apron and lugging a basket of folded hemp cloths out of a back room.

Without even looking around Kris smacked him on top of his bald head. "Behave," she said. "I'm not sure you can say everybody likes her. She comes off as kind of stand-offish, and can be stubborn as a jug-head mule. But she does a power of good for the ville, not much disagreement about that."

"What sort of good?" Mildred asked.

"You mean other than providing invaluable public services like whores and beer?" Wilson asked jauntily, hoisting the cloths onto the sturdy wooden counter. "Well, the place serves as a lending library. Not many intact books are around Deathlands these days, and people come from far and wide for a chance to borrow one. The name's not just for show. And she gives free reading lessons to anyone who needs it."

"Mebbe half the people in Amity Springs can read," Kris said with pride. "Wilson and I knew how before she got here, but she taught a bunch of folks. He's the avid reader in the family. I don't find much time, myself."

"She does handle a lot of our salvage operations," Wilson said. "You know about those, right?"

Mildred nodded.

"She came here mebbe five, six years ago, nobody knows where from," Kris said. "Little frail-looking wisp of a thing, with those big black eyes. But smart, and without an ounce of back-down in her."

"Her and pretty much that huge steamer trunk of old books she used to start her library with," Wilson said.

Mildred wondered just how a "frail little wisp" managed to drag a whole steamer trunk full of books along with her into the Basin—Nukem Flats. Given that she had to bring them across the mountains to the east, bluffs north and south, or up the cliffs the Río Piojo apparently hurled itself off of in an endless suicide dive beside the ville of the same name. But Mildred let the question go. She had more pressing concerns, and limited time to indulge raw curiosity.

"We were just starting to realize what we were sitting on top of back then," Kris said. "She had the idea of making a focused effort to scavvy the primest stuff out of the trash beds, and use the proceeds to build up the ville, which you can see has worked out double-well."

"But she's not the baron?" Mildred asked.

Husband and wife looked at each other. "Never felt much call for one of those," Wilson said, "lording it over us and all."

"Dark Lady is what you might call a leading light of the community," Kris said. "People just naturally go to her for advice on help on all manner of things. She gives it if she can. And she's right at least a bit more often than she's not, which isn't a bad record."

"She sounds too good to be true," Mildred said. "Things like that have a bad way of turning out not to *be* true. Or good."

Kris shrugged. "We're not much given to borrowing trouble here. All we can go by is what we see. And now if you'll excuse the two of us, I have to get to pestering this lazy man of mine into making something useful of himself."

Chapter Seventeen

"Dark Lady's a witch," the kid said in a confiding yet confident tone.

"Oh, she is, is she," Mildred said.

"Uh-huh."

"So you're scared of her?"

He was a slat-skinny boy of about ten, with a mop of muddy blond hair, freckles, a red shirt and blue canvas pants. He squatted, peering intently into one end of a stack of weathered wood poles, four inches thick and ten feet long. Firewood evidently.

His right hand darted the long-hafted implement he held into a gap near the bottom of the pile. She heard a squeak, then frantic chittering.

He pulled out a large brown rat, impaled, writhing on the barbed tines of what she'd thought was a frogging gig.

"Sorry, little guy," the boy—he'd said his name was Billy—told the rat. He laid the gaffe on the ground and crushed the animal's skull with a decisive stomp of a boot heel. Then he pinned it and yanked out his two-pronged spear.

"Nope," he said. "Why should I be scared of Dark Lady? She likes kids. Now, if you try to *hurt* one of us kids, then she gets stone scary."

"Um," Mildred said. "Yeah. I've seen her do scary."

A tiny triangular face sleekly furred in white and silver

poked out of the pile of poles where Billy had gigged the rat. Beady black eyes stared at him from a black bandit mask.

"Good girl," he told the ferret approvingly. "Go get me some more, Angelina. I hear 'em in there."

The face vanished.

Picking the now-still rat carcass up by its tail, he tossed it onto a heap of a dozen or so others lying eight feet away from his stakeout. A brief shift in the slow noontime breeze told Mildred why: they were starting to get ripe in the warm sun.

"I get paid for bringing in so many tails," he explained.

"I see. So why do you apologize to the rats when you chill them?"

He hunkered down again, leaning forward, then left and right and frowning as he tried to see into the spaces between the poles.

"Rats are actually intelligent and sociable," he said. "Did you know they cry when they're alone?"

"I don't believe it." Mildred didn't want to believe it.

"True as glowing nuke death, ma'am, cross my heart and hope to die," he said. "See, Dark Lady had us kids raise us some rat pups. We kept 'em as pets until they died—they don't live long. We found out when they were kept alone, without other rats or us for company, they'd whimper."

"So, how can you bring yourself to chill them now?"

He shrugged. "Well, we got to, I guess. The ones we kept were our friends. These ones are our enemies. Same as human coldhearts. They take what we need, because they need it, too."

He glanced up at her.

"They're not really to blame, though. Not like coldhearts are. Rats got no choice. They want to live and raise their kids same as we do. If they got to do it by stealing our food, that's what they do. But when they do that, they threaten our lives. So we get to fight back, and that's just too bad for them."

He speared another rat and finished it off with the same cold-blooded yet merciful efficiency.

"I wanna hurry and grow up and start chillin' cold-hearts," he said. He looked at Mildred again. "Just like you and your friends do. Because when they hurt and rob and kill, they *do* mean it. They're double worse than rats that way."

His words chilled her. More than they should have. In her own time she'd known of children growing up in such close-to-the-bone situations—and not just with regard to rats. Or not just the four-legged kind. She'd *worked* with some of them, as an intern.

She realized he'd given her a clear snapshot of two seemingly contradictory sides of Dark Lady's nature: compassionate and cold-blooded. Just like the way the boy finished off his prey.

"You say she's a witch?" she said. "But you seem to like her."

"She's not a scary witch," he said. "Not if you're her friend. But how else can she know the things she knows, or do the things she does?"

Mildred had no ready answer.

"You know, she's got a soft spot for muties," he said, deftly spearing and dispatching yet another rat. "You know how she's got a soft spot for that big two-head mutie who always talks to himself?"

"Yes," Mildred said. "But he's not a mutie. He's—never mind. Go on."

"Some folks say the reason why is, he's her brother. My older sister Maggie says it's because he's her lover. But when she talks like that Mama always threatens to wash her mouth out with soap."

"I should say so."

"Anyway, she used to roll with that traveling freak show that just left town. Some people say mebbe she's even a mutie herself. She sure comes down hard on anybody picking on 'em."

"You know this for yourself? That she was with Madame Zaroza, I mean?"

He shrugged. "Well, that's what people say. Some people whisper she's got a dark secret, too."

"What is it?"

He looked at her as if she were the triple stupe to trump all triple stupes.

"Well, if they knew that, it would hardly be a *secret,* now, would it?" he asked with abundant pre-adolescent scorn.

"Oh. I guess not."

He turned back to his task.

"Some people do say it has to do with Baron Sand."

"Baron Sand?"

"Yup." He nodded, though his eyes never left the logs. Or the spaces in between. "They got history together of some kind, and that's a fact. As to what—some folks say they're sisters. Had a falling out over a lover picked one over the other. Some say the Dark Lady, some say Sand. Dunno how anybody'd pick the baron over Dark Lady though. She's funny-looking."

"That's not nice," Mildred said. "She has a very pretty face."

"Well, she is funny. I mean, make-people-laugh funny. The kind of funny a body wants to be. I gotta give her that."

He didn't sound convinced anyone would pick the baron over the gaudy owner, though.

"Some other people even claim Dark Lady and Sand was lovers themselves."

"Goodness gracious!" Mildred exclaimed, scandalized. "Was that your sister Maggie, again?"

"Oh, no, ma'am. But my aunt Blanche has been known to say it once, or more than once, when she'd had a little too much summer beer or Towse Lightning to drink of an evening. Mama always tells her to hush her mouth. I guess she can't wash her mouth out with soap, being as they're both adults and all."

"I suppose not."

"There's even some as say Dark Lady and Sand are in cahoots," he said.

"Cahoots?" Mildred asked. "To do what?"

"Never heard that part, rightly. Usually when they start talking that way they get quiet, then chase me off. Don't put no stock in that, myself."

"Who says that about her?"

He shot her a narrow-eyed suspicious look. "Why do you wanna know?"

"Forget I asked," Mildred said. "I take it there are people in this ville who don't care much for Dark Lady?"

"Some," he admitted.

"I really don't believe it, though," she said. "I think you're making that up."

"Am not! Are too! There's Sarah Walker. And the Mormons—they don't live here rightly. And there's Mr. Sinclair. He runs the wag yard and he's almost as important as she is."

"Is he indeed?" Mildred said.

"Billy!" a woman's voice cried from around the corner of the building. "Billy Cohen, you come right now!"

"But, Ma!" he called back. "My tails!"

"You leave those nasty things for now. I need you right this moment."

He made a clucking sound. Angelina poked her pointy,

piquant face out, higher up than she had before. He scrabbled a couple fingers on the ground. She jumped down. He gathered her up and, standing, poured her inside his shirt.

"You won't take my rats, will you, ma'am?"

"I wouldn't dream of it," she said. "Cross my heart and hope to die."

"They're pretty tasty when they don't get too high in the sun," he said. "Hope the cats don't—"

"Billy!"

"Yes, Ma!" Clutching his ferret against his belly, he raced away out of sight.

"So you want to know about Dark Lady?" asked the man who sat in a small office with his boots on the desk.

She sat across the paper-piled desk from him. Inside was dusty and dim, and smelled of sweat and tobacco smoke from his cigar. Outside, the Sinclair and Sons Wag Yard creaked and whinnied and clattered and shouted with activity.

He took a last drag on his cigar and stubbed it on a copper tray on his desk.

"Some might call it a mite strange for the hired help to be taking a poll about their boss."

"I reckon, if we put our butts on the line for a person, it behooves us to know as much as possible about that person," she said.

Even she had long since started to wonder why she was dragging this out like a murder investigation. It wasn't as if she'd insisted before that everyone they took a job from had to be a Mother Teresa. She had stayed in plenty of gaudies before and had encountered many gaudy owners. For some reason Dark Lady just rubbed Mildred the wrong way.

Now she wondered why, aside from her innate bulldog perseverance, she insisted on taking things so far. She was starting to wonder if it was a reaction to the frequent sense of powerlessness that gripped her since she awakened from the cryosleep.

Sinclair was frowning at her speculatively. He was a man of early middle age, still mostly lean and lank in a tan vest, matching trousers and a white shirt. He had a red mustache, and receding red hair cut short. His eyes were green in a face lined and weathered like his boots.

He looked just like a character in a cowboy movie from Mildred's childhood. Except for the matte-silver Beretta M-92 holstered at his left hip.

"All right," he said. "Reckon that's fair."

He swung his boots down, scooted his secretary's chair closer to the desk, and dropped his elbows on the scarred hardwood surface.

"What is it you care to know about her, Ms. Wyeth?"

"I've heard you don't like her," she said, feeling even less inclined toward tact than usual. "Pretty unusual stance, given that the rest of the ville seems to think she spends her spare time walking on water."

By the brief lowering of his brows she wasn't sure he got the reference.

"Dark Lady doesn't go far out of her way to *be* likable," he said. "She's not the sort to suffer fools gladly. And she regards those who don't share her vision of what's best for Amity Springs as fools."

He sat back. "Since I and certain of my associates most emphatically do not share the vision—well, you can draw your own conclusions."

"So you don't like her."

He shook his head as if he were trying to clear water from his ears.

"Like, dislike—that's of no consequence. The important thing is, anybody who doesn't respect Dark Lady is a stone stupe. I honestly don't know of a person in this ville who fails to respect her, or to acknowledge the power of good she's done the community."

"Okay," Mildred said. "So, is she the baron, or what?"

"No. We have no baron." He shook his head. "Better by far if we did. I hope the people of the ville awaken to the fact that it's long past time for us to grow up and accept that we need proper governance."

"So, how exactly is Dark Lady preventing you from doing what you want to, then?"

"Moral suasion. People listen to her. Enough, frankly, that if we openly defied her wishes we would face ostracism at best. Business would drop."

"I thought you said she didn't go out of her way to be likable."

"Ah, but being *likable* and being *charismatic* turn out to be entirely different things." He tipped his head briefly to one side. "That and the fact she does have a habit of being right tend to tip the balance of opinion consistently in her favor. For now."

"What's your beef with her, then, exactly? What's she *not* right about?"

"I and several other substantial members of the community feel Dark Lady's desire to keep a low profile is not serving our interests in the long run," he said. "It's not protecting us. It's actively dangerous. By spurning the opportunity to grow the ville's resources as hard and fast as we have the opportunity to, she's putting us all at greater risk in the future."

"Harder and faster how?"

"By selling as much scavvy as we can dig up as fast as we can dig it up," he said as if that were the most self-evident thing there was.

Maybe he doesn't exactly understand the risks of

flooding the market, she thought. *But I* damn *sure didn't come here to discuss economics with this dude.*

"And in the process casting off this pretense of poverty and weakness," he said. "It's growing threadbare anyway. Rather we should acknowledge our wealth, and use it to build up our strength. Rather than hunkering down and hoping stonehearts won't notice we have anything here worth stealing."

"I take it the whole idea is to fly under the coldhearts' radar, by making the ville look a lot poorer than it is."

"Yeah. And that's already breaking down. This Diego and his Crazy Dogs know well what kind of value Amity Springs has to offer. They've started in threatening the drivers of wags coming from the east again. I've been hearing about it all day as they roll in."

That makes our services more valuable to Dark Lady in terms of taking the bastards down, then, Mildred thought. Is that rotten cynical? Well, tough, I guess. I long ago decided to do what it took to survive in this brave new world. If I want to live, I have to live with *that.*

But she said nothing.

"Even if we manage to deal with this bunch, others will come after," the wag yard owner said. "What Diego's figured out, others will, as well. They'll come against us in a force greater than we can handle, all too soon. Unless we start making the proper preparations now."

"Such as?"

He leaned forward intently. "Such as establishing proper central authority, for starters, and then letting go of all this silliness about wasting resources to make our ville look shabby. Focus on making it *strong.* And appear strong, as well."

"Uh-huh," Mildred said.

She agreed with the need for central authority, as far

as that went. Though she wasn't sure Amity Springs really needed anything more formal than what Dark Lady provided.

But Mildred knew that he had no idea of what the Deathlands could bring to them.

She shook her head.

"Do you disagree?" he asked.

"Not really," she said, which was true enough.

The fact was, she wasn't sure what the right answer was to the dilemma he'd proposed. She certainly knew it was real.

"Understand," he said. "Dark Lady cares deeply for the people of Amity Springs. In action as well as thought. That is a given. What we can and do differ over is how best to secure their future."

"So what's your solution?"

"To the Dark Lady problem?"

"Yes."

"Ideally, to buy her out and let her do whatever she chooses, go or stay," he said.

"She'll never sell," Mildred said before she realized that was what she thought.

He sighed and looked pained. If that was fake, Madame Zaroza was missing out on a gifted performer.

"We shall try our best to get her to do so," he said. "After that, well, I think we'll shoot that catamount when it comes to us."

Her eyes narrowed. Just another vivid shit-kicker figure of speech, or was he telling more than he intended?

It could be that lethal threats to Dark Lady didn't all come from outside Amity Springs.

He stood. "And now, if you'll excuse me... Yes?"

The last was directed past her, at the door that opened

out toward the main yard and the street beyond. Mildred turned in her chair.

A wild-haired figure with shabby work clothes and a scraggly beard stood apologetically half in the doorway. Mildred recognized the ville's loquacious coffin-maker, who chose to go by the named Coffin.

"Sorry to bother you, sir, ma'am."

He looked at Mildred.

"You're wanted back at the Library Lounge pronto. Your friends been looking all over for you."

THE SUN WAS heading for the far end of Nukem Flats when she followed the Asian-looking carpenter into the yard. It bustled with activity as drivers and stable hands unhitched horses from several wags, to lead toward the barn in the back to pass the night. The drivers themselves would doubtless end up in the Library Lounge, sooner rather than later.

Something brushed up against Mildred's arm. She turned to see Coffin trying to measure her with a length of cloth tape.

She batted the shabby fabric ribbon away as if it was glowing radioactive. "Hey, now, what the Hell do you think you're doing?"

"Just taking your measurements, ma'am," he said. "You know—just in case."

"Thanks for the vote of confidence."

"The end comes to us all. No shame in being prepared."

Chapter Eighteen

"Baron."

When Trumbo walked into what Sand called her Grand Salon, the room was full of the reek of pot, wine and glandular secretions. The smoke hung in a greenish haze from waist height to the dark brown rafters.

The Baron of Joker Creek was lounging in her regal chair, with that repellent oily Arcane draped over one side of her and a half-naked redheaded woman named Silky on the other. Trumbo tamped down his disgust hard. He had a mission.

Sand lolled her head over her shoulder to blink myopically at him. Her lips were soft and moist, her cheeks flushed. Her eyes were bloodshot. Disgusting, he thought. If only you knew what you were doing to yourself....

"What?" she demanded. Arcane giggled. Silky peered coyly around her baron's bulk.

"I just received a report of a possible Crazy Dogs' patrol sneaking around on the bluffs," he said.

She blinked at him twice, slowly. Her eyes were huge.

Then she popped to her feet. Silky melted away from her. Arcane was unceremoniously dumped on his skinny butt on the maroon tile floor.

"Then what are we waiting for?" she demanded hoarsely.

She glared around at her hangers-on. They looked at her with a mixture of fear and partly repressed amusement, as if they wished to believe this was a joke, and didn't want to be seen not to get it, or laugh at the right time.

Arcane whimpered. She tapped him on top of his curly haired head.

"Stop feeling sorry for yourself," she said. "I knew the Dogs would try us again, after our deliciously dark and mysterious friends made their spy disappear. They need to be taught a sharp, hard lesson now. Because if they somehow take over, they'll really give you something to snivel about."

Trumbo wrestled to keep his emotions off his face. Feelings were unmanly anyway. Showing them was as bad as dropping your pants and showing a scar where your balls should be.

He loathed this den of repulsive muties—and degenerates who were worse freaks than even muties were. Yet he adored this baron.

How I wish I could take her away from all this, he thought. Make her see this isn't the right way to live.

She'd lacked a strong man's hand guiding her life for so long she'd come to imagine she didn't need it. He knew he was the man to help her see light.

Arcane got to his feet with surprising speed.

"The farmers' dogs've been barking for a while now," he said, pouting only a little. "Mebbe that's the Crazy Dogs they're responding to."

"Likely," Sand said, turning and putting her hands on her hips as if to evaluate him. Trumbo wondered why she couldn't see he was worthless.

"Will you fight them for me?"

"Of course."

She reached out and pinched his cheek, lightly furred with what it disturbed Trumbo to have to call a beard.

"That's my good boy," the baron purred. "I knew I could count on you."

"Always."

Sand turned away and bent. From somewhere in the tangle of cushions and wisps of fabric and smoke she produced an ebony cane. She flourished it in the air.

"Gather your troops, Trumbo," she commanded. "I shall lead you into battle personally. As soon as I find my boots. And some pants."

He nodded. "Yes, Baron."

And hoped she didn't see the secret smile he couldn't keep off his face.

"Okay," said Krysty, lowering Ryan's Navy longeye. "I see Ryan's signal. They're ready to move on the house."

"I hear dogs barking down below," Ricky said worriedly. "Might they give them away?"

"Then we'd best get to using these toys Dark Lady gave us, shouldn't we?" Mildred said, picking up a firefight simulator from the dirt beside where she, Krysty, Ricky and Doc crouched or lay on the ridge overlooking Sand's domain. It was basically a string of firecrackers rolled into a ball and rigged with an initiator that would start them going off in series. It was meant to mimic the noise and flashes of a serious shootout.

They had concealed themselves a bit east of the baron's big house, not far from where Ryan had shot the Crazy Dogs' spotter.

There was no moon this night. It was a waving sliver and had set early, which was to their advantage.

"J.B. will be eating himself with jealousy that he doesn't get to light these puppies," Mildred said.

"Doubtless he is sufficiently occupied at the moment to overcome that emotion," said Doc, who was crouched back from the lip of the cliff with his big LeMat clutched in one bony hand.

"Are we ready?" Krysty asked softly.

She wasn't happy at having to split up like this, but staging a diversion was the best shot at letting Ryan, J.B. and Jak get in and out safely.

"Oh, yeah," Mildred said.

Doc nodded. "Indeed."

Ricky was facedown beside Krysty, pointing his DeLisle into the Basin. Though he could be high-strung in some ways, she had learned to trust his steadiness where blasters were concerned. She wasn't worried he'd loose off a shot out of overeagerness, or worse by accident, and alert the baron and her sec men prematurely. And anyway, the long-blaster was so effectively sound suppressed they'd never hear it if he did.

He twisted around and looked at her. His head moved slightly up and down as he swallowed in nervousness. Clearly he was crowding his mind with everything that could go wrong for their three friends below.

It was a lot, but Krysty had practice putting that knowledge out of her head. It was a necessary skill to lead the life she had chosen. She gave him a smile of encouragement.

"Yes, ma'am," he said.

She looked at Mildred and grinned.

"Do it," she said.

Mildred pulled the string initiator hard. The device in her hand began to fizz. She stood and heaved it as far west as she could, aiming it to land as close to the cliff top as she dared.

They all hunkered down then, and waited. In a moment all hell broke loose. Lights flared and danced. Smoke roiled. The noise made Krysty wince.

She grinned at Mildred. The stocky woman was already

prepping a second simulator. She was clearly having a lot of fun.

And then from the night, off toward the stream cut that flowed down past the big house, more dancing lights appeared.

Unmistakable muzzle-flashes were pointed their way.

Krysty ducked in alarm as a bullet cracked over her head.

"We're under attack for real!" she shouted, hoping to be heard above the din.

THE TOP OF the bluffs, a good quarter mile away, suddenly lit up with bright flashes, and it sounded as though several blasters were shooting.

"Right," Ryan said, leaning back around the front of the small shed he crouched behind. "Time to move."

He signaled to Jak. "We best go with a purpose. People will be starting to rouse and look outside any moment."

The albino had already slipped around the far side. They had crossed the creek downstream from the settlement and had made their way near the foot of the bluffs before Ryan signaled they were in place. They had avoided detection so far.

Except by the rad-blasted dogs. There was one barking vigorously at them from not forty yards away. Apparently folks around here weren't suspicious of such—no doubt coyotes, armored or otherwise, visited on a regular basis, and they knew by the sounds of their watch animals just how immediate a threat was. That had led Ryan, J.B. and Jak to take longer than they otherwise might have, steering wide enough of barking dogs that the animals didn't take it up from general alert to condition red.

"They're putting on a good show up there," J.B. murmured, nodding toward the bluffs to the north.

There certainly was a lot of racket going on. It really did sound like blasters.

"Dark Lady gave us enough of those things," Ryan said. "They must've found the old arsenal."

"Yeah," J.B. said a bit wistfully, and slipped around the corner of the shed. Ryan knew he wished he could be setting them off, but his real talents were needed down here.

Trotting bent over, Ryan followed him toward the big house. Light was pouring out of every window. He had his Steyr longblaster strapped across his back, where naturally the muzzle banged him on the kidneys with every step. Couldn't be helped; he didn't know he'd have call to use a scoped long-range blaster, but then, he couldn't know he *wouldn't*.

Ahead of him J.B. was running along the same way. He had his Uzi strapped over his back and his M-4000 scattergun in his hands. Ryan hoped they wouldn't be spotted before they reached the main house, or things could get loud down here, too, in a hurry.

The farmers could be another issue. They ran along the bank of an irrigation ditch flanking a field full of rows of low mounds of what had to be some early rising crops. Ryan had no idea what. He wasn't any dirt farmer.

But even the lowliest sodbuster could chill you deader than dog dirt, if he blasted you from ambush with a shotgun, or caught you in the head with an ax. Ryan, J.B. and Jak just had to hope Sand's subjects had the sense not to go sticking their heads out like triple stupes when blasters were barking nearby.

They made it away from the last huts into the fifty yards or so of cleared space between them and Sand's Casa de Broma without being gunned down, having their heads split or actively chased by dogs. Nobody sounded any alarms, either.

Ryan and J.B. crossed the creek just short of the house. The water wasn't deep but it was cold.

Jak waited for them around the nearest corner from the front. They joined him and pressed close against the house to minimize visibility, although there was nothing like cover here. The yard-thick walls were cool and smelled like cool earth.

"Out back," the albino said as Ryan leaned close to hear above the noise. "Watching."

By which Ryan understood him to mean some of the house's occupants were behind the house gazing up at the heights. Great, he thought. The fewer people inside, the less chance of discovery. Or of serious resistance if they were discovered.

Of course they had no way of knowing whether Trumbo and his sec men had risen to the bait. But if they hadn't gone charging out to engage an intruder making that much noise, how big a threat were they?

At least as far as Ryan could tell, no shots were coming from the house. If Trumbo or the baron had decided to hunker down and defend the place, that would likely be the case.

He looked at J.B. and gestured toward the front door. Then he signed for Jak to keep watch toward the rear of the house.

J.B. went to work on the lock on the massive front door. Ryan may have been the one to carry an emergency lock-pick kit in the heel of his boot, but it was J.B. who possessed true artistry with locks, as he did with most things intricate and mechanical.

Ryan stood beside the door, facing out. He had his Scout unslung and gripped in both hands now. With the light from the front windows, little dimmed by the filmy curtains that nonetheless made it impossible to see inside, he was as concerned with someone farther down the creek spotting and firing on them.

It took J.B. scarcely more time to open the lock than that taken by inserting his tools. He straightened and gave his friend a quick grin.

Ryan grinned back and nodded. J.B. put his lock-pick away and took up his shotgun.

The one-eyed man gestured Jak over. The albino was next to Ryan in an eye blink. Even if it hadn't been for the Hell continuing to bust loose from above and echoing along the bluffs, Ryan knew he wouldn't have heard him come.

"First?" Jak asked with ill-concealed eagerness.

"I go first," Ryan said. "Then J.B. Watch our backs until we give you the sign to come in."

Jak nodded.

Holding his Steyr by the pistol grip in his right hand, Ryan put his left on the door handle. J.B. asked a question with his cocked eyebrow: Why not your handblaster?

Ryan just grinned. After an instant J.B. gave the minutest of nods.

Gently, Ryan twisted the knob until he felt the latch disengage. Then he yanked it open and thrust himself into the front room, leading with his blaster barrel.

Chapter Nineteen

"Shit!"

Even under heavy fire Mildred felt a stab of annoyance at herself for losing track of how many shots she'd fired. She'd not only dropped the hammer on a spent cylinder, she'd pulled the double-action trigger of her Czech-made target revolver again in her frenzy, which was *not* the kind of shooter she was.

She ducked and popped open the cylinder. Fortunately, Krysty had picked out a spot with some rocks to offer some cover from which to launch their diversion. Even if it wasn't *enough* cover for Mildred not to regret the flesh she continued to carry on her sturdy frame in spite of several years of long miles and lean rations.

She still had some speed loaders charged with fresh .38 Special rounds. She dropped the spent shells into her pocket by touch as she looked west to take stock of their situation.

Short form: it sucked. It sounded and looked as if the firefight simulator—long-since burned out—was still going. Except louder and brighter because it was all focused on them.

Her friends all had cover, too, and were popping up in the lulls to shoot back. From the occasional outcry she could tell they were scoring hits.

From the corner of her eye she caught a stab of muzzle-flare from Ricky's DeLisle carbine. She saw a form straighten about thirty yards away, then keel over. Like the rest of them, the kid was shooting for muzzle-flashes.

Ricky promptly rolled to one side. No return fire came his way, so far as Mildred could tell before she snapped the cylinder shut and started looking for targets herself. But they were also lucky Trumbo's sec men were too stupe to do what the boy did, and instead just stayed in place, advertising just exactly where that was every time they pulled a trigger.

The firestorm abruptly cut off. Mildred heard a high, commanding voice calling for a cease-fire. She was more impressed that it actually got one.

Sand does have a presence to her, she admitted.

She actually saw the large shadowed form stand bolt upright and brandish a cane.

"Surrender!" the baron called in a brassy voice. "We don't want to have to hurt—urk!"

The last came out involuntarily as another, shorter, blockier form low-tackled her out of view.

Ricky's blaster thumped.

Mildred thought she heard the boy mutter, "Mother-fucker," under his breath. Despite their desperate situation she almost laughed out loud. The kid was normally so pious.

Out of sight, Sand was squalling like an angry cougar.

"Pipe down!" Trumbo bellowed. "What were you thinking, making a target of yourself like that? That was triple stupe!"

Sand did pipe down, possibly because she was unaccustomed to her sec boss talking to her like that. Or anybody.

Illogically, Mildred felt pleased somehow that Ricky hadn't chilled her. Despite, or maybe because of Sand's unabashedly alternate lifestyle—by the standards of Doc's, Mildred's, this, or pretty much any day—she felt more affinity toward her than Dark Lady with her show of rectitude as a respectable community pillar and businesswoman.

But the other sec men promptly started up their barrage once more. Even after a couple went down to the companions' blasterfire, there were at least a dozen of the sec men out there. And even if they couldn't do much more than burn holes in the night with their bullets, so far, they sure seemed to have lots of bullets to burn.

"They are flanking us inland!" Doc cried out in alarm.

Mildred set her teeth in dismay. Sure enough, she saw shadowy shapes moving out to her right. She lined up a shot and fired. The figure went down, but she was sure she'd missed and the sec man was just ducking. Dire experience had taught her that, no matter how ace a shot you were, your unaided aim was lousy at night. And neither Mildred nor any of her friends had so much as luminous sights, much less night-vision equipment.

This blows, she thought. If the enemy started cross-firing them, they were as good as staring up at the stars already. Or at best captives—and while Mildred also caught no hint of actual sadism from the baron, as flamboyant as she was, she was no more sure of that ugly bulldog sec chief of hers than she was of Sand's ability to keep him on his leash.

"Simulator," Ricky shouted at her over the gun-storm.

She blinked at him.

"Throw it! To scare them back!"

She looked down at the remaining firefight simulators, sitting on the dirt beside her. "Oh."

She stuffed her ZKR back in its holster and snatched one up. She yanked the string, hard, waited for the fizz to indicate it had taken and pitched it.

A moment later, it appeared to the flanking quartet of

sec men as if all the blasters in the world were firing at them from their other flank. They immediately made themselves one with the Earth.

"Good move," Krysty called. "But that won't keep them off us long."

"Ladies," Doc called.

They looked at him. He had the largest rock between him and the enemy, and had his back to it as he stuffed a fresh shell into the shotgun tube slung under the regular barrel of his commemorative LeMat handblaster.

"I shall hold them," he called. "You rejoin the others."

"But we don't leave anybody behind—"

"Then live long enough to rescue me!" he called. *"Go!"*

Krysty looked at Mildred. Even in the dark Mildred saw tears glimmering in those huge emerald eyes.

The redhead nodded. "Right."

"Okay, kid," Mildred called to Ricky. "Time to go."

"But—"

She grabbed his collar and hauled him around. When she saw the others moving, Krysty started crawling briskly away east on all fours.

"Come at me, you caitiff rogues!" Mildred heard Doc roar from behind as she, making sure Ricky stayed with her, followed her friend toward what they all hoped was safety.

Go with God, you crusty old bastard, she thought. And felt like the world's worst coward.

A sec man lounged in Baron Sand's special chair, and at least a couple of her courtiers cowered in corners, apparently terrified of the racket outside. Smart move, Ryan thought as he sized up the room in one glance.

The sec man's eyes got huge. He started out of the chair, grabbing at a holstered blaster.

Ryan skip-stepped across the room. A hanging swatch

of some filmy cloth caught him around the face but gave way. He could still see through it well enough to butt-stroke the sec man across the chops with his Scout.

The longblaster's synthetic furniture didn't give it the heft of good old hardwood; that was the *point,* actually, to keep weight down, which most of the time was a good thing, as it meant less to carry.

But that didn't matter much. Ryan gave it ample energy to sprawl the guy cock-eyed on the cushions. On his way down he got well and truly entangled in some strands of filmy lavender and dark green fabric. They pulled loose from whatever held them up and fell to swath him.

"Jak, secure the far door," Ryan said, nodding toward the back of the house. "J.B., take the left."

As they moved to comply, he looked menacingly from one retainer to the other. The woman was a not-bad-looking bottle blonde, although her eye makeup had begun to bleed down her clownishly pale-painted face from fear tears. A somewhat saggy breast hung out of a filmy negligée. Though she didn't seem to have underpants on, she wore combat boots, for no known reason. The male wore a loose white shirt with lacy cuffs and knee britches over some kind of shiny stockings. He was a mutie, apparently, or wearing a triple-strange costume. Instead of hair he had a crest of yellow and pink feathers above a bony pallid face, and his eyebrows seemed to consist of the same.

"Over here, you two," he said, gesturing with the longblaster. As he reckoned, they were too frightened to take note of the fact that if he blasted one, he'd have to cycle the bolt before he could shoot the other. Or at least to act on that knowledge if they had it. "Gag this bastard with some of this foofy stuff."

As they hastened to obey, Ryan gave a quick eyeball to the sec man, who lay with eyes half closed, moaning and feebly stirring. He was probably concussed, though Ryan wasn't about to rely on the fact.

J.B. and Jak reported the doors clear and no sign of life from elsewhere in the house. Given the noise outside and the absence of more visible sec men inside, Ryan was starting to feel concern over Krysty and the others. But he was committed now. What happened to the rest, happened, and they'd pick up the pieces afterward.

"Now," he directed the fancifully dressed pair. "Tie his thumbs behind his back. Tight. If he gets loose, you'll be the second and third chilled after him."

They did that.

"Why not chill?" Jak said, turning briefly from the door to the rear of the house to nod at the three.

"No need. Now, you two, pick him up and drag him. You're all coming with us."

"What if we won't comply?" demanded the feathered guy. Apparently that much exertion was one too many for him.

"Then there's a need. *Move.*"

They moved.

THINK THE LAST one's a chill," called the sec man as he advanced cautiously along the nighttime cliff top with a Ruger blaster clutched to his chest.

"Careful, there, Wiley," called a voice from behind. "He was a tough one."

"Ha," Wiley said with a sneer. "He was just an oldie. You turds are just soft—"

Doc sat with his right knee beneath him, right ham on heel and his back to his sheltering boulder. He clutched the freshly reloaded LeMat in both hands and took a deep breath.

Then he pushed up from the cold, dusty ground, twisting

in place with the knee still down. He thrust out the huge handblaster.

Wiley had just turned his dark-stubbled hatchet face forward. "Fuuu—" he began.

The shot column from the underbarrel shotgun tube tore his lower jaw clean off.

As he fell, strangling on his own gore, Doc heard curses from the darkness, scarcely twenty yards west by the sound. He lowered himself behind the rock, just peering around the edge of it. A risk, he knew.

But what of that? he thought. It is not as if I expected to survive the night when I volunteered to delay the pursuit.

Muzzle-flares blossomed, huge and bright, yellow with blue cores. Bullets passed over his head with *wheet* sounds. One, more rapid than the rest, cracked. Another struck fragments off the face of Doc's rock and whined away tumbling into the night.

Bracing his revolver against the side of the rock, Doc switched the barrel to blaster shots, drew a bead on an enemy on a blaster-flash and fired. He heard a yelp, then a thrashing sound.

"Rad-blast it!" Doc heard the unmistakable bull-roar of an angry Trumbo from somewhere behind the shooters. "Wing out to the left and pin the prick against the cliff."

So this is how the game ends, Doc thought, curiously without regret. I hope Krysty, Mildred and Ricky have made it to safety by now.

He heard rustling and pounding steps. Shots cracked.

Dearest Emily, Rachel and Jolyon, I am coming.

Doc fired at flitting shadows, ducking as best he could to keep cover between him and his enemies' blasters as long as he could. His aim was uncertain in the dark. But he did see one shape drop, in a way that suggested it was not to rise again.

The hammer clicked on a spent chamber. And a figure sprang to the top of the rock he sheltered behind.

"Got you, old bastard!" a sec man whose face was fringed in unkempt hair and beard exclaimed in triumph. He raised a pump shotgun to aim at Doc's face.

Doc had already dropped his empty handblaster and snatched up his swordstick. Now he swung it in a whistling arc. It cracked against the sec man's left hand, on the blaster's pump foregrip. Whether the hand was broken or not, it let go. Impact jarred the shotgun aside the instant before it roared and vomited a giant orange-and-yellow flame over Nukem Flats.

Because the shooter was unexpectedly holding on to the powerful blaster when it went off with only one hand, the weapon kicked its way out of his grip.

"You prick!" the sec man screamed in fury and probable pain. He grabbed the gleaming black cane.

Doc pulled back. The long, slim sword blade slid free of the ebony sheath. The sec man's already wild eyes grew round.

Then he shrieked as Doc thrust hard, punching the tip of his blade through his staring left eye and into his brain.

The man toppled. Doc stood. No point in cowering now. He would meet death as a man ought, on his feet and facing his foe with final defiance on his lips.

He flourished the sword with a snap of his wrist to clear blood and aqueous humor and brains from it.

"Who next wants to dance with Death, you rogues?" he cried.

Half a dozen blasters were pointed at him from almost close enough to reach out and touch. But something about his manner—most likely the manifest sheer madness of his bravado—stayed the sec men's trigger fingers.

"What's the holdup?" Trumbo demanded, walking up

with jaw and torso thrust forward, as forcefully as if the night were a door and he meant to put his shoulder through it. "Blast the old bastard and then let's go hunt down the others!"

"Wait!"

The voice was feminine, contralto, and trumpet-ringing with command. Trumbo's bulldog face fisted in irritation and he turned.

"What is it?" he asked, going from anger to servility in the space of three syllables.

Baron Sand strode up as if the night were her personal possession that she deigned to let other people use. She was dressed in blouse, jacket and trousers of some dark stuff, possibly velvet, mannish in cut but closely tailored to her distinctly and amply feminine form. She flourished a walking stick of her own as she approached.

"Call your dogs back, Trumbo," she said. "I'll handle this."

For a moment Doc thought her sec boss would defy her and order his men to blow Doc down where he stood. Then his puffed-out chest seemed slightly to deflate, and his head to hunch down on the neck it seemed to lack.

"All right," he growled. "You heard the baron."

Sand stepped into the open space on the far side of Doc's rock. Realizing he had little to lose at this point, he rose, slowly, then stepped to his right around it.

"So do you like to fence, Doc Tanner?" she asked. "Or do you just stab the unsuspecting?"

"I prefer the latter, when it is feasible," he said.

"I took you for a man of honor."

He shrugged. "In this day and age, what is that? And in any event, whatever honor I once had was thoroughly stripped from me."

Into his mind flashed an image of Jordan Teague, immense and gross in every sense.

"I don't believe that," Sand said. "I myself am a man of honor—when it suits me, anyway. And one honorable man can recognize another."

"'Man'?" he said.

She laughed.

"Why don't we just chill him?" grumbled one of the sec men standing faceless in shadow.

Doc heard a smack and a whimper.

"What'd you go and do that for, Trumbo?"

"You don't know this Baron, Elliott," the sec boss growled.

"My sec boss," Sand said with a lilt. "He knows me so well. You do not. And my choice of word appears to have taken you aback, Doc Tanner."

"Well, do you consider yourself—"

"Something I doubt you have referents for." She tossed her short sandy hair away from her face. The rising breeze ruffled it like a lover's fingers. "You have a curious manner to you, like a man out of time. And I myself find myself out of step with this age."

Keep talking, Doc thought, with a faint flame wisp of hope beginning to curl and dance inside his dark soul. Perhaps all my friends will accomplish their tasks and make good their escapes.

"I identify myself with a gentleman," she said, with surprising earnestness that made her seem somehow vulnerable despite her assured manner. "A lord of the manor, a prince who takes seriously the welfare of his people—unlike most."

"I thought a prince, like a baron, found it better to be feared than loved?"

"Machiavelli, Doc Tanner? An unfashionable bit of

knowledge in this time when reading is a rarity. Anyway, that was all parody. He was a devout republican who sought to expose the baseness of the royalty and self-made magnates of his day. And consequently was misunderstood by roughly everybody, forever."

She made a flipping gesture with her cane. "I can identify. And now—"

She took a step forward with her left boot and assumed the en garde position. "Enough foreplay. Let's do it for real."

Doc mirrored her. "Ah, but this seems hardly gentlemanly," he said. "Mine is of fine steel, and pointed. Yours, alas, is a stick."

She cocked a sculpted eyebrow. "So, you haven't abandoned honor entirely, then, have you, old man? If you truly know how to handle that toothpick, you know that a properly wielded stick is nearly as formidable as a bared blade. And also—"

She whipped the stick upright in front of her face as if saluting. She gripped the wooden cane, twisted slightly and pulled. It slid free to reveal a slender upright blade with starlight jittering on its well-polished length.

"I have one, too."

He barely had time to register surprise before she stamped her lead foot and lunged. The wickedly pointed tip of her blade darted toward his face like a striking adder.

Chapter Twenty

Ryan grunted as he labored to pull aside the steamer trunk at the foot of Baron Sand's canopied bed. The bed itself was a remarkable construction, enormous, massive, with a canopy hung with pink and purple, and satin sheets piled high with cushions. Big black iron rings were set deeply into the stout oak at the corners of the frame.

"Impressive," said J.B., standing by examining it. The Armorer was a man who appreciated good craftsmanship, no matter what.

Jak stood by the door, his big knuckle-duster hilted trench knife in hand. The concussed sec man lay with his face to the foot of a low chest of even stouter construction than the bed frame, of some kind of age-weathered wood and carved with odd exaggerated Maltese crosses. He breathed with soft gurgling sounds around his gaudy silken gag, and showed no signs of resuming consciousness. Ryan judged either he was a triple-good actor or that Ryan had nailed him harder than intended. He thought the man's jaw was possibly broken.

"Fireblast," he said. "Does she make all her sex toys out of lead?"

The two courtiers now sat on the floor with their backs to the closet, clinging to each other. The bleach-blonde's eyes were blue and as round as saucers. At closer range she looked to be at least Ryan's age, and not having weathered the years well.

The feathered man had regained a little bit of his attitude. "Why don't you open it and find out?" he asked challengingly.

"Oh, Ike," the woman said, "don't make them mad. They're so brutal."

Feather Dude laughed. "Relax, Arabelle," he said. "If they meant to chill us, we'd be dead."

"We could change our minds, though," J.B. said mildly.

The feathered man's eyes got as wide as Arabelle's. They were yellow, Ryan noted.

With a final heave and groan of effort, he got the chest free of the foot of Sand's absurd bed. The floorboards where it had been didn't look all that different from those around them, but J.B. smiled slightly. Pulling his knife, he knelt and thrust it between two of them.

A four-foot slat came up readily. J.B. laid it aside as Ryan, who had stepped away to give his friend room to work, shifted his Scout on its sling so that he could hold it by the pistol grip, ready for use at need. Naturally he hoped not to have to do any blasting. It would bring anybody left in the house right down on their necks. And in the confines of these sturdy whitewashed walls the report would make his ears ring for a week.

In a moment J.B. had a four-by-two-and-a-half-foot space opened in Sand's floor. On his knees he bent in, taking his lock-pick kit out of one pocket.

Ryan became aware of something that prickled his nape beneath his shag of curly hair. Jak stiffened.

"No shooting," he said from the door. His ruby eyes looked up at a corner of the room, toward where Krysty and the others had presumably been staging their diversion.

"Not good," J.B. said. He frowned with concern. But small clicking sounds indicated he was still at work on the lock of the strongbox sunk in the hidden well in the floor.

"Weren't you wondering why there's hardly anybody here?" Ike asked.

"Heard a bunch of folks were out back watching the light show," Ryan said without much conviction.

"But that's just our friends who like such things," the mutie said. "Arabelle and I have sensitive ears. But Sand and that surly, burly sec boss of hers took off with most of his team long before all that horrible racket started."

"Fireblast," Ryan breathed.

"Your friends are chilled or captured now," the feathered mutie said with grim satisfaction.

"Ike!" Arabelle said in horror. "Don't tell them that!"

"Chill now?" Jak asked.

"Shut it," Ryan growled. It felt as if a clammy hand had closed on his heart and was squeezing. Not just because of the dreadful danger to his life-mate Krysty. The others, too—even the new kid Ricky. He was as ready to lose even one of them as he was to lose a part of his body.

The scar down the left side of his face and the vacant left eye socket twinged. Another one, he mentally amended.

"Got it," J.B. said. He bent and a moment later brought out a sturdy box. It looked to be made of some presumably fairly light-gauge metal. It was right about the size, Ryan thought, to hold a human head.

He stood, holding it. "Hefty."

"Right," Ryan said. He gestured to the two captives with the barrel of his longblaster. "You two. Into the hole. Be a tight fit, but you look like you know each other."

"What?" the feathered mutie said.

"You can't—I'm claustrophobic!" Arabelle wailed.

"Shut it," Ryan said. "You can go in still breathing, or otherwise. Your choice."

With the woman sniffling and the mutie glaring defiance, the two complied.

J.B. set down the metal box to help Ryan push the steamer trunk back over the opening. They didn't bother replacing the floorboards.

Even if the two inside were stronger and more determined than Ryan reckoned, he and his friends should be long gone from the house by the time they managed to push it far enough aside to free themselves.

J.B. picked up and reslung his shotgun and his Uzi, which he had shucked to work on the lock. Tucking the box under his arm, he turned to Ryan.

"Ready," he said. "You reckon—"

"Got no time to reckon," Ryan said. "Jak, take point."

Jak opened the door, which had been open a crack to let him peer out, and slipped into the corridor.

"Shitfire!" a voice exclaimed.

STEEL RANG ON steel, and sang as it slithered clear.

"'Vous auriez bien dû rester neutre,'" the baron recited, smiling, as they fought. *"'Où vais-je vous larder, dindon? Dans le flanc, sous votre maheutre? Au coeur, sous votre bleu cordon?'"*

Taken by surprise by the baron's sudden attack, Doc had barely managed to bash her blade aside with his own in time. Then he'd danced a long-legged step back and engaged his foe with form more befitting his skills.

He'd understood what she'd said, of course. "You'd best have stayed neutral. Where shall I hit you, turkey-cock? In the side, beneath your sleeve? In the heart, beneath your blue ribbon?"

He also knew where the quote came from.

Of necessity he concentrated his attention entirely on his foe and her oddly graceful bulk. He was too skilled to narrow his focus to her point alone, or even her blade. That was a quick path to perdition. Or whatever awaited such a lost soul as he.

He realized all too well that he was practically inviting any one of the semicircle of watching sec men to back-shoot him, whether with his opponent's sanction or not.

But that's mere bagatelle, he thought. Inasmuch as my life is already forfeit, why should I concern myself with the precise manner in which it is claimed?

At least being back-shot was likely to be quicker than what awaited him should he be taken captive.

As they fenced back and forth there on the edge of the bluffs overlooking Nukem Flats and the farms and huts and manor of Joker Creek, he finished the verse.

"'Les coquilles tintent, ding-dong! Ma pointe voltige: une mouche! Décidément...c'est au bedon, qu'à la fin de l'envoi, je touche.'"

Meaning, "The sword hilts ring, ding-dong! My point flutters: a fly! Decidedly—the belly, where at the last verse's end, I strike."

At the last she smiled ruefully. She was heavier than he, and if she was a hair shorter he couldn't see. But she was as light on her feet as a ballerina. Her wrist was strong, her blade was fast, and her form was excellent. If a little showy.

"You are clearly a man of culture," she said, stepping back and saluting him, "to match me quote for quote from *Cyrano de Bergerac*."

"And you, as well," he said, "to know your Rostand in this lost age."

He didn't see fit to mention that the play had debuted in Paris just a year or two before he was time-trolled from the bosom of his family. For one thing, it would've taken too much breath to explain. And would have been as likely to distract him as his foe.

As for breath, she seemed to have it to spare. She launched

a lunging thrust for his face. From her body's motion he knew it was no feint. He parried *seconde,* turning his blade counterclockwise and up, rolling his hand on its back. He riposted, striking back at her face, which even in starlight he could see was lightly sheened with sweat.

She parried prime, counterclockwise and down, dancing back. She laughed and, stamping her right foot once again, launched an attack.

He had his opponent's measure now. He gave ground rapidly, sidestepping the rock that had sheltered him. He sensed the sec men around him, surly shadows, half seen and out of focus. He could spare them no attention. He was luring her on, inviting the baron to press her attack. She did, stamping, thrusting from low to high and high to low, her round face getting redder and redder.

As a man who knew a thing or two about the science of fisticuffs, Doc was familiar with a phenomenon called punching oneself out. It referred not to literally hitting yourself, but to attacking with such a fervent flurry that you spent all your wind and energy.

Even as she was calling him a scullery servant and inviting him to hang on tightly to his spit, she exhausted herself striking air and his singing blade.

He danced back away from a final thrust for his face. Her point stopped quivering in air a hand span from his nose. And he beat her blade down and counterattacked.

"Prince," he roared in triumphant French, "ask God's forgiveness! I lunge, point-high, I skirmish, I thrust, I feint—"

He did, stamping himself in a lunge, clashing blades briefly in a flashing exchange. He dropped his wrist to his left to attack upward from the inside low line. She parried in desperate *octave,* counterclockwise and down again.

The blades met almost too late to stop him from puncturing her right side under the short ribs.

He withdrew and stabbed for her face. Her blade whipped up clockwise into high position: *quarte* again.

But it was a feint. His point was already withdrawing. He slashed his blade around hers, struck it from inside to out.

Worn down from her flurried attacks, she had let her grip grow slack. His swift stroke knocked her sword out of her hand and sent it spinning end-for-end into the chaparral.

Her blue eyes grew huge in her flushed face, which now streamed sweat. Her nostrils flared as he placed the tip of his own sword at her throat.

Then lights exploded through his skull from a hard sudden blow at the back of it.

His sword dropped from his lifeless fingers, the cold hard earth hit his knees and brutal arms pinioned his behind him.

Chapter Twenty-One

"Ryan!"

The one-eyed man turned. He and J.B. had just emerged from the front door, Jak having slipped out first to confirm the way was clear.

It was Krysty, flying out of the deeper shadow of the big, windowless building next to the barn from which he'd sniped the Crazy Dogs' spotter. Mildred and Ricky trotted behind her.

"Where's Doc?" he asked. He could see in the glow from the house that she was unhurt.

Krysty ran up and hugged him tight. The air oomphed out of him. In times of stress she forgot her own strength.

"Taken," she said quietly.

"We got hit the second we launched the diversion," Mildred said. "They were all over us. Caught us wholly unprepared."

Ryan grunted.

Krysty pushed off and looked around.

"Are you all right?" she asked.

"We're fit to fight, yeah," Ryan said. "Got what we came for."

"Where is everybody?" Mildred asked. "I know where all the sec men are. Up there presumably dancing on poor Doc's head. But how about the mobs of peasants with torches?"

"We best move and talk," J.B. said. "Not give them a chance to form the idea, so to speak."

Ryan led them away from the Casa de Broma toward the southeast, back toward Amity Springs pretty much on a line. It meant they slogged across furrows and trampled barely sprouting crops. Ryan wasn't of the mind to care.

"Nobody's come out to see what the ruckus is about," Ryan said as Jak trotted past into the lead. "Reckon they're more prudent than curious. I wasn't exactly yearning to have to fight our way clear. Whether it was people sniping us from the shadows or the angry mob thing."

"Ho, there!" a feminine voice, brassy and bold, rang out like mythical angels' trumpets on high. *"Ryan Cawdor!"*

"Don't stop," Mildred urged as the words echoed off the cliff face. Jak called the same warning, less grammatically.

Ryan stopped. He turned and gazed back at the bluffs behind the big house. They were about a hundred yards off at this point.

On the heights just east of the baron's manor a rude dome of garish yellow light thrown by driftwood torches wavered against the black sky and banished the stars. In the middle of the glow stood the baron. Beside her stood Doc, his head thrown back defiantly, his gray-white hair wild. The squat form of Trumbo stood beside him, ostentatiously pointing a pump shotgun at the old man's skull.

"Now that I've got your attention," Sand called, "I'd wager you have a little something of mine. And it appears I have something of yours. I believe that forms the basis of a trade, wouldn't you say?"

"Do not do it, Ryan!" Doc cried.

"You shut up!" Trumbo bellowed. He whacked Doc in the kidney with the butt of his scattergun.

Doc dropped to his knees with a groan Ryan could plainly hear.

"I meant to sacrifice myself that the others could escape," Doc managed to say. "Leave me to my fate."

"I'm not making any deals," Ryan called back.

"Ryan!" Krysty exclaimed.

"What?" Baron Sand called out.

"It's just a payday, Ryan!" Mildred exclaimed.

Ryan shook his head. "We worked hard for this," he said. "And I don't negotiate with hostage-takers."

Krysty put a hand on his arm. "Ryan," she said softly. Her eyes glinted with tears.

"Don't worry, Krysty," he said.

Then up at the cliffs he shouted, "I'm calling your bluff, Baron. You keep him awhile. I don't reckon you're the sort to chill for chilling's sake. And you don't strike me the sadistic type, either."

Sand put her hands on her generous hips. "You presume much, Cawdor."

"Always."

For a moment she glowered down at him, then she seemed to deflate.

"For such short acquaintance, you know me too well. Very well. You win this round. Your friend will be safe—but he's staying here with me."

"What are you talking about?" Trumbo demanded hoarsely. "This old taint chilled some of my best men!"

Sand took a pinch of his cheek. "I pay your men handsomely to get thrown away," she said. "I pay you even more handsomely to throw them away. And also—" she released his face, leaving him rubbing his cheek as if afraid she'd left marks "—I'll thank you to watch throwing around those anti-mutant slurs. Some of my nearest and dearest might take offense."

"This isn't over, Cawdor!" Trumbo shouted down from the cliff.

"For once I agree with you," Sand said.

"You're both right," Ryan called back calmly. "It isn't."

He turned away and led his friends off into the night.

"THEY HAD TO have been warned, Ryan," Mildred said. She was up front, though as usual Jak roved out on point, invisible now in the scrub. "They were all over us like white on rice the moment I threw the firefight simulator. We never had a chance."

"We would've been overwhelmed," Krysty agreed, "if Doc hadn't told us to run while he stayed behind to hold them off."

"We should never have run away," Ricky said miserably.

Ryan frowned. He carried the metal box on his shoulder. It was heavy, and the edges dug into him uncomfortably.

Somehow he reckoned he didn't have anything to complain about.

"Sure you should," he said. "You did the right thing."

"But…but Doc's one of us!"

"And he still is, son," J.B. said. He was walking alongside his protégé. "But you heard Baron Sand say she was going to treat him right."

"And I believe she will," Ryan stated.

"Seriously, Ryan?" Mildred asked in disbelief. "You, of all people—trusting a baron?"

"Ryan trusts barons to act according to their nature," Krysty said.

"Right."

"But isn't it the nature of barons to be rapacious, sadistic and just plain evil?" Mildred demanded.

"Usually," Ryan said.

His throat rasped. He took a canteen from his hip with his free hand. Krysty promptly took it out of his hand, unscrewed the cap and handed it back. He drank deeply with a grunt of gratitude.

"It's not like I think Sand is straight," he said. "Not at all. Just don't reckon she's bent that way."

"Anyway," J.B. said, "she can always chill Doc later if she changes her mind. What? Why are you looking at me like that, Mildred?"

"Stop reassuring us," Mildred said.

"I think he means that's actually a reason to take her at her word," Krysty told her. "She always has that out in her mind. And, anyway, I agree with Ryan. I don't think Sand's a good person. But I don't see her as that kind of bad."

"Trumbo, though," Mildred said, "is bad clean through."

"Sand's got him on a tight leash," Ryan stated. "For now."

"But what happens if he decides to chew through the damn leash? What if this is the final straw?"

"Isn't that mixing metaphors?" Krysty asked.

"Got no more reason to presume it'll happen this time than any other time before," Ryan said. "Looked like that was an old familiar game for Sand and her sec boss. Anyway, I'm not talking about leaving Doc back there for a month-long vacation. We get back, get paid, take stock of the situation. Work out a plan to get the old man back."

"A better plan," J.B. suggested.

Ryan uttered a noise halfway between a grunt and a laugh. "Better be, yeah."

They walked along in silence except for the crunching of sandy soil under their boots. The breeze pushed gently at their backs.

"Anyway," Ryan said eventually, "we've got a more immediate problem, the way I see it. Dark Lady has—"

Jak suddenly materialized out of the night, standing

stock-still in front of them with a white hand upraised. He looked like a warning ghost.

"Listen," he said in a soft voice.

J.B. and Ryan exchanged looks.

"Dark Lady has trouble, is what she got," J.B. said. "That's blasterfire."

Ryan held up a hand for a halt. He could already tell J.B. had called it right.

The noise was like a woodpecker working up a far-off tree trunk. A *lot* of woodpeckers.

The lights of Amity Springs were plainly visible here. Ryan reckoned they were no more than a quarter mile from the wag yard on the west edge of the ville.

The shooting, he could tell now, came from the east.

"That's the other side of town," J.B. said, frowning in concentration. He took off his glasses and began to polish them.

Ryan thought he could see lights flash between buildings on the ville's far side. And from the flats father along, the faint flicker of incoming fire.

"What now, lover?" Krysty asked.

"We earn ourselves a nice fat bonus," Ryan said. "Come on."

RICKY RAN HUNCHED over. He clutched the fat barrel of his DeLisle with its built-in suppressor, which was slung muzzle-down across his back for quick access into firing position. He'd learned the trick from watching Ryan, to keep it from prodding his kidney painfully as he ran.

That did nothing to stop his lungs from feeling as if they were being torn out of his chest by handfuls with every gasping breath he heaved. After walking in Deathlands for months, he figured he should have been in better shape. To their south the Flats flashed and crackled and boomed like a fireworks display. From the snarling of engines there were both motorcycles and motor wags in play. Evidently the Crazy Dogs were a well-equipped gang, which they surely hadn't seen evidence of at that roadblock on their way into the Basin.

"You think…these are…the Crazy Dogs?" Ricky panted in rhythm to his slogging footsteps. They were traveling through some soft sand right now, which made it at least triple hard. Ricky hated walking in soft dust or sand. But it wasn't as if the others loved it, either, so he'd learned to stop whining about it.

"Are you stupe, kid?" demanded Ryan, still churning in the rear. "Who else would it be, the Cub Scouts?"

Ricky didn't get the reference, but the rebuke made his eyes sting almost as bad as his lungs did.

"I hope we're in time," Krysty said. She was running elbow-to-elbow with Ryan, and seemingly having no trouble with the footing at all.

"Fire's going both ways," J.B. said.

He was just moving along at his usual dog trot, as if nothing bothered him or ever would. His main concession was to hold his hat on his head with his left hand. The right held his Uzi by the pistol grip; apparently the M-4000 bouncing around on his back didn't bother him.

"Ville folks seem to be giving good as they're getting. And then some, mebbe."

Strain as he could, Ricky couldn't tell which way the fire was going by listening. All he could hear was that there was blasting—hard to miss unless you were deaf or dead.

"What's the plan?" Mildred huffed.

Ryan raised his hand for the group to slow up.

Gratefully, Ricky did. He fought the urge to bend over and just stand there sucking wind.

"Automatic fire," Mildred remarked at a sharp snarl. "These are some well-heeled coldhearts."

"Full-auto's not going all one way," J.B. said. "Ryan?"

Ryan scratched his head and surveyed the scene to the south of them. To Ricky's eyes it was confused. Mostly he saw lights moving left and right and getting brighter and fainter east of the ville, as if the machines that carried the Crazy Dogs were maneuvering. There was a stationary pool of brightness some distance away from Amity Springs.

"Wish we had something like cover here," Ryan said. "As it is, we're going to need to get closer through this scrub before we can calculate what to do. Or even whether to do anything."

"Is it really our fight?" Mildred asked.

"After that little scene in the gaudy," J.B. said, "looks like it's ours whether we want it or not. Unless we just shake the dust of this whole Basin off our boot heels."

"We'll see," Ryan said. "Follow me. Best to hunker down somewhere. It's unlikely anybody'll be looking this way, or even see much if they do. But it's triple-stupe to take extra chances with that much lead in the air."

He led them forward several hundred yards, then held up his hand in the signal to stop. Next was a signal for his companions to come up alongside him and go to ground. But not spread out.

Ricky was almost sure. The hand signals the group used for silent comms were simple and straightforward. Still, he was deathly afraid of screwing up and endangering his new family.

Holding his carbine unslung in front of him, he duck-walked forward to join the group nucleated on Ryan. The tall curly haired man had his single eye pressed to the eyepiece of his Navy longeye.

Ricky could make out the gist of what was going on. For

whatever reason the scrub petered out a couple hundred yards from the road, both to the north and south.

From Amity Springs in the west flickered the flames of a number of blasters. They were widely spaced in a ville that looked darker than usual. The shots came sparsely now, although he did see a brief burst of automatic-weapon fire. A moment later the reports hit his ears with surprising force.

That's at least a .308 there, he thought in surprise.

"I'd say our friends in Amity Springs are the ones who are surprisingly well-heeled," Krysty remarked, squatting at Ryan's side.

She had her right hand on the cool ground, her fingers splayed, as if to support herself. Ricky knew she had perfect balance; it was a gesture he'd seen her use frequently, though. As if she liked or even needed to reaffirm her connection with the Earth, to which she felt a mystic affinity.

"I seem to recall hearing something about them finding the armory for the predark lab they built on," J.B. said.

"Plus this may be where a lot of the proceeds of selling their scavvy goes," Ryan said without looking away from his target.

He seemed to have fixed on the unmoving glow east up the road from the ville. With his unaided eye Ricky could see there were a couple wags parked with their headlights on, aimed toward Amity Springs. He saw dark figures moving around the vehicles; they were smart enough to stay out of the lights.

"Why haven't the ville people shot out the headlights?" Ricky asked.

"Long shot," Mildred said.

"Likely they're just as happy for the coldhearts to keep silhouetting themselves against them," Ryan said.

A number of bikes and open-topped wags were driving between the parked wags and the ville. Counting multiple occupants in the wags, Ricky guessed there had to be at least a hundred of the coldhearts. At first he thought they were burning gas and rubber to no purpose, then he picked out the pattern.

They kept moving to make themselves harder targets. Every once in a while one or a group would make a run right at the ville. They'd open up and then turn away and scoot back from the inevitable return fire.

"What do you see, Ryan?" J.B. asked.

"The bastards are playing it cagey," he said. "But I reckon Diego isn't missing this little party. And if he's anywhere, he's there."

He passed the Navy longeye to J.B. and unslung his longblaster.

"And if I chill him," Ryan said, "could be the Crazy Dogs might have a change of heart about messing with the people of Nukem Flats, and move on in search of greener pastures."

"Seems like a long shot," Mildred said. "You're not usually guilty of wishful thinking, Ryan."

J.B. chuckled. "Nor is he now. If nothing else it'll disorganize the bastards plenty."

Ryan popped off the caps that protected the lenses at both ends of his longeye-relief Leupold scope and stashed them in a pocket. Then he raised the longblaster, turned the handle and opened the bolt just enough to confirm the chamber was loaded.

"Anything gives us an edge," he said, closing the bolt and locking it again, "I like. So here's how—"

"Ryan," Krysty said, her voice urgent and low.

She pointed toward the ville. A mixed group of bikes and wags, about half a dozen in all, had converged on a point on the road perhaps fifty yards from the town. Yet no shots were being fired at them.

Their behavior reminded Ricky, unpleasantly, of swarming wasps.

And then a single headlight, mounted on a bike like a giant staring eye, swept across a solitary female figure, walking the road toward the parked coldheart wags.

Chapter Twenty-Two

"Isn't that Lucy from the Library Lounge?" Mildred asked. She was peering through Ryan's longeye.

Kneeling, Ryan shouldered the Steyr and swung it south. "Fireblast!" he exclaimed.

It was Lucy. She still wore her finery from the Library Lounge: tight bodice and short flouncy skirt. With his scope dialed up to full power, it still didn't give triple-good detail at his range, which he estimated as 250 to 300 yards. Had it not been for the shine of the parked wags, and the headlight glow from the wags and bikes full of jeering Crazy Dogs orbiting her, he wouldn't have been able to identify Dark Lady's star entertainer.

The gaudy slut walked with head down and shoulders slumped, ignoring the jeers of the coldhearts. Her feet were bare, or perhaps in stockings, which would've been well-ruined at this point. She seemed determined to walk that road, no matter what.

A bike swerved close to her. Either its fat gas tank or the rider's knee brushed her hip. She stumbled.

"Back off, dickholes!"

Ryan swung his scope back around to focus on the parked wags. A man stood there with a microphone to his face. Ryan reckoned sound gear in one of the wags had amplified and broadcast the command in his harsh whiskey baritone. Far enough, no doubt, to be heard by the defenders in Amity Springs. If not clear to the Library Lounge.

The vehicles sheered away from the lone walking woman. They continued to dart at her, and their occupants kept jeering and shrieking obscene abuse.

"Take the shot, Ryan!" Mildred hissed. "Blast the bastard! What're you waiting for?"

"I want to see what the nuke this is all about," Ryan said. "Could be important."

He focused his scope on the man. He could make out a tall, powerful frame dressed all in black, with wide shoulders and a visible paunch lopping over the belt of his tight black pants. He had a rough-hewn handsomeness to him: a brutal long-rectangle of a face, well-busted hawk nose, and bushy black brows over squinty eyes. His mustache swept down either side of his mouth onto his jut of a chin. His hairline receded to a black brush on top; the sides and presumably the back hung to the shoulders of his black leather jacket.

"A mullet?" Mildred murmured. "Jeez, I hate that that shit came back."

He was flanked by a pair of big guys, a man with a fist of a face and a shock of brown hair, and on the far side, his left, by a bald man with an impressive reddish beard spreading over an even more imposing belly. The nearer wag was parked so that its front end obscured the lower bodies of the coldheart chieftain and his companions.

"So what's the deal, Lucy?" Diego demanded in his booming god-voice. "Or did you forget we had one?"

She had made it halfway between the outskirts and the parked wags. Turning his blaster west to look at her, Ryan was impressed with her fortitude and courage, if not her sense.

"Yes," she screamed. "We had a deal! You said nobody would get hurt!"

"We lied," Diego said. "It's just politics. You make a piss-poor omelet if you don't break the bastard eggs."

"What about my daughter! Give her back to me! You said you would if I did what you told me!"

"Well, see, there's a problem with that. She's dead. Had a bout of cholera come through. She wasn't tough enough for the Deathlands. Sorry. That's just Darwin, you know? But mebbe if you ask double nice I'll help you get started in on cooking up a new one."

"You bastard! I'll see you in Hell!" Her face twisting in rage, she began to run forward, heedless of the vehicles circling her like sharks in bloody water.

"Mebbe," Diego said, "but you'll get there first. Such a waste."

He had to have made some signal. Ryan saw something flicker from a bike that passed close behind the running Lucy. Something thin passed in front of her face, then she was yanked backward off her feet as the motorcycle wheeled and accelerated back toward Amity Springs.

A lariat, he realized.

"Right," he said, not bothering to keep his voice down for the noise. "Spread out either side of me. I'll start the show."

"What's your plan, lover?" Krysty asked, her voice curdled with rage.

"We're going to beat the bastards so hard they leave. Keep them off me, and stay alive. Jak, you guard my back."

He had taken his face away from the scope to look at the others as he gave his instructions. Jak flourished his paired leaf-bladed knives and grinned. The others slipped into position lying prone in the brush to Ryan's left and right.

"Here we go," Ryan said.

He put his eye behind the glass and lined up on Diego. He aimed for the chest. The head was too dicey a target.

It moved around too much, especially since the bastard kept turning left and right to joke with his crew. If the coldheart's arm got in the way, the jacketed 7.62 mm slug wouldn't much mind, as long as it hit a bone that would flatten it or make it tumble. And that'd just blast a bigger wound channel through his body.

Ryan breathed in deeply, let half the breath go, caught it. His finger squeezed the trigger. The Scout roared and bucked.

Even before recoil kicked the scope upward, Ryan knew he'd missed the shot. For some triple-bad luck reason the coldheart boss had leaned back, twisting his head to talk to somebody behind him even as the trigger broke.

He still followed through properly, throwing the bolt even as the carbine's rise peaked, riding the recoil and expertly bringing the longblaster and scope down to almost precisely where they'd been when he'd taken the shot.

The red-bearded bull of a man was still in the act of crumpling against the pickup truck to his left. Diego had his head turned toward him. His right arm reached to his waist, undoubtedly to draw a blaster. Much good that'd do him at this range.

Ryan fired again. This time the guard to Diego's left turned to face Ryan, bringing up a handblaster of his own. Diego was already throwing himself back. No doubt the sound of the first shot had just reached his ears. The second bullet hit the lesser Crazy Dog in the left shoulder, staggering him.

Mostly out of frustration, Ryan lined up and shot again. The brown-haired top of the man's head blew off. Behind him the red-bearded guy threw up both hands and sank out of sight. Apparently the blow-through nailed him a second time.

Of Diego there was no sign. Ryan carefully scanned the two wags. The Crazy Dogs' boss was still the ace target.

Headlights played across Ryan's face. He ignored them, as he did the sounds of engines getting louder and higher.

Around him he heard his friends begin to fire as the parked wags' lights went out.

A RAGGED SKIRMISH line of bikes and one wag rolled toward the party. Krysty held her Smith & Wesson 640 straight out in front of her in both hands, cursing the fact the snub-nosed .38 didn't have much range.

At the far left end of the line, where Ricky had taken up position beyond Mildred, a biker abruptly slid from the saddle of his machine. It veered promptly to the left, causing another to have to swerve violently to avoid being taken down by the unpiloted machine. Krysty had heard no shot from her vicinity. That meant Ricky had blasted the cold-heart with his whisper-silent carbine.

To her right J.B. reared up on his knees. He cut loose with the Uzi held by his side. He ripped off three short but brutal bursts, two to four shots—Krysty couldn't be sure.

Two bikers went down. One was enveloped immediately in a yellow flower of flame not forty yards from Ryan's firing line. The other bikers faltered and turned away from the unexpected firepower of their still-hidden opposition. A couple turned back.

"What the nuke do you think you're doing?" Krysty heard Diego roar. "Get back after them, you chicken guts! Or you'll wish you'd taken a burst in your bellies when I'm peeling off your yellow hides in inch-wide strips!"

The wag, which was stripped down to frame and roll-bar with engine exposed, kept onward. It had followed the first line of bikes by about twenty yards. A man stood beside the driver with long hair streaming, firing a small semiauto longblaster with sharp reports over the raggedly padded bar.

Suddenly the goggled driver's head lolled aside. In front of it a starred hole had appeared in the windshield. The wag slowed to a stop as the dead coldheart's foot slid off the gas pedal.

The shooter looked down in consternation. Then he howled and doubled up in response to a sharp blast from Ryan's left. Krysty realized Mildred, the crack handblaster shot, had expressed her opinion of these Crazy Dogs by shooting the rifleman squarely in the nuts.

Whipped by their leader's chilling words, the other fifteen or so riders turned and accelerated toward Ryan and the companions once more. Krysty held down on the closest and waited for the Mohawked woman leaning her goggled face low over her handlebars to get in range.

Krysty felt no more compunction about blasting a female enemy than Ryan or J.B. did. Only Ricky seemed still to hesitate. Even Doc, raised to the mores of a more courtly day, had gotten used to the bitter reality of chill or be chilled.

Krysty had heard the force of personality in Diego's voice, and, in a way, could understand how Lucy had become caught up in all of this. She realized that no one went to work on her back without being broken in some pretty basic ways.

Lucy was a lost soul, lost by Deathlands standards. She had little to rely on but her looks and wits. She knew that one was a wasting asset and the other an uncertain shield against the brute force of a face punch by a man with greater strength than her body could support. To survive for her meant cultivating a powerful will to believe—and a sense of denial.

The former had actually served her well when she hap-

pened to end up at the Library Lounge. She'd bought in to
Dark Lady's vision and found shelter and redemption. But
that very willingness coupled with denial had already betrayed Lucy, it seemed. It was clear as new ice to Krysty
that the woman had been sent as a spy into Amity Springs
not by Baron Sand, but by the force-of-nature bravo who
ruled the Crazy Dogs.

She became aware that Ryan was shooting toward the
parked wags again. He fire-aimed measured shots, trusting
his companions to shield him from the Dogs as he was lost
in the glass, as he sometimes put it. She fervently hoped
his bullets would find and chill Diego. But she doubted
they would. For all of Ryan's skill, at this point the coldheart boss held all the cards: distance, night and cover. And
clearly he had a coyote's gift of sheer survival.

The attack in front of Krysty had slowed like an old-
days vid. The angry snarl of engines rose around her as if
out of the Earth herself. The biker woman's face grew large
over the nubbed front sight of Krysty's 640. She squeezed
the trigger.

She saw blood spray out behind the hair-crested head.
The front tire turned sideways and the motorcycle somer-
saulted. The rider was flipped, limbs sprawling, end over
end through the air to land not ten feet in front of Krysty.

She winced in unwilling sympathy as the woman's
body hit. She was already seeking other targets, blasting
at roaring, moving shadows. She heard J.B.'s machine pistol
shredding the air, saw falling tangles of limbs and hair and
mechanism. Another bonfire burst to life not twenty feet
from their position, with at its core a flailing figure, pinned
under a burning motorcycle's weight, which flailed and
shrieked intolerably until a stray bullet ended the suffering.

The bikes were almost on top of them. Krysty blasted a
shaved-headed male rider in the chest, then ducked as his

riderless machine roared past. Her piece empty, she hugged the ground and reached into a pocket for a speed-loader.

She saw a rider with upraised hatchet ride down on Ryan, who still ignored the near anger for far targets with a courageous resolve that even in this heart-crushing crisis thrilled Krysty with pride. J.B., his Uzi's 30-round magazine exhausted, grabbed up his M-4000 and blasted the hatchet man, whose blaster arm exploded away from his shoulder in a black splash of blood. He shrieked and rolled through the line, steering his heavy machine with his remaining hand by sheer reflex, as the life pumped out of his body from severed arteries.

Another bike, coming at high speed from behind to join the attackers, hit a clump in the mostly flat ground off to Krysty's left and soared into the air. Its engine rose in pitch as the driving rear tire free-wheeled.

Krysty heard what she had learned to recognize as the bang of Ricky's antique Webley handblaster, which fired the same .45 slugs as his DeLisle. The flying motorcycle suddenly burst into flames.

The rider let go of the handlebars to bat at the flames as his ride flew over Ricky's ducking head, but his leather-jacketed arms were already wings of searing orange flame. The bike's front dropped before it hit ground. It slammed its several hundred pounds of metal mass right down onto the burning man before bouncing away, drawing crazy trails of firelight in the night.

Its rider didn't flop and scream the way the first man did. In Krysty's peripheral vision blasterfire flashed off to the west, toward the ville. As the distinctive sound of fully automatic weapons as well as the booms of single shots reached her ears, she realized some of the Amity Springs defenders had to be skirmishing forward to take advantage of the surprise flank attack by Ryan and the others.

She had no time to think about that, far less to confirm her flash impression. A wave of noise enveloped her. A hunchbacked, malevolent shadow grew huge, right in front of her face, which hung just above the sweet-smelling soil.

A motorcycle rushed by Krysty to the right, so close she had to roll to her left to avoid its flesh-ripping tires. It immediately slewed broadside, expertly halted by its rider as its big tires dug deep into soft soil. The Crazy Dog, grinning beneath goggles and a topknot hanging over the left side of his face, raised a sawed-off double-barrel shotgun to point at Krysty.

"You lose," he said.

But with presence of mind even Ryan couldn't better, Krysty had slammed the snub-nosed revolver's cylinder shut on a fresh load of five .38 Special cartridges even as she dodged the burly bike. From her back she held both arms out straight and blasted all five rounds into the cold-heart.

Both barrels of his scattergun vomited fire and noise, but it was at the stars. He toppled backward, mortally struck by Krysty's fusillade.

With her handblaster empty and useless again, she saw a sight that gripped her heart like a fist. Another motorcycle had skidded to a sideways stop right behind where Ryan lay, still single-mindedly focused on his sniping and completely vulnerable.

In an ecstasy of terror Krysty fumbled for a fresh reloader. The others on the firing line were still engaging the attackers. They couldn't help her doomed mate, either.

The Crazy Dog turned his bike to line up right between the prone Ryan's outstretched legs. Grinning diabolically through his beard, the shaved-headed man gunned the engine to alert his prey as to the awful fate that awaited:

having his bones and flesh pulped and ground beneath tires of seven hundred pounds of malice.

Then a slight figure with streaming white hair appeared astride the bike behind the hunched-over figure. Two hands as pale as the stars themselves crossed beneath the driver's chin. Slim shards of steel flickered outward. The biker's head snapped back in a gargling scream as blood geysered from a throat doubly severed to the neck bone.

Jak jumped lithely clear as the bike fell onto its side well behind its intended target. Its rear tire spun futilely as its former driver attempted to breathe through a clean-cut airway. The engine died away with no hand on its throttle.

Down on the road the nearer of the parked wags suddenly blew up in a yellow ball. Ryan had pierced its gas tank and then managed to light the spilled fuel fumes.

But the pickup was already peeling away into the darkness. "Pull out, boys and girls," Diego shouted into the night. "We'll let these ville rats and their shitbag mercies broil in their own fear of when we'll come back to pay them off—and where!"

Ryan was up on his knees, cursing. He had just fired his current 10-round detachable mag dry. As fast as he could reload the Scout, there was no chance of getting another shot off before night and distance swallowed the biker chieftain.

"Well," Mildred said, standing.

Five feet from her a figure lying on its face in the grass started to rise, a cowboy-style six-shooter in a fingerless-gloved hand. Barely looking, the stocky black woman shot the Crazy Dog in the head.

"I guess that means we're off his Christmas list."

"We wish," Ryan growled.

Chapter Twenty-Three

"Poor Lucy," Dark Lady said. She had her head down with her black bangs hanging in front of a face that looked paler than usual in the turned-down lamplight of her office. Behind her Mikey-Bob loomed outside the lamp glow like a shadow colossus.

The Great Whatsit in its box had been duly delivered and paid for. Dark Lady proved as good as her word. For all his mistrust of barons—which Dark Lady was to his mind, regardless of what she or the Amity Springers might say—he wasn't surprised.

Neither Ryan nor J.B., who had naturally stopped on the way back to Amity Springs to pick the box's lock and peer inside, had the remotest clue what the Whatsit or its nature might be. Ryan's rad counter showed it was only slightly hotter than background, which settled their only practical concern.

And *practical* was commonly all Ryan concerned himself with.

"She betrayed you," Mildred said. "Why waste your tears?"

The giant rumbled deep in his outsize chest. Ryan wasn't sure which head was responsible. Both, likely enough.

"I long suspected she was spying for Sand," she said. "I never could have imagined she was also working for the Crazy Dogs."

She raised her head to look at Mildred, calm despite the tear trails glimmering on her cheeks.

"I care about my people," she said. "Because the rivalry between myself and Baron Sand has not descended to killing—so far—I believed that her spy's motivation, whoever he or she might be, would be non-malicious. But to learn that she also served Diego—and the reason why…it breaks my heart."

"But how do you know Sand and Diego weren't together on this spying thing?" Mildred asked.

"Aside from the fact she offered to pay us to chill Dogs?" Ryan asked. "Plus paid us when we did?"

Dark Lady was shaking her head.

"For all her flaws," she said, "Sand would never be in league with the likes of the Crazy Dogs."

"You seem unusually charitable toward your main rival," Krysty said.

"I stand for truth," Dark Lady said. "I strive to be honest, with myself or others, which is one way Baron Sand and I differ."

"She does seem to have a double-loose notion of where other people's stuff ends and hers begins," Ryan said.

With visible effort the gaudy owner pulled herself together.

"Right now I'm more concerned at the risks Jim Sinclair led the others into," she said. "He was a fool to risk leaving the cover of the ville and going out in the open against a mobile foe. If the Crazy Dogs had rallied, he and the rest would have been cut to pieces."

"That little move did help save our asses," Ryan reminded her. "Just as we helped save yours."

He couldn't help recalling Mildred's misgivings about the wag yard owner, though. Sure, he helped them then.

But he was no supporter of Dark Lady's. Might he be playing a double game, too?

Dark Lady sighed. "Much as I have grown to admire you and your companions, Mr. Cawdor," she said, "I must admit my overwhelming imperative is to protect Amity Springs and its people. Not you and yours."

Ryan laughed. "Understood," he said. "I do the same sort of arithmetic. I throw that little reminder in for free."

"That's triple generous of you, mercie," growled Mikey.

"Don't mind him," his brother said wearily. "He's just bitched because Lucy got chilled."

"She was one of us," the black-haired head said sullenly. "She always treated us decent. Instead of as some two-headed monster."

"We *are* a two-headed monster, dimwit. In the end she sold out Dark Lady. And that means all of us."

"She didn't realize the full import of what she was doing," Mikey said. "Anyway, she didn't have much choice."

"There's always a choice," Bob said, starting to heat up.

Dark Lady held up a slender hand. It looked so frail and tiny against the shadowed bulk of her helper and friend— and whatever else. But both heads immediately shut up.

"The other people may need to be reassured after all that's gone on," she said. "Go and make sure they're all right, won't you, Mikey-Bob?"

The giant sighed volcanically through both throats. "Of course, Dark Lady," Bob said.

As Mikey-Bob lumbered past, she grabbed his left hand with her right and squeezed it briefly. He paused a step and then went out, with Mikey sweeping Ryan and his band with a final resentful glare.

"What I'm wondering," Mildred said when the door shut, "is how Lucy was able to get to Joker Creek to tell Sand we were coming, then get back here so fast."

"No mystery there," Dark Lady said. "Sand used a system I myself use—and may have taught her. Thinking about it, Diego may also have employed the same technique."

"How do you mean?" Ryan asked.

"People come and go freely from Amity Springs," Dark Lady said, "as you have seen. People regularly travel between Joker Creek and here. Sand makes no effort to stop such traffic, any more than I do. Trade between the villes benefits us all, which she may not like but accepts.

"People carry messages to and fro all the time. Lucy probably found someone headed that way and gave them a letter for someone in Sand's domain. That person would have been instructed to pass the message along to the baron."

"You mean you have other spies here?" Mildred asked in alarm.

Dark Lady smiled. "No doubt we do," she said. "But that's supposition. This system requires no collusion between the intermediaries and the opposition. Lucy's messenger need have no idea what he or she carried, nor its import. And when instructions or other communications came back for her, they would be delivered to a third party on whom Lucy would call to pick them up."

"Again, you seem very trusting."

"Not at all. It's simple security. The fewer people who know a secret, the likelier it is to stay secret."

"She's got you there, Mildred," Ryan said.

"Perhaps the time has come," J.B. said, stirring in his chair, "to talk about compensation for those Dogs we put down."

"I shall pay on the terms agreed, and gladly," Dark Lady said. "I don't believe in binding the mouths of the kine that tread the grain."

"First Corinthians 9:9?" Mildred said in obvious surprise. "You know the New Testament?"

Ryan remembered she was a preacher's daughter in her prior life.

Dark Lady smiled wanly and waved a hand at the book-filled shelves that surrounded her.

"If I get my hands on it," she said, "I read it."

"Read *all* books?" Jak asked in something like awe.

"Not all books," she said. "But most of what I have, yes."

"That's what he meant," Mildred said. "All these. Got a stingy way with demonstratives, the boy does. Pronouns, too."

"Mikey-Bob will provide you your reward," Dark Lady said. "You did substantial hurt to our foes. So what will they do now, in your professional estimation?"

"Maybe we hurt them bad enough that they'll look for easier hunting grounds," Mildred suggested.

Ryan snorted. "Dream on. I reckon we hurt them just bad enough they're pissed off way past nuke red. They'll come back and come harder. Triple sure.

"But Diego's no stupe. He won't try again until he's got a better plan. We bought you some time. No more."

Dark Lady nodded. Then she leaned back in her chair and eyed them appraisingly.

"What are your intentions? Will you be leaving us, now that you've fulfilled the mission I originally hired you for? No one could fault you for fleeing the wrath to come."

J.B. glanced at Ryan. "Baron Sand still has Doc," the Armorer said. "Isn't our way to leave a man behind. Nor woman."

"You could go elsewhere to plan your rescue of your associate. Even leaving the Basin proper might lessen your danger."

Ryan shrugged. "I don't think Diego's a dog ready to let

go of a bone just because it gets moved a little farther away. These are mobile coldhearts, as you yourself pointed out.

"And anyway, as long as you're willing to pay for Crazy Dog scalps, that's sweetening the pie. Mebbe Sand'll pay for them, too, come to that."

Mildred turned her head to look at him in surprise. "Why would she honor that deal, after what we just did to her? It wasn't just the Dogs we laid the wood to tonight."

"Just like before," Ryan said. "Different business. And business is business."

"She may indeed agree," Dark Lady said. "Sand has her own code, and its core is as inflexible as its outer extremities are flexible. Plus she loves the game for its own sake. She may well choose to honor that agreement because it's separate."

She shook her head and frowned disapprovingly. "Or on her whim. She hates being bound by sense and reason as passionately as any other rules."

Ryan stood.

"If your kitchen's still open, we need to get some chow," he said. "Or else our rumbling bellies'll keep the whole house awake all night. And then mebbe get cleaned up so we don't soil those nice clean sheets of yours."

"Absolutely!" Krysty said. Mildred nodded eager agreement.

Ryan grinned.

Chapter Twenty-Four

"Who are these people?" the ice-blond woman asked as Mikey-Bob ushered Krysty, Ryan and Mildred into Dark Lady's office.

The kids, as Mildred couldn't help thinking of best-buds Ricky and Jak even though Jak was a chronological adult even by the standards of her day, were out prowling the ville on this bright morning after their night's adventures. This was the sort of thing that at best would bore them. And at worst, their volatility couldn't help.

The Mikey head seemed more sullen than usual, Mildred thought. Bob looked pensive.

"They're my new sec consultants."

It was a cool day. Dark Lady wore a black turtleneck over black jeans. Mildred wondered if she had any other colors in her wardrobe.

"Your prices are excessive," the blonde in the blue tunic declared. She had dismissed the newcomers with a brief look. She had a haughty supermodel look, with prominent cheekbones, a straight nose and blue eyes. Mildred tried not to hate her for her looks alone. That was racist.

I need to concentrate on hating her for her attitude, she told herself. *Not that that should be hard to do.*

"What Mistress Devere means, Dark Lady," said the man at her side, "is, don't you think you could bring your asking price down slightly? Inasmuch as we are long-time loyal customers."

He was shorter, older, and clearly didn't spend near so much time keeping himself in shape as the woman did. He had a homely, saggy, middle-aged face with a wart on his prominent nose. His graying brown hair was cut as if around the rim of the bowl, with a bald spot on top. It put Mildred in mind of the popular conception of medieval monks and their tonsures. The fact he wore a baggy brown smock that hung down to the thighs of his tan pants did nothing to dispel the resemblance.

"You are certainly free to seek elsewhere," said Dark Lady. Her voice was calm and conversational, but her black eyes were fixed tight on the other woman's ice sculpture of a face. "Just as we have other parties who are eager to purchase our wares."

The woman flashed her eyes in what was clearly not meant to be a friendly, reassuring gesture. Her nostrils flared.

"Now, now," the man said, patting air toward Dark Lady with his hands. "I'm sure we can work something out."

"Indeed we can, Mr. Lowenstein. You can agree to meet my price. Or you can return to the barroom below and enjoy a refreshing beverage. On the house."

"Um," Lowenstein said. He wouldn't look at his mistress, which was just as well, because she was giving him a bug-shriveling look, as if she were the sun through a magnifying glass.

"Are you whitecoats, then?" Krysty asked. She crossed her long legs.

Ryan gave her a sidelong eyebrow-raised look. Usually she was the tactful one. But her major antipathy toward whitecoats sometimes cramped that.

Lowenstein's eyes got wide. "No, no, no!" he said, wagging his hands in horror.

"We are representatives of a research facility," Devere

said, enunciating each syllable in an overly crisp way. She actually talked like a not double-good speech synthesizer. "Nothing more."

"I'm sure you are," Krysty replied, smiling sweetly.

Dark Lady dropped her curved fingers and thumb on the hardwood desktop in front of her with a precise rap.

"Have you made your decision?" she asked.

Devere looked blazing blue death at Dark Lady. Unlike Lowenstein, the gaudy owner declined to shrivel.

"Yes," the blonde said, as if the word were being torqued out of her with a pair of pliers. "But you may expect us to explore…alternate arrangements."

"Good luck with that," Mildred said. And gave the anticipated Death Look a big toothy smile.

"YOU ARE A man of parts, Doctor Theophilus Tanner," Baron Sand said. Then she purred like a big cat adding, "Some of which are astonishingly durable for a man of your age."

Doc lay with his weary head supported by a soft feather pillow on Baron Sand's enormous canopied bed. The baron lay beside him on top of the pale-green satin coverlet with her bare pink rump in the air. The room smelled of sex, lilacs and cigar smoke.

"I suspect you might find me surprising in other ways, as well," he said.

It was the second day of his captivity, which was shaping up in an extraordinarily unexpected way.

"You know so much history," she said, shaking her head. "It's almost as if you lived through it."

"Indeed," Doc said with an indulgent chuckle. "I have been on intimate terms with much of it. And I have taught history here and there to so many students."

"I wish I knew more," she said, clasping her knees and

resting her cheek on them. It made her look like nothing so much as a schoolgirl. Albeit a more naked schoolgirl than Doc would have expected to encounter in his original lifetime—he scarcely counted the times he'd helped Emily bathe Rachel.

My poor lost loves, he thought, overcome by sudden desolation. How fresh those wounds still feel.

But Sand was lost in herself once more. "I try. I can't even recall whether the Battle of Waterloo was in 1814 or 1914. Well, I don't have the resources my beloved enemy Dark Lady does. And knowing that sort of thing is her job."

That flicked him out of his sad reverie.

"What do you mean?" he said, raising his head. "My impression was most distinctly that she was what an associate of mine rather inelegantly described as a 'flesh-peddler.'"

"Here, now." She tut-tutted and pressed a fingertip to his lips. "That's neither fair nor strictly accurate. To be sure, she provides the opportunity for her people to pay for their keep through selling that which my children give away purely for love. Whereas I provide for them by, for example, certain *exactions* upon travelers through my realm. Especially those with overdeveloped senses of credulity, or underdeveloped senses of the odds. But she doesn't *peddle* anybody. Any more than she'd peddle her own tight and narrow fanny."

"You paint her as quite the innocent."

"That's precisely the word. I like you, Doc. You know things."

He smiled. "It seems as if you draw an elusive distinction between what she does and flesh-peddling," he said. "But, back to the question of her real occupation—"

"Ah, but see, that's more of a sideline for her. What she's really about is both gathering and disseminating knowledge. It's what she was trained for, you might say. In a most boringly rigorous fashion. Among other things."

She lay back down on the bed and smiled at the round heavy rafters. "I could do you stories that would curl your hair," she said. "For example—"

A ham-fisted knock sounded from the door.

"Go away!" she sang out sweetly.

"It's Trumbo, Baron."

"I know. Trumbo, my sec boss. Whom I left explicit instructions I was not to be disturbed except in case of alien invasion or unless the funhouse was on fire. And I don't smell smoke."

"There's someone here to see you."

"Tell them to go away. Tell them to come back during my next open office hours, which if I recall occur next Tuesday—the twelfth of never."

"Double funny," the sec boss growled. "It's them."

Sand sighed. "Why didn't you say so?"

She sat up. Her breasts were so small they scarcely bounced, their tips almost covered by areoles surprisingly wide and dark brown, given her fair coloration. Doc had found little to complain about with them, though.

"I'll be there in half a mo," she said. Then she balled her hands into fists and slammed them down on the bed. *"Bother."*

She looked at Doc. "So you still won't extend your parole, dearest Doc?"

He shook his head. "I fear I cannot, madam. I have stretched the elasticity of my conscience and my duty to my friends as far as it will reach by agreeing not to attempt to escape while directly in your presence, nor to harm you in any way, nor attempt to use you as a hostage or otherwise to secure my liberty."

"And I'm so glad you did," she purred. "Admit it. You are, too, you randy old goat!"

"Well, I admit that I have found the results of those concessions amply gratifying. But not so much I can vouchsafe more."

"You're no fun."

"You said otherwise, not so very long ago."

She chuckled, then hopped up from the bed with surprising alacrity in one so large. Though she was far from slender, he had learned she was not so much fat as large, which among other things concealed a surprising bodily strength.

I shall have bruises for a week as it is, he thought. Not without a certain smugness.

She dressed quickly in white linen and a blue-velvet shirt and breeches. He stirred himself and retrieved his long johns from where they were thrown on a chest of drawers and pulled them on up his naked bony shanks.

"I'll have to secure you, then, you know," she said. She knelt beside the bed and pulled open a drawer built into the massive frame. It clanked when she rummaged inside it.

A moment later she came up with a large iron shackle lined with fine black-and-silver fur on the inside, to avoid chafing the limbs of a captive. She turned and affixed the non-shackle end of the chain to the corner of the bed nearest the door.

"There," she said, sitting back on her heels. "You'll be able to reach the door but no farther."

He didn't ask her how she knew. He was quite certain that she did.

"Be a love and bring your ankle over here, Doc."

Obedient to the limited parole he had eventually given her, he did. At this point he saw no point in trying to resist or make a break for it anyway. Trumbo and his giant shadow Lobo had beefed up security considerably after the other night's raid. He had to bide his time in any event.

There was no reason he could see not to enjoy his captivity as much as possible. He was morally certain his friends were scheming feverishly as to how to get him back. Though he himself could see no practical means of doing so.

But then, he wasn't the cunning one in the group, nor the tactician. He felt quite confident leaving those roles to Ryan and the taciturn but exceedingly competent J. B. Dix.

The cuff felt like a sweet embrace as she clicked it home around a pink-and-white ankle and locked it.

"These are truly lined with mink?" he said.

"Yep." She stood and kissed his nose. She didn't have to stretch on tiptoe to do it, nor even raise her face. "They grow wild in what used to be Oregon. There's quite a lucrative trade in trapping them for their pelts."

"Indeed."

"Be good," she said with a twinkle. "But only until I get back."

She was gone. The door closed with authority. Baron Sand was a woman who did little by half measure. Least of all live that way.

Doc took in a deep breath, then, putting his hands on his thighs, he rose and made his way to the door.

He paused; pressed his ear against it. He heard nothing, which he found reassuring, if only mildly so. If the baron caught him eavesdropping, she was likely to regard it as a sign of spirit; the woman had a love of mischief for its own sake, and that was a fact. But he felt less sanguine about the prospect of opening the door to find himself staring into the brutish face of Trumbo as its habitual sullenness turned to sadistic glee.

Ah, well, Theophilus, old man, he told himself. Nothing

is more certain in this world than that we shall one day leave it. Though my efforts in that direction have admittedly thus far come to naught.... He turned the knob and pushed the door open two finger-breadths.

He saw nothing but a slice of the corridor, whitewashed walls dim in the afternoon. But he could clearly hear voices from the main salon. And that was his goal.

"Mistress Devere means," a masculine voice said, oozing obsequiousness, "is that the time has come for you to take decisive action, Baron."

"We are out of patience," said a female voice like icicles snapping. "The time has come when you must act. Or we shall."

Doc Tanner raised a brow. And who, or what, dares speak thus to Baron Sand in the heart of her very stronghold?

He already knew the answer would portend little good— for himself or his friends.

Chapter Twenty-Five

Ryan sat against the back wall of the big barroom of the Library Lounge. He ignored the setting, which was lazy with midafternoon, and even his companions, who sat around the table murmuring among themselves. The head he rested against the wood paneling was filled with storms and darkness.

Two days, he thought, and we're still no closer to calculating a way to get Doc back.

"Well," said Ricky, crossing his arms on the table and resting his chin on them. "At least the Crazy Dogs haven't made a play for us yet."

J.B. took off his glasses and polished them with a handkerchief not only laundered but pressed by Dark Lady's employees.

"Reckon that's a worse sign than a good one," he said. "Means they're up to something."

"If only we were," Mildred stated.

"Now, Mildred," Krysty said sharply, "you know that's unfair."

"I'm sorry! I didn't mean to criticize. It's just— I feel so frustrated. And this feeling of helplessness…"

"Tell me about it," Ryan growled. It was something he had little familiarity with. He wasn't enjoying getting to know it better.

The problem was that the Casa de Broma was a pretty fair little fort. And even if Trumbo's large and well-armed sec force hadn't managed to keep them from stealing back the Great Whatsit, they wouldn't be caught with their pants around their ankles a second time.

And reports from people traveling between the two villes indicated the population of Joker Creek was on the alert, too. However popular the baron was, her subjects seemed determined not to let intruders impose on them again.

Leaving aside their employer's squeamishness, Ryan wasn't the kind of man to try blasting his way through a load of civilians even to *get* to sec men hunkered down behind bulletproof walls. It would eat up a power of bullets, for one thing. And no matter how badly outmatched the sodbusters were by his seasoned crew of chillers, there was always the drunkard's chance of a stray round taking one of them out. Even Krysty.

So Ryan, if not content, had consented to bide his time and scheme. He was at least slightly soothed by Dark Lady's assurances that Sand was unlikely to harm Doc, nor allow harm to come to him. Not without provocation.

Mebbe he wasn't as calmed by all that as his companions were. But he had to admit Dark Lady's assessment of the blonde, anomalously self-named lady Baron dovetailed his pretty neatly.

"Why not drink?" Jak said. He was especially bored and disaffected. Inaction galled him like a pebble in his shoe. He'd tired, at least for the moment, of exploring Amity Springs. And Ryan had strongly forbidden him to venture past the outskirts without permission.

"You know, Jak," Krysty said.

She shot a worried look at Ryan. She knew he was worn down until the nerves stuck out of his skin like invisible porcupine quills. Even if the others didn't see it. He hoped.

The door opened. Always alert, Ryan flicked his eye that way.

Then it went wide. He stood and stepped out from behind the table, reaching for his SIG handblaster.

"Good afternoon," Baron Sand said, sweeping in as grandly as if she owned the gaudy. "I trust everyone's having a good time."

"I am now," Ryan rasped. "I didn't reckon on you making it so easy."

"Blasters down, boys."

Ryan froze as a voice cracked out of the stairway like a whip.

"And girls," Dark Lady added. She stopped a few steps from the bottom of the stairs.

"Don't make me use this," Mikey rumbled from behind the bar, where an eye blink before he had been lazily washing glasses.

Ryan only needed to flick his eye that way to see what it was the two-headed giant was aiming at him and his friends. A giant-ass SPAS 12-gauge battle shotgun, as it happened.

"I was starting to sorta like you folks," Bob said in a tone less menacing, if not exactly friendly.

"But not enough to lose sleep over," his twin added.

"What's going on?" Ryan asked Dark Lady.

She had put on her finery for the evening: off-the-shoulder black dress with its skirt puffed out by petticoats, also black-and-white-striped knee socks, tall lace-up boots with high but blocky heels and little skulls and crossbones picked out on the toes in either steel studs or fake gemstones. And a blaster, still black, in either fingerless-gloved hand. Not hidies, either; a matched set of CZ-75s or some license-built version.

Over her shoulder Ruby aimed a lever-action carbine

from a couple steps upstream of her employer. The entertainer had a low-cut bodice and a look on her lovely coffee-with-cream face that said loudly to Ryan that she was gut frightened.

Of the situation. But not to shoot.

"The bitch betrayed us!" Mildred yelled.

"Wait!" Ryan shouted. He knew Dark Lady had a few raw spots, and calling her a name like that dug a dirty thumbnail straight into one.

"Everybody calm right the fuck down and let her have her say," he said in a voice that even to him sounded as if it came out of a throatful of ground glass. "It's not like we've got anything to lose from that."

"*Thank* you," Dark Lady said tautly. She took a deep breath and visibly composed herself. "Nothing has changed, including my absolute policy that guests of this house are sacrosanct."

"What about those Crazy Dogs you chilled?" Mildred demanded.

"They broke D.L.'s absolute policy," Bob said.

"You don't threaten the lady in her own house," Mikey growled. "Not and live."

Sand was standing alone in the middle of the sawdust scattered on the floor for the evening not ten minutes before. Even her two sec men hung back. It seemed to Ryan she wasn't failing to enjoy being the cause of so much strife.

"Really," she said, pulling off a long black glove. "Such melodrama."

"Don't press your luck," Dark Lady said.

The baron smiled. She wore a man's suit of what looked like purple crushed velvet, with a lilac-colored shirt beneath. She also wore Lobo, her sec boss Trumbo's giant shadow, and a second sec man on invisible leashes two steps behind her—flanking the now-closed door.

"What do you want?"

"A cool, refreshing beverage would be nice," Sand said. "A mug of your fine dark that Ms. Chavez brews up for you. Cider for my men—the non-hard variety."

Lobo's blunt Indian face showed no more response than the statue he resembled. His partner, a wiry Mex-looking guy, medium height, made a small sound of disappointment.

"And drinks for the house on me," Sand finished with a grand sweep of her arm.

"No one count on a second round," Dark Lady said. "The baron won't be tarrying."

"Stand down," Ryan said to his companions. He didn't take his eye off the baron, though he kept his focus soft, so that if either of her chillers made a move, it'd register. He had no more attention to pay to the blasters aimed at him and his people. If they even still were.

"Seems like you're taking an almighty chance marching in here like this," J.B. said.

"Why, Mr. Dix? Don't you think I know Dark Lady well, her qualms and her curiously archaic sense of honor? Not so much different from my own, I grant, but where hers is arbitrary, mine's capricious."

She pulled off the other glove. "Also, as a practical matter, and just in case you chose—or choose—to disregard your employer's clear wishes, please let me remind you we have a hostage."

"What have you done with Doc?" Ricky asked.

She smiled. She walked up to the boy and briefly caressed his cheek. He held his ground, though it visibly cost him effort.

"Treating him better than would be suitable for you to know," she purred. "See, D.L.? I do have *some* scruples."

"Say your piece," Dark Lady said.

"Well, as I was saying," the larger, paler woman said, stepping back out of the kill-zone of the leveled blasters, "we do have your Doc Tanner in hand, back at my Casa de Broma. A truly lovely man, really. He is, as I intimated, well. Doing well indeed. Still—"

She shrugged.

"As I suspect, my narrow-bottomed dear rival here has assured you, wanton cruelty is not my style. I dislike inflicting pain. Unless it's strictly necessary. Or—for pleasure, but granted that tends to different, in degree if not in kind.

"However, my sec boss—these gentlemen's superior, Trumbo—feels quite differently. Especially in regard to your friend, inasmuch as you and he chilled several of his men during your nocturnal visit to my home."

"You don't sound too broken up about it," Mildred said.

Sand shrugged. "Trumbo and his men are hirelings," she said. "I hire them to do things like die so that I and my retinue don't have to. It's a dirty job, and they are handsomely paid to do it."

Wanda June, a short, nervous redhead with disproportionately large breasts pushing out and weighing down the front of her filmy red top, came from behind the counter carrying a tray with the drinks for Sand and her guards.

Sand picked hers up and drank deeply. "Ah," she said, wiping her mouth with the back of her hand. "My compliments to Leticia. An excellent batch."

Behind her, the door opened. The smaller guard spun to face it. Lobo just stood with his leg-size arms crossed over his keg-size chest.

Blinking and disheveled, Coffin the coffin-maker shambled into the gaudy. He stopped just inside. Then shaking his wild-haired head and muttering, he stepped the rest of the way in and closed the door.

Sand gestured imperiously. The smaller sec man stepped

back. He continued to give the shabbily dressed carpenter the fish eye.

"Isn't it a little early for the usual, Mr. Coffin?" asked Dark Lady. She still held the blasters. But now their muzzles were pointed upward with her fingers off the triggers and outside the guards.

"Well, I saw the way the wind was blowing," he said. "And I come in looking to see if, you know, my services are needed."

He brightened and dug into his pocket. The smaller sec man started to reach for his holstered sidearm.

Coffin's hand came out clutching his ragged cloth tape. "I was all ready to measure folks, and everything."

"You seem disappointed at not having had any custom drummed up for you, Mr. Coffin," Sand said.

"Well, you know. Not wishing harm on anybody here or anything—well, you know, business is business."

"Indeed," Sand said. She turned back to Ryan. "And just to confirm what you and your colorful and handsome associates have doubtless figured out, given how astute and quick-witted you have shown yourselves to be, if I do not return, safe and sound, by sunset, I am afraid Trumbo will mishandle poor Doc quite severely. And I hope that you will believe me when I say I want that no more than you do."

"Ace," Ryan said. He held his hands out to his sides. "We won't make a play. Not now."

"You needn't belabor the obvious, you lovely curly wolf," Sand murmured. "And, Mr. Coffin, I have news that might cheer you. If only you, perhaps."

He had shuffled up to the bar as if nothing was out of the way at all. Mikey-Bob stood behind it with his right hand holding the beefy Franchi scattergun pointed upward by the pistol grip, as if it were no more than a pistol. Once there, Coffin put a loose-soled shoe on the brass rail and turned an inquisitive whiskery look back.

"You might want—as soon as you finish your drink—my treat—to scurry back to your shop and get to work. Because come tomorrow, should matters not proceed as I desire, you may well have more customers than you readily know what to do with."

"What do you mean, ma'am? Sir? Uh, Baron?"

"Simply this." She turned a bright, beaming smile back on Dark Lady. "If you do not accept my offer to purchase your entire ville, tonight—now would of course be preferable—at the crack of dawn tomorrow I shall destroy it."

"You wouldn't!" Dark Lady said.

"Oh, no?" The baron showed white and even teeth. For no particular reason Ryan suspected they were triple-clean dentures. "Look into my eyes, my love. Do you really think I'm bluffing."

For a moment Dark Lady's eyes bored into her like black lasers. Then the gaudy owner dropped her gaze.

"Damn," Mildred said under her breath.

"Just as a matter of professional interest, Baron," J.B. said, "how precisely do you mean to go about doing that?"

"That would be telling." She struck a girlish pose, chin down, finger alongside nose.

"I will point out that *all* of the interesting scavvy from the days before the Megacull is not necessarily lying beneath our little pink toesies as we stand here exchanging witty repartee."

She pulled on her gloves with crisp, practiced ease. "I shall await your reply at my funhouse, my dear girl. And you know what silence shall mean."

She gestured with a forefinger at Mikey-Bob. "Remember those drinks for the house, boys. Just put them on my tab."

Chapter Twenty-Six

Heart in his throat, longblaster gripped tightly in both hands, Ricky Morales faced the predawn flatlands.

Somewhere out there in the dark and lonely, a bird whistled a long, plaintive call.

Ricky and his companions stood with Dark Lady and a dozen or so of the ville's defenders behind a barricade across the east-west road, improvised out of two wags loaded with crates and barrels. It was a cool morning—night still, so far as Ricky was concerned, at least until he saw the sun or any way a lightening in the sky. Dark Lady wore a black turtleneck sweater over black jeans, which emphasized her trim figure in a way that would've distracted Ricky more if his heart weren't in his throat.

If their employer knew what to expect, she showed no sign. And if Ryan had any speculations, he wasn't letting on.

"Sun's coming up," said Wyatt, a young employee of Sinclair's wag lot, which lay beyond the barricade and to the left.

Ricky glanced back. The sky above the Deadfall Mountains had begun to lighten.

"Well, the baron's ultimatum just ran out," Mildred said, as if anybody had forgotten it.

"It doesn't matter," Dark Lady said tightly.

"Dark Lady—" Sinclair said. He wore a sheepskin jacket, which even the tropical boy Ricky thought was a bit of overkill, and held a big black Browning automatic rifle in his hands. Ricky was totally envious of the BAR, but he thought the wag yard owner would not look too kindly if he asked to fondle it. Especially not now.

Standing next to Ricky, Jak cocked his white-haired head to one side. "Hear something," he said.

A heartbeat or two later, Ricky heard it, too: a rumbling growl that seemed to rise like a slow tide all around them. He had no idea which direction it was coming from.

"See something moving out there," Ryan reported. "Something big."

Ricky aimed the DeLisle over the crates weighting down the wag bed. It was mostly to reassure himself. While in the dark he didn't have double good depth perception, he already sort of understood that as far as his eyes could resolve anything, it was out of range for the thrown-baseball trajectory you got from a .45 handblaster round, even fired through a carbine barrel. Then he saw it: a vast humped shadow, seeming to materialize almost atom by atom from the dark ominous air into the scrub. It was unquestionably approaching the ville. But his mind couldn't quite make sense of the vague form.

"Oh, are we screwed!" Mildred exclaimed.

"Looks like that's on the agenda, all right," J.B. drawled.

"WHEN IS THE sun coming up?" Mystery asked sullenly, turning back from the front window and letting the chintz curtains fall back over. The wispy hanger-on's round cheeks were brushed with early beard growth too delicate to call stubble.

"Still an hour yet," Baron Sand said. She sat as if lounging in her grand chair among all the swatches and sweep of fabric and the scattered cushions, with a steaming blue mug of real coffee in her hand. But perched less than comfortably on a chair beside Sand's throne, Doc could tell she was anything but at ease.

"So why did you roust us all out so early?" Mystery whined.

"Because I want to be ready in case a messenger comes from Amity Springs," Sand said. She lolled her head around to look at Trumbo.

"Nothing yet, I take it?" Sand asked for the fifth time.

Trumbo shook his head. "Still no word," he said. "You'll be the first to know."

Doc's sense of honor restrained him from taking any action. Not that such was readily available. Not unless it was to throw his life away to the baron's brutal sec boss and his men. And little as Doc Tanner might value his own life, he could not do that to his companions.

They valued his life, paradoxically, far more than he. And he valued them.

So I will continue to sleep on kindling and lick gall, as our Japanese brethren say, he thought, and bide my time until opportunity presents itself to take meaningful action.

And if such action involves meaningful sacrifice—so much the better.

"You really think she's gonna go for it, Mistress?" Trumbo asked, rubbing his jowls.

He stood by the side door that led eventually to the kitchen and the back door of the big, thick-walled house. His gigantic lieutenant, Lobo, loomed silent as always beside him, partially obscuring a gigantic painting on black velvet of a voluptuous nude raven-haired woman kneeling, apparently supplicating a gigantic, muscular demon with extravagant horns. Despite the lurid palette—Doc had long since overcome, or had burned out of him, his Victorian revulsion for such subject matter—and naïve presentation, it had been executed with a certain undeniable skill.

Pursing her lips dubiously, Baron Sand slowly shook her head. "It depends in large part on whether she thinks I'm bluffing," she said. "Which, admittedly, I've been known to do."

"The Dark Lady seems to be of a nature but little inclined to accommodate threats," Doc said.

He saw no harm in candor, since he doubted he was telling the baron anything she didn't know about her rival in Amity Springs. During his captivity it had become blindingly apparent the two women had a history stretching back years. Apparently long before either had assumed her current role, or even come to the Basin.

"And that's the root of the problem," Sand said with a wry little shrug. "She's the sort to burn in her house with those beloved books of hers before she'd give in. She's always been a bitter-ender—unwilling to trim her sails to even the most drastic shift in the wind."

A blowsy blonde named Arabelle and a spindly mutie with a crest of yellow feathers in lieu of hair sat side by side on a bench by the other window. He rejoiced in the unlikely name of Ike, Doc knew.

Now Arabelle glanced at the grandfather clock standing by the wall across the room from the dining room door.

"It's five o'clock," she said.

Sand produced a noise: half growl, half groan. "Well, at the very least the little minx is determined to see my hand."

She tossed her short hair back defiantly. "So be it!"

"Shall I fire up Old Snort?" Trumbo said with unconcealed eagerness. He ran his tongue over his wide, coarse lips. His murky gray-brown eyes showed what Doc deemed an unholy gleam.

Sand nodded. "Get your team and go," she said.

"So we get to crush the bitch at last?"

She rounded on him with fury in her pale green eyes.

"Don't ever call her that! Or if you do, call it to her face, which will be the last thing you see. No. Make a show of it. Let her see what we hold over her head."

"And when she says no," Trumbo said, "then we smash the ville, right?"

"No." Sand's head sank into her double chin in a defeated slump. "Then we look for—something else. Because it is a bluff, in the end. I'm bad to the bone. But not bad in that way."

"The whitecoats won't like that," Trumbo said.

Sand laughed with a wild bitter skirl. "Nuke them. They have to deal with one of us, Dark Lady or me. They'll find I am the easier to deal with. But I don't have round heels when it comes to intimidation, any more than that sexually repressed little ferret Dark Lady does!"

"Donaldson," Trumbo called.

"Boss." With a clatter of the beaded curtain that covered the door to the dining hall, a sandy-bearded, older sec man came in, blinking behind round glasses that most poignantly reminded Doc of his friend J.B.

"You got this. Drive the machine…. Martin. Andrews."

Another pair of sec men entered behind Donaldson.

"You lead the blasters. Take half the boys with you. The rest'll stay here with me. You know the job."

The newcomers smiled and nodded.

Sand turned in her chair, whose festoons seemed unusually tawdry in the turned-down lamp glow, with the first tentative dawn light just beginning to stain the curtains gray. She crossed one purple-velvet-clad leg over the other.

"Excuse me," she said. "I told you to lead this mission, Trumbo. What's all this talk?"

"Change of plans, Baron," Trumbo said with a wide, greasy smile. He pushed his big shoulders off the stuccoed wall.

"By whose authority, little man?" Sand demanded imperiously.

In the past when the tall blonde who liked to play at being a man—while still being, as Doc could well attest, altogether a woman—had taken that tone, her sec boss had cringed like a whipped dog.

Now his smile broadened.

At the window to the front door's left, the feathered mutie cocked his narrow smooth-sided head to one side. With his gaunt cheeks and bony nose he really did resemble some kind of giant bird, albeit a most lamentably bald one.

"I hear engines," he said. "Many, many engines!"

The windows commenced to rattle to a rising many-throated snarl of *mechanism*.

"Whose authority?" Trumbo asked.

His eyes bulged from their sockets in what Doc took for unholy glee. He laughed.

"My own!"

LIKE A SHADOW mountain it squatted, perhaps three hundred yards from the improvised barricade to the main street of Amity Springs.

"That has got to be the biggest bulldozer I've laid my eye on in my entire life," Ryan said. He stood upright behind where the wag-tongues crossed in the middle of the street. "That's got to be a Komatsu D575A-3 Super Dozer," J.B. said in tones of open admiration. The little man stood at Ryan's side as gray light filled the world around them. "I've seen pictures of them before. One hundred, sixty-eight tons. Biggest production bulldozer ever."

"Where the nuke—" Ryan's tone grated "—did it *come* from?"

Dark Lady laughed bitterly—and a bit wildly, Ryan

thought. She had stepped around and out in front of the makeshift barrier.

"Where else?" she cried. "Sandy—Sand herself said we weren't the only ones who could find scavvy of the old research facility in Santana Basin. We got their trash—and their armory. She got that!"

"Tell me you got a wag-chiller missile or two out of the arsenal," Mildred pleaded.

Dark Lady shook her head. "No. Explosives, small arms. Even Mr. Sinclair's BAR. Nothing heavier than that, I fear."

"You there, Dark Lady?" a voice demanded. It was electronically amplified, the way Diego's voice had been when his Crazy Dogs had attacked the ville.

"Trumbo?" Krysty asked. She had come to stand on Ryan's other side.

"Sounds like," Mildred said.

Ryan raised the longeye.

"Fireblast," he said. "That beast's so huge it has a safety rail around what looks like the deck over the engine compartment. That's Trumbo standing there on it in front of the rail, sure as glowing nukeshit."

"You got an answer for us?" the Joker Creek sec boss demanded.

Dark Lady stepped forward alone.

"Be careful, there, hon!" Mildred called. The gaudy owner ignored her.

She cupped her hands in front of her face. "Do you hear me?" she shouted. For such a small and quiet person she had a pretty loud voice when she wanted to.

"I hear you," Trumbo said. "Loud and clear. We got a paraholic mike here and everything."

"*Parabolic,* dimwit," Mildred said.

"I heard that!"

Mildred raised a hand and shot him the bird.

"So what's it to be, Dark Lady?" Trumbo said in his artificial demigod voice. "You sell out? Or do we get to smash the whole shit-pot of a ville around your ears, including that gaudy of yours?"

"Dark Lady," Sinclair said, sounding worried. "Mebbe we should consider this a little more—"

"Come and try," Dark Lady shouted. She spun on her heel and stalked back around the barricade.

"Right," Ryan said. He dropped the longeye and picked up his Scout carbine from where he had it leaning against the hitch pole of the wag to his right.

When he shouldered the longblaster and looked through the scope, the deck was empty. "Bastard ducked right off," he said. "Not that stupe."

He couldn't make out a driver through the smoked glass of the cab, which was probably doubly roomy despite looking tiny, perched way back there past a blade as broad as the street and an engine housing the size of a house. But he reckoned if he even put one close to the operator, the Joker Creek sec man might start having second thoughts about how ace an idea this whole thing was.

He fired.

When he brought the scope back in line with his eye with a fresh round chambered, he saw nothing different. No surprise. In this light, at this distance, he couldn't make out enough detail to see if he'd punched a hole in the windshield, even if he starred the whole bastard thing. He sighted in, let out half a breath and squeezed the trigger again.

With a rumble and a gout of black smoke rising into the paling western sky, the mountainous machine started forward.

"I don't think you're getting through to him, Ryan," J.B. said.

"Fireblast!" Ryan slung the weapon and took up the long-eye again.

Even in this light and at this range he could instantly see that the cab's windshield was completely intact and unholed.

"I know I hit," Ryan said with the simple certainly of a triple-skilled marksman. "Both shots, clean."

"I wonder if a Lexan windshield came standard on those puppies," J.B. said. He sounded more interested than alarmed—though even Ryan's hard heart was beating a touch faster at the approach of that metal monster, slow as it was. "Reckon the old-days whitecoats had their reasons for springing for one, if it didn't."

"Men come," Jak said. He seemed to be vibrating like a hunting dog that smelled the quarry. He was a close-in fighter; he hated having to wait to get to grips with an enemy like this like poison.

"Not just men," Krysty said. "Wags. And—motorcy-cles."

She turned to Ryan with wide eyes. "Ryan, it must be the Crazy Dogs!"

"Well, that just made our whole day," Mildred said. "Sand sold us all to that bastard Diego."

"No," Dark Lady said.

Everybody looked at her. She stood near Ryan, staring into the scrub. Her face was paler than usual, and her fists were knotted at her sides.

"Sand would never do that. She knows what it would mean for her people. For *her.* She'd no more submit to an animal like Diego than would I. She's been betrayed herself."

"None of that loads any blasters for us," Ryan said. He lowered the longeye again and took up his longblaster. "These bastards aren't bulletproof."

He raised the Steyr and began to scan for targets. Men strode on foot to either side of the massive dozer. They trotted, their weapons across their chests. The machine itself moved at no more than a few miles an hour.

Before he could pick a target, a yellow flare flickered.

Wood splintered to thudding impacts. Somebody screamed.

Chapter Twenty-Seven

Baron Sand shot to her feet.

"What in the name of sweet, sweaty *fuck* are you talking about?"

"See, Baron," Trumbo said with a triumphant smirk, "there's been a slight change in administration of this barony. Grab her, boys!"

Andrews and Donaldson grabbed Doc by the arms. Lobo came away from his station by the painting. He moved with alacrity surprising for his mass of bone and brawn. He seized Baron Sand from her chair and picked her up as if she were a four-year-old girl.

"No!" Mystery screamed. He launched himself at the stolid giant, fingers clawed as if to gouge out his dark Indian eyes.

A shattering blast erupted from the side door. The retainer spun, a look of surprise in his wide kohl-rimmed eyes. Then he slumped to the floor. His blood added a new, darker stain to the hues of an ancient throw rug already discolored by various exudations.

Another of Sand's courtiers, a frail woman with short black hair named Gayle, fell to the floor flopping and shrieking behind Mystery.

An immense handblaster, glinting chrome, protruded through the beaded strands that covered the side door. A thread of blue smoke trailed upward from its muzzle. It pushed through, followed by a man so tall he had to bend to clear the arched top with the brush of thick black hair atop his head.

To the sides of his dark face the hair hung like glossy raven-wing curtains to broad shoulders. He grinned with rotten teeth through an extravagant handlebar mustache.

"Diego!" Baron Sand exclaimed.

"Right in one," the Crazy Dog chieftain said. "Did you miss me?"

"I haven't shot at you yet," Sand said frostily. "An oversight I will certainly correct."

"Yeah," Diego said with a laugh. "Hold that thought. And you—"

The last was an aside to one of several sec men who had entered the room when Lobo grabbed the baron.

"Shut her up."

The man looked at Trumbo. Trumbo flicked his eyes at Diego. He licked his fat lips, then nodded.

The man withdrew a handblaster and shot the woman, who lay on her side curled up in a knot of pain around her stomach or possibly pelvis, in the side of the head. The flash briefly filled the room, along with a shattering noise that seemed to make the windows bulge outward. The air, which was already thick with musk and hemp and incense smoke, took on a ripe reek of spilled bowels.

Trumbo stared at the chill for a moment. A trickle of sweat ran down his fat face from his receding hairline.

Sand tossed her short hair back from her face.

"So the worm turns," she said, sneering. "How could you do this to me, Trumbo?"

He covered his face in his meaty hands. "I did it all for love of you, my lady!" he sobbed.

"Really?" She cocked an arch brow. "Well, that's rather sweet. If cloyingly sentimental and somewhat trite."

"No," Trumbo said, raising his face and grinning. His

eyes and cheeks were dry and showed no sign of weeping. "I'm lying. I hate you. And I want to watch you die!

"But first, I want you to *suffer.* I'm going to make you watch while I torture, defile and break all your pretty play toys."

She yawned ostentatiously. "Be my guest," she said. "I've grown bored with them, anyway."

Some of her retainers, pressed against the walls in fright, registered shock at the baron's attitude. Especially with Mystery lying dead or dying heroically, if not effectually, at her very feet.

"No time now," Trumbo said, rubbing a cheek and glancing at Diego.

The coldheart lord stood by watching silently and sneering. The sounds of his followers' rides was very loud. Doc, who had been yanked rudely to his feet next to the baron, reckoned Diego had to be bringing his whole force into Joker Creek.

"Now's the time to go put wood to that tight-ass Dark Lady," Trumbo said. "If she survives long enough to get hauled back here, mebbe her ass won't be so tight anymore. Leastways, not when me and the boys are done with it. And you—"

He shot Doc a bloodshot glare of hate.

"I owe your friends, too. Not forgetting about them."

He signaled some of his men. "Donaldson. Andrews. Like I told you, lead the group to the Springs with the chill dozer. Time for me and my man Diego to start consolidating our hold here."

"No," Diego said.

Trumbo gaped at him. "Huh?"

"You go," Diego said. "Take who you want. I'll send some of my wags along—the sound setup and the dozer should come in double handy."

"What about Joker Creek?"

"I can take care of the situation here."

Trumbo went red. He tried to cover his apparent shock and dismay with bluster. "What are you trying to pull? We had a deal—"

The room was full of Trumbo's blasters. Diego was here on his lonesome. But the tall, powerfully built coldheart was on the sec boss in a long-legged stride and grabbing him by the throat with one hand.

"Yeah," he said. "The deal was, you got to run this place. But I run the whole nuking Basin. When it comes to Nukem Flats, I am the President-King-God-Emperor. So you'll do what I tell you to and never talk back again. Ace?"

"Ace," Trumbo croaked.

"Fine." Diego let go of Trumbo and turned to face his sec men.

"Anybody got questions about the chain of command?" he asked.

He gestured with the immense shiny silver handblaster in his left hand. Doc thought he recognized a Desert Eagle, a late-twentieth-century semiautomatic blaster designed to fire cartridges normally too powerful for such actions, such as .357 and .44 Magnum and something called .50 AE. Doc had run across a few of them before. The Armorer said they were good pieces, well-designed and solidly made. But he'd also said they were so heavy only a stupe would carry one, when for only a trifle more weight one could pack a lightweight carbine like the M-4.

Doc suspected Diego didn't do a lot of long hiking. And that he was mindful of making a strong first impression. He certainly had on Doc.

"Enough bullshit," Diego said. "Get the dozer and get your ass gone."

Trumbo went out the side door with the sec men he'd

called out trooping after. Lobo handed the baron off to a couple of others and walked after his boss.

"What will you do now?" Sand demanded.

Diego gave her a raised eyebrow. For a moment Doc feared he meant to strike her.

Then he grinned. From the way Sand blanched, Doc suspected she actually would've preferred the blow.

"I'm gonna tell my boys and girls what someone told me the great conqueror Genghis Khan once said, 'The hay is cut; give your horses fodder.'"

He laughed at the unalloyed horror of her reaction.

"See, we've been working a long, hard time trying to pry out a toehold in this valley," he said. "I reckon everybody has worked up quite a head of steam to blow off. Plus it should serve to cut the ice, you know? Get everyone acquainted double-good. And get your people so they know their rad-blasted *place*."

He waved the blaster. "You heard the fat man," he snarled at the remaining sec men. "Get the bitch and the beanpole out of here. We'll sort their asses out later. After we get done with the prime stuff!"

WHEN THE DOOR to Sand's bedroom was locked from the outside, the baron turned to Doc and collapsed in his arms. For all his wiry strength, which had surprised so many others—some lethally—he barely managed to avoid collapsing under her not inconsiderable weight. As it was, he sagged lamentably at the knees and felt something twinge in his back.

"I'm so sorry!" She wept into his shoulder. "I tried to save you. I tried to save everybody. And instead I just got poor Mystery and Gayle killed!"

He got her turned so he could brace his back against the door to help hold them up. As he did, he felt her straighten her knees, taking up her own weight again. Still she clung to him and wept inconsolably while he stroked her short hair and wondered what to do.

"Now it's all gone to pieces," she moaned.

"Still," he said, "we live. And where life is, is also hope."

She pulled back and smiled at him faintly from a puffy tear-sheened face.

"Really? That's pretty trite too. Yet there's a certain daffy sincerity when you say it."

"Believe me, dear lady, it is based upon experience," he said.

She took in a deep breath and sighed.

"Well," she said. "Nothing we can do now."

She turned away from him and rested the back of her head against the door.

"We'll just have to wait our chance."

"MACHINE GUN!" J.B. shouted. "Get to cover!"

Crouched behind the wag to the right, and hoping the kegs inside it were full of nails or something else that would slow a machine-gun bullet, Ryan looked left. A townie lay in the dirt past the other wag's far end, kicking and clutching himself and howling. A couple of people dragged him back into cover of the wag.

Mildred crouched behind the wag, over the prone body of a young woman in a flannel shirt and jeans. The woman had her face turned toward Ryan. He recognized Ruby, one of the handfuls of Dark Lady's employees whose name he'd retained.

Her amber eyes stared at him. From the small dark spot above her right one he reckoned she didn't see him. Mildred glanced at him and shook her head sadly.

Another burst rocked the wag. Ryan clenched his jaw as a bullet cracked right over his head.

When it cut off, he came back over the top and leveled his longblaster. He got a flash sight through the scope on the blaster wag, and fired. He missed, but as he brought the weapon back down he saw the gunner duck behind the tailgate.

It wouldn't stop one of Ryan's 7.62 mm slugs. But he didn't dare waste a shot on a target he couldn't see. Instead, having bought himself a few heartbeats to aim with, he shifted the field of view to his left.

The loader had also flinched from the bullet, wherever it hit. But he hadn't hidden fully the way the gunner had. Ryan lined up a shot on the dark blur of his head as somewhere to his left Sinclair let loose a burst from his BAR.

Even as he triggered the shot Ryan saw the gunner start to rise. With machine precision he jacked the action and brought the Scout back down onto line.

The loader was falling, shooting a fan of dark spray from what had to be a blown-out carotid. But at the edge of his circle of vision Ryan also saw the gunner hunched behind the butt-stock of his M-60.

There was no time to line up another shot. Even as he ducked behind the rear wheel of his sheltering wag, his glass lit with the garish yellow flame of the big blaster.

The Crazy Dog kept spraying until Ryan reckoned he meant to just saw right in through to him. Fortunately what was weighting down the wag bed did stop the bullets. Most of them—at least the ones that would've hit Ryan, although he did wince a bit as one ripped out through wood about eight inches to the left of his head.

"Keep it up, prick," he muttered. "Burn out that barrel." Even if the Dogs had a spare it would take several minutes to change. That was one of many flaws of the M-60 design; it lacked a true quick-change barrel.

The bullet stream cut off.

"Burned the barrel," Ryan heard J.B. call in satisfaction. "Stupe."

Ryan moved to the end of the wag before poking his blaster back around. As he did, he swapped in a new 10-round mag. The old one still had two cartridges left, if he counted true. But experience had taught him even the coolest head didn't always count straight when the bullets were flying—and never to pass up a chance to reload.

He saw the gunner hammering in rage on his piece even before he got the scope to his eye. Unfortunately the bulk of the slowly advancing bulldozer promptly blocked his view.

Ryan glanced around. A kid had just rolled up a wheelbarrow from somewhere. Defenders were wrestling the still-thrashing wounded man onto it. With nothing better to do, Mildred was overseeing.

"Dark Lady," Sinclair called as he swapped mags in his big automatic longblaster. "Are you sure you want to do this? Can't we at least talk to them?"

Behind the other wag Dark Lady stood looking grim. "No," she said.

She gestured toward the screaming man. "Bring him," she said, turning to walk back up the street toward the center of the ville and the Lounge.

"Wait," Sinclair called. "Where the nuke do you think you're going? You running out on us?"

The half light streaming up the street silhouetted her slim shape. Ryan saw her shoulders twitch as if she'd taken a bullet. She stopped.

"You won't stop them," Dark Lady said flatly, turning. A burly male entertainer from the Lounge continued wheeling the barrow, while a sturdy townswoman walked alongside trying to keep the still-thrashing and wailing occupant from turning it over. "Not even the highly resourceful Mr.

Cawdor and friends. You won't even hold them long. I'm going to go prepare the inner defenses."

"What good will that do, if we can't slow them down?" Mildred demanded.

Dark Lady showed the ghost of a smile.

"I believe I have a few surprises for our enemies," she said. "Perhaps Mr. Dix and young Mr. Morales might accompany me? I have some items they may find useful."

"She's right," J.B. said. He hefted his Uzi. "We might as well be waving our di— That is, might as well be chucking rocks at that big bastard."

He nodded toward the bulldozer, still several hundred yards off but inexorably advancing. The Crazy Dogs and their Joker Creek sec men allies were sheltering behind it.

"Then go," Ryan ordered.

"Ryan," Mildred said, "do you trust her?"

"You got a better idea? No? Then shut it."

"Here they come!" screamed the boy who'd brought the wheelbarrow.

Ryan looked back around the end of the wag.

A dozen motorcycles and at least three wags had appeared to the left and right of the monster machine. Winging out to either side, they accelerated toward Amity Springs.

Yellow flames danced in the mouths of coldheart blasters.

Chapter Twenty-Eight

"Take them down!" Ryan shouted. They had a chance to make these bastards eat it, until and unless the coldhearts got the machine gun blazing again.

He saw Sinclair, his face red and streaming sweat behind his ginger mustache despite the morning chill, frown at him. He wasn't taking kindly to some outlander mercie shouting orders to him, a big dog in the ville.

Nuke him. There was no time for pissing matches. Ryan came up over the top of the wag looking for targets.

He found a prize one right away: an old muscle car bristling coldhearts and blasters out the cut-off top, barreling right toward him. He let himself smile as he lined up on the driver's shaved, goggled head.

He saw blood and brains spray even before recoil kicked his longblaster up.

When he had the Steyr leveled again, he saw the driver's head lolled back and a snake-ball of confusion behind him. Apparently the slug had blown through his head and hit at least one of the coldhearts behind. As the vehicle, unsteered, slewed off to his right, he put another shot right into the middle of things. Just to keep them *interesting*.

To his left he heard blasters cracking from the barricade. The BAR snarled and Ryan saw a brief yellow glare light the flats. He heard wild shrieking, smelled burning gas and barbecuing flesh. Apparently the auto-blaster had lit off the fuel tank of a second Crazy Dog wag.

There were half a dozen Amity Springs residents still behind the wag barrier, along with Ryan, Krysty, Mildred and Jak. They were all shooting at the Crazy Dogs driving fast toward them across the open. He heard what had to be other locals open up from the buildings to either side, as well.

He noticed a coldheart out front of the others and only thirty yards away, hunched over handlebars with a cloud of dark hair streaming out from behind a goggled face. Ryan couldn't tell if it was a man or woman, especially with the light sporadically flashing in his eyes as the speeding motorcycle bounced over land that wasn't as dead flat as it looked. He swung the Steyr onto the rider, lined up the ghost ring iron sights beneath the scope, and fired.

Rider and bike went down sideways. Spinning wheels gouged up a mighty spray of dirt and grass.

The other coldhearts had had enough. They turned and sped away from the barricade, leaving half their number chilled or wounded on the cold ground. As Ryan tried to line up another shot, he saw a last fleeing rider throw up his hands and fall backward out of the saddle. His bike continued on for twenty or thirty feet before falling over.

The defenders raised a ragged cheer, but that was the last of the good news. The dozer was barely fifty yards off, and the sec men on foot and the riders alike were sheltering behind it.

Off to Ryan's right of the bulldozer—the north—and several hundred yards back, a huge yellow flame bloomed and pulsated. A spray of bullets smashed into the barricade. The Crazy Dogs did have a replacement barrel—and had managed to swap it for the ruined one.

Rendered cautious by the fates of the original gunner and loader, the Dogs had opted to hang well back from the ville to resume fire. And this gunner was smart enough to keep his bursts short.

"Time to go!" Ryan shouted, mostly to his own people. "Pull back and snipe the bastards! Krysty and Mildred, go south. Jak, with me!"

"That's right," Sinclair shouted, firing a burst from his Browning. "Run, mercies!"

Ryan ignored him. If he wanted to stand his ground and get chewed up by the M-60, or ground into gore-oozing paste by the Komatsu, that was his look-out.

With Jak right on his heels Ryan raced down the street toward the center of town. He quickly saw what he was looking for and cut left into a skinny space between two frame buildings. Jak followed.

Just in time: a burst from the machine gun cracked down the street behind their backs.

It was the first three-story building on this edge of the ville. Or the last, depending on which way you were going. It had a rickety-looking set of stairs leading to the door. Signaling for Jak to hang in the narrow yard between it and the single-story building just west, Ryan pounded rapidly up the steps.

At the top was a landing and a locked door. The one-eyed man didn't like being up here in the open where the blaster man in the wag could plainly see him—if he happened to look. But the dozer was getting close to the barricade, its blade shielding its colossal engine from the defenders' bullets, its thick hydrocarbon windshield continuing to shed them like spit droplets.

And the M-60's ripping bursts were starting to smash holes in the barricading wooden wags. Ryan saw a young man in canvas pants and suspenders fall backward, the front and back of his white shirt showing fist-size red stains where jacketed rounds had punched right through the plank shielding him.

There was no time to waste. Slipping his left forearm

into the loop on the shooting sling, Ryan turned and knelt, presenting his carbine over the wood rail. He'd get one shot before the machine gunner spotted him and raked his perch with blasterfire. He had to make it count.

With practiced skill he pointed the longblaster at the distant wag. When he put his eye to his scope, the pickup was almost centered in the reticule. He saw the loader, a burly shaved-headed guy in thick gauntlets, slap the gunner's arm frantically and point. Dead at Ryan.

The gunner, a youthful-looking man with goggles pushed up on a wild shock of hair, looked up.

Just in time to see the flash of the shot that sent a bullet through his forehead, a finger's width to the right of the centerline and two fingers above his wide, astonished eye. The bullet punched a wound channel through his brain and drilled a neat hole in the back of his skull. It was still going so fast it sucked about a quarter of his brain mass right out with it before smashing into the truck's cab.

The driver was hard-core, Ryan had to admit. He tossed the chill out of the way and grabbed for the pistol grip of the M-60.

He had turned clockwise. Now he turned slightly counterclockwise to work the weapon himself. As he did, Ryan's second shot, aimed for his temple, hit the side of his bearded lower jaw right below the hinge and tore it clean out of his face.

He dropped, covering his ruined face with both big-gloved hands. Ryan saw blood fountain between the futile fingers as he vanished from view into the bed. If he was hard-core enough to come back from that to try to take another shot at Ryan, the Deathlands warrior reckoned he'd earned it. Most likely he'd bleed out in a couple minutes.

Anyway he was out of sight, and Ryan had more targets to mind. The wag's passenger door opened and a skinny guy in a leather jacket open over a pale T-shirt got out and turned to face the ville. Ryan didn't know whether he was making a move to hop in the bed and take over the blaster or simply was looking to see what was going on. He didn't care. He put a bullet through his sternum and saw him slump as if the bones had dissolved within him—the mark of an instant chill.

The driver slammed the wag in gear and started to drive west. For a millisecond Ryan considered letting him go, clear back to Joker Creek, if running was on his mind. But he also didn't want the guy finding his balls again once he was out of range and circling back with yet another set of Dogs to work that damned blaster. He and the ville folk were going to have their hands more than full without having to worry about that.

He punched a hole through the rear of the cab at about the center of the driver's broad back. The driver jerked and his head slumped. The wag, which had barely started, slowed to a stop.

The driver's head lolled to the right. Since it was clearly visible, Ryan put another bullet into it. He didn't want the driver simply *playing* dead.

Then he shot out the right rear tire, just to be safe.

"Ryan!"

It was Jak, calling from the street. Ryan didn't look at him—he had too good an idea what the albino was warning him about.

Instead he pulled his head back from the glass in time to see the bulldozer slam into the wag barricade. He saw Sinclair with his full-automatic longblaster shouldered, still shooting as one wag was pushed over right on top of him.

The remaining defenders bolted. Or tried to. One thick middle-aged man got his heel trapped as the giant machine smashed over the right-hand wag. He shrieked horribly as a wide track rolled over him.

Ryan saw blood squirt out from beneath the tread. There was enough light it showed red.

The sec men, at least twenty of them, began fanning out on either side of the dozer as it rolled into the ville. Sure were a lot of those bastards, even for a ville as large and populous as Baron Sand's, Ryan thought. It occurred to him that the baron had been augmenting her sec force to respond to the growing Crazy Dog threat.

And also that it was triple likely that more than one or two of Trumbo's recent hires were Crazy Dogs themselves. He doubted this was a partnership that sprang into being overnight. Although naturally such betrayals were anything but uncommon when it came to the twisted power structures of villes.

He blasted a sec man using his ghost-ring iron sights. Realizing he was exposed if they or the Dogs beginning to roll into the ville noticed the roar and flash of his powerful blaster, he slipped his arm out of the shooting loop. Holding the weapon by the front stock, he started down the wood steps.

He heard the Komatsu's enormous diesel engine roar. Looking around, he saw the hundred-sixty-plus tons of yellow metal and malice making straight for him.

Quickly slinging the Steyr over his back, he vaulted the rail and crouched on the landing below.

The smell of diesel fuel and the earthquake growl of the house-size engine filled the air around him. Wood splintered. He looked again to see the dozer's blade clip the building just west of the one he was on. The dull-steel machine was as wide as the rad-blasted building itself.

He could clearly see the operator through the tinted Lexan windshield. It was another burly, shaved-headed

Crazy Dog, with gigantic arms sticking out of a denim vest. He and Ryan briefly exchanged looks. The coldheart grinned through a massive beard and threw the monster into lower gear for more torque.

Building-eating torque.

Ryan turned away to the rear of the doomed three-story structure. The dozer's path took it right over the spot where Jak had been guarding the base of the steps. Ryan spared his friend scarcely a thought. Of all the people on the scorched, scarred Earth the wiry little albino once known and feared under the name of the White Wolf was approximately the very last to let himself get squashed by a lumbering mass of metal the size of a nuking warehouse. Ryan's own narrow ass was plenty enough for him to worry about.

An empty wag was parked below and behind the building in a little yard behind. It wasn't much, but it was better than dropping the full two stories. Slightly.

It was also something of a jump. Ryan had motivation. As the vast blade struck the corner of the building and the stairs began to splinter beneath him, he coiled himself on the railing and sprang for all he was worth.

"FIREBLAST AND FUCK!"

Even over the unbelievable din of the monster engine, and the screams and blasterfire and general Hell breaking loose, Ryan's cry was clearly audible across the street as he made his leap for life off the collapsing structure.

"Ryan!" Krysty cried from the open window next to Mildred.

Mildred took aim and shot. The Crazy Dog driving his big motorcycle barely twenty feet from the window let go of the tall ape-hanger handlebars and went down. Mildred had shot him through the chest with a .38 Special slug. Whether it was a mortal wound or not, he was conscious enough to howl when the several hundred pounds of his ride crushed his left leg.

"He'll be fine, Krysty," Mildred told her.

Of course she had no way of knowing for sure whether that was true. She knew perfectly well—too well—that he was every bit as mortal as any of them, that he could get dropped at any time by a mere meaningless accident—a stray round, or just a rock turning beneath his boot at the right moment to throw him down and break his neck. Much less something like the biggest machine Mildred had ever seen smashing the very building he was standing on to matchsticks and dust bombs.

The dust rolled across the street like a tsunami. It hid an already crazy scene: the bikers and sec men invading; the locals blasting at them from windows and alleys; the chills lying and the wounded rolling on the street, screaming.

"Time to go, Krysty," Mildred said. She took a quick look around. They stood in a dim parlor, sparsely furnished with mostly late-twentieth-century scavvy, yet still managing to retain a Victorian sensibility somehow. The occupants seemed to be long gone when Mildred and her taller redheaded friend ducked inside for shelter.

"Right," Krysty said grimly. Her heart had to be breaking for Ryan, but her jaw was set firm when Mildred glanced her way.

Then her emerald eyes widened and she straightened her arms in front of her.

A Joker Creek sec man—Mildred had a vague flash impression of familiarity—had come in the open front door with a blaster in hand. It was an old Smith & Wesson Military and Police revolver, a cheaper but infinitely rugged and reliable cousin to her own match-grade .38 double-action blaster.

It was even closer to Krysty's S&W 640 snub-nose—

with which she blasted the man twice from eight feet while he was still looking around the room.

He dropped to the floorboards, his blood gushing out to stain a tatty throw rug set just inside it for visitors to wipe their feet.

Across the street the whole three-story building collapsed. The monster dozer crunched right on through, turning right to take out the next building toward the center of town.

"Out the back," Mildred said.

Krysty went to the man she'd shot. He stirred feebly. She put a boot on his outflung blaster hand and stepped down. Bones crunched. He moaned.

Stooping, she twitched the blaster out of his mangled fingers with her left hand.

"I'm ready."

Chapter Twenty-Nine

Half stunned by cracking his head on the front of the wooden wag bed, Ryan lay still a moment. He was completely enveloped by thunder and crashing and dust and diesel fumes as the bulldozer shrugged off the wreckage of the building he'd just bailed from as if it were no more than snowflakes. The machine then smashed its happy way into the neighboring structure.

He heard coughing. As if of its own accord, his right hand came up holding his SIG handblaster.

A pale hand waved at the dust. A lean white face appeared over the edge of the wag. Jak saw the 9 mm and grinned.

"No blast," he said.

Moving his right hand to stop pointing the blaster at his friend's skinny nose, Ryan reached his left hand. Jak caught his wrist and with his surprising wiry strength helped Ryan get up enough to get a boot beneath him.

"Break bones?" Jak asked. Ryan as much as read his lips as heard him over the racket.

Ryan blew out a breath. "Think not," he said. "But my bruises got bruises."

With more effort than he was pleased to have to expend, he clambered out of the wag and dropped to the hard-dirt yard beside Jak. His first move was to tuck the SIG back in its holster. The second was to pull the Scout around by its sling and check it quickly.

"Ace," he muttered. The quality of noise produced by the Komatsu changed. Jak grabbed Ryan's arm.

"Going other way," he shouted.

Over the top of a mound of kindling that had been a reasonably well-made three-story structure about two minutes ago, Ryan saw the yellow back of the cab. The beast was crossing the main street. As he watched, it rolled free of the rubble of its latest victim and ground onto the street at an angle. Dust obscured it. A moment later the sound of window glass exploding announced its arrival at the false front of a building across the dirt street.

"Having fun," Jak said.

"Yeah," Ryan agreed. "Looks like he aims to maximize damage before taking down Dark Lady's precious gaudy. Amping up the pressure, I guess. Plus pure meanness."

He cracked the bolt on his Steyr. He saw what he knew he would, the yellow gleam of a chambered cartridge. But a wise blaster always made *sure*.

"Hope Dark Lady was right about being able to help J.B. and Ricky surprise the puke," Ryan said.

He slammed the bolt closed.

"Let's go spoil the fun for some of these other bastards."

THE MAIN BARROOM of the Library Lounge was a hive of busy action around J.B. and his young apprentice as they stood in the gloom waiting for Dark Lady. Some of the employees were busy loading blasters. Others were shoveling books into crates and handing them off to others who carried them downstairs to the relative safety of the basement. Dark Lady's giant factotum, Mikey-Bob, went by holding a double-size crate that had to have been loaded with a hundred pounds of cracked and ancient hardbacks in his arms. Both his heads looked as grim as death.

The sounds from outside were distant and muted by

the walls. But it was clear that Hell was coming to Amity Springs with a bloody vengeance, and it was getting closer.

Down the stairs came Dark Lady. She seemed oddly calm. She carried a metal briefcase.

She laid it on a table next to J. B. and Ricky.

"Gentlemen," she said, snapping the latches with crisp metal sounds, "I promised you what I hope will prove the means of providing an unpleasant surprise for our visitors and their monstrous machine."

She opened the lid.

"Will this serve, do you think?"

J.B. looked into the case. He felt his eyes go wide.

He looked at Ricky. The kid was staring, too. A look of sheer delight spread slowly across his face. Warms the cockles, it does, J.B. thought. He wasn't an overly sensitive man. Or a regularly sensitive man, come to that. But for just a moment he allowed himself to savor a moment of pure pleasure shared with his pupil.

He looked at Dark Lady and smiled.

"Yes, ma'am," he said. "I do believe we can make some use of this."

SIDE BY SIDE Mildred and Krysty fought their way back through the ville of Amity Springs.

They stopped when they could to snipe at the Crazy Dogs and their Joker Creek allies. The locals were fighting back, too.

And they were laying serious hurt on the invaders, though they were also taking hurt themselves. Mildred understood just why there had been no successful assault on the wealthy ville before. It seemed every adult had at least a longblaster, and a bunch of the kids had blasters, too. And more than a few of them were full autos, M-16s or their little brother M-4s.

But there were more attackers than Mildred had realized at first, and they kept coming despite their losses.

She guessed the fact that they had an ace in the hole in an invincible yellow metal monster tended to keep up morale.

The Amity Springs folk tried to fight it, too. She saw a pair of youths clamber onto the front of the dozer as it angled across the street, halfway along its crooked path of destruction toward Dark Lady's HQ at the center of town. One actually ran up to grab the door handle outside the cab.

A storm of blasterfire from the sec men following on foot swept them off the dozer like rubbish, streaming blood as they fell back to the street. The bulldozer continued its grinding, crushing, all-destroying way.

A pair of sec men stalked past the alley where Mildred and Krysty sheltered. Seeming intent on targets already, they didn't notice the two women crouching behind some piled refuse.

Not until Krysty stepped up, put her claimed M&P blaster almost to the side of the nearer one's red-bandanna head, and fired. He jerked and went down.

His partner whirled, bringing up a sawed-off double-barrel shotgun. Mildred double tapped him. As he went down, Krysty deftly twisted the scattergun from his hand.

After cutting back around behind the building, the dozer burst through a building to their left.

From across the street scuttled a short, stocky man with a bald head gleaming in the early morning light. Mildred recognized Wilson, the shopkeeper. He hurled something that trailed orange fire against the side of the bulldozer.

It was a Molotov cocktail. It burst, sending a reverse cascade of garish orange flame up the machine's track and yellow flank. It didn't take; it barely scorched the paint. But the driver shied the huge machine away. Instead of smashing Wilson's general store it turned back to the north.

And a Crazy Dog rider put a boot down, turned his bike sideways and shouldered a Mini-14 longblaster. He fired three quick shots. The slugs cut down the shopkeeper before he could race back to cover.

Muzzle-fire flashed from the doorway of his store. The Crazy Dog rider jerked and fired a shot into the street.

Another 3-round burst ripped out. The Dog started to slump. Wilson's wife, Kris, walked from her shop firing an M-16 from one generous hip.

Another bike roared along the street toward her. Deftly she shouldered the weapon, turned and fired another burst. Mildred saw the rider's head come apart and he went over the rear of his ride.

Continuing to fire short bursts west along the street one-handed, the red-haired woman grabbed her husband by the collar and started to drag him.

"You help," Mildred said. "I'll cover."

Krysty darted out. Mildred came around the mouth of the alley and opened fire on a knot of sec men. Already cowering from Kris's shots, they dived out of sight, through a broken window or between buildings.

Krysty helped Kris drag Wilson into the shop. Then she emerged, shooting the M&P as she crossed the street.

"Is he alive?" Mildred asked. Krysty shook her head.

They headed back to the other street.

"Ryan!" Krysty called.

In the far alley, half obscured by shadows, stood a familiar lean figure in a long coat. Mildred thought she saw teeth flash in a grin. Then he vanished.

The two women came to the corner and looked cautiously up and down the main street. The dozer smashed through yet another building and continued irresistibly at an angle across the street. It was almost to the center of the ville and the Library Lounge now.

Mildred looked left. Jak suddenly appeared on the board-walk across the way. He shot a double bird at an approaching coldheart motorcyclist, then ducked down the alley in which the women had briefly glimpsed Ryan.

The burly bike roared in after, then it halted. Brandishing a big double-action revolver, the rider looked around in confusion. His quarry had simply vanished.

But Krysty and Mildred had watched Jak scale a rain gutter as agilely as a monkey. He was perched on a ground-floor roof. When the motorcyclist stopped, he leaped lithely onto the saddle behind the Crazy Dog.

The coldheart roared in surprise. Jak reached his hands around the man's throat, then yanked them quickly back to the sides.

A fan of blood sprayed dark from the biker's scissored-out throat. The small but lethal blades of the leaf-bladed knives in Jak's hands glinted in the light that filtered off the street.

He leaped off the bike as it toppled and disappeared.

"Oh, no!" Krysty exclaimed.

She was looking right. Mildred leaned out to see past her in time to watch the bulldozer accelerate through a sleet of blasterfire to punch in the false front of the Library Lounge.

Chapter Thirty

There was an avalanche of rumbling and creaking. Blaster-fire crescendoed, muffled from the upper floors and blasting Ricky's eardrums in the barroom.

Through his ringing ears and the holocaust roar he heard Dark Lady shouting in a startling brassy voice from somewhere overhead, "Everybody out! *Now!*"

"Move!" Mikey-Bob added his two-throated bull bellow from the back by the exit. He tucked a box of books under his left arm and, snagging a young busboy by the collar, flung him bodily through the swing doors to the kitchen.

J.B.'s calm was unruffled, as always.

"You heard the man," he said, slinging the backpack he'd just finished stuffing with the contents of the metal case. "Men. Time to go."

Without seeming to hurry, but making good time just the same, he made for the back door. Ricky scuttled after him, wondering what the older man's secrets were.

Other employees, including both male and female entertainers, ignored the commands of both their boss and her giant lieutenant to continue cranking rounds out the front windows. The noise from outside was so cataclysmic even blasters going off in the saloon's echoing confines were getting overwhelmed.

"Dark Lady!" Ricky shouted as J.B. hit the doors.

"She's got to fend for herself now."

The front of the gaudy imploded.

Despite the fact that both reason and fear told Ricky to bolt through the kitchen and out the door and Devil take anyone and anything in his path, he stood in the open door rooted to the spot.

With fatal fascination he watched the defenders at the windows thrown down as a vast gray object like a metal wall pushed through the wood of the façade. It was the blade of a bulldozer, clearly. But before now he'd had no grasp of how freakishly huge this one was.

The monster's progress stopped. The engine growl subsided. One end of the blade jutted at a slight angle into the barroom on Ricky's right. The other was actually out of sight beyond the interior wall to his left. And the top of it was invisible *above* the ceiling, whose wood rafters sagged and whose planks rained dust and debris to join the chaos of smoke, dust and fragments that swirled in the room.

And screams.

"Come on," J.B. said. He almost sounded urgent this time.

"People are hurt! We've got to—"

He felt his own collar grasped, then he was being towed inexorably back through the kitchen.

"We've got to do our jobs," J.B. said, as if that explained everything and answered all objections.

Ricky Morales realized that, if he wanted to continue as the Armorer's apprentice—it did. He turned and ran for the outdoors as the earthquake noise of the house-size diesel began to rise again.

THE FRONT OF the Library Lounge buckled to the Super Dozer's impact. Krysty sucked in a sharp breath as she saw people fall from the upper floors to land in the street.

"I hope J.B. got clear," Mildred said. "Ricky, too."

"I'm sure they did," Krysty replied. "You know how J.B. is."

Both women ducked back as a shot cracked over their heads from up the street. They looked quickly west.

Emboldened, the invaders were pushing hard for the center of the ville. A knot of Crazy Dogs rode by, hooting triumphantly and waving their blasters. Joker Creek sec men jogged along both sides of the street. Or at least Krysty judged them to be sec men, by the fact they weren't riding. It wasn't as if they wore uniforms, or dressed any more sedately than the motorcycle-riding coldhearts.

Bent low, Ryan and Jak darted out of an alley and across the street toward where the women crouched. Ryan blasted two quick shots up the street. Though her heart jumped into her throat, Krysty saw no evidence of shots thrown at them.

"Power on out of here," Ryan called as he approached. "Circle north, then east to where we can see the gaudy."

The four did so. Krysty felt concerned they might run afoul of the invaders, but the coldhearts and sec men seemed focused entirely on whatever the massive Super Dozer was doing to the Library Lounge, which entailed a power of crunching and engine-roaring, though thankfully no screams.

That she could hear.

Ryan led them two blocks north, then turned west onto a street that showed no sign of intruders. They slowed to a walk as they approached the corner that should afford them a view of the Lounge.

"Bastards don't seem really worried about leaving locals with guns in their rear," Mildred said.

"They see no need, likely," Ryan said. "They've got the giant wrecking machine. Looks like they hope the ville will just surrender if Dark Lady's headquarters goes down.

But if they got to, they can make good on Trumbo's threat to scrape Amity Springs right off the face of the Earth."

They reached the corner. Jak sprinted ahead the last few steps to peer around first. Krysty saw Ryan's face tighten at the albino's impetuousness, but he said nothing. This was no time to waste words.

Jak signed it was safe to approach.

"Keep an eye out behind us, Jak," Ryan said as he came up to look.

Krysty joined Ryan, hunkering down to look with her face beneath his.

The monstrous machine was using its treads to turn left and right, mostly in place. She frowned. She didn't understand what the point was.

"Probably trying to take out structural support without going in too far," Ryan said. "Or, just rubbing it in."

"Why doesn't that thing get stuck when it just drives right through buildings? I mean, I know it's big. But come on."

"A tank might," Ryan said. "But this isn't a tank. It doesn't need armor—though it's got some, especially that bastard blade—nor a big blaster. Anyway, this is what it does. But it still can get stuck, so the driver may not want to take unnecessary chances."

Even as he said that the engine's growl got louder. With one final side-to-side wag it straightened itself and backed out of the hole it had made in the front of the Library Lounge. It pulled back up the main street about twenty yards, so that its rear was invisible from where Krysty and her friends were. Then it stopped.

A man appeared in front of the engine, right behind the blade.

"Trumbo," Ryan said. He pushed his left hand through

the shooting loop of his sling and got ready to shoulder the
Scout for a shot.

The burly treacherous sec boss held a fist to his face.
"Had enough yet, Dark Lady?" His amplified voice
boomed.

"Didn't their sound wag make the trip?" Krysty asked.

"Putting on a show," Ryan said.

"Or do you want us to knock the whole place down
around your sweet little ass cheeks?" the sec boss asked,
warming to his role.

Though the floors above the gaudy's main barroom had
begun to sag in the middle toward the hole the dozer had
made, a spatter of blasterfire crackled from one or two of
the upper-story windows. Trumbo promptly dived back
off the dozer, out of sight down the far side, the way he
had climbed up.

"I may not be sure of her judgment," Mildred said, "but
I have to say I do like Dark Lady's style."

Ryan shrugged. "She knows how much mercy she can
expect from Trumbo—or from Diego, who's no doubt the
one holding his chain. So she might as well hold out to
the end."

He flashed a grin at the women. "But I like it, too."

Krysty saw something that made her heart jump.

"Look," she said, pointing into the gap between the
dozer blade and the doomed gaudy house.

"It's J.B. and Ricky!"

"OKAY, KID," J.B. said to his apprentice as they crouched
behind the northwest corner of the Library Lounge. "Stick
close to me, keep the coldhearts off my ass and try not to
get squashed."

He thought that covered everything, so he ran out into

the open intersection. Straight toward the idling 168-ton bulldozer.

He ran bent over, but not because the backpack weighed anything to speak of, but to reduce his silhouette to the Crazy Dogs and turncoat sec men who were gathered behind and to the sides of the dozer.

A couple shots flew his way from his right, where sec men had shifted north from the main street. He put on a little extra speed and hit the dozer's blade sideways. The steel plate was warm from the sun and smelled of dust and, incongruously, perfume.

Ricky thumped into the blade right behind him.

Holding his Uzi in his right hand, J.B. leaned out around the blade. He saw several sec men on foot and Crazy Dogs on their bikes. He fired a short burst to make them flinch.

Ducking back, he nodded to his apprentice.

"Thin them out for me," he said. He had to raise his voice to make it heard above the rumble of the giant engine just the other side of the massive blade. The monster dozer itself stayed put. For now. "Need some breathing room to do the job."

Ricky grinned and nodded. He tucked the Webley revolver he'd been holding in its holster and unslung his DeLisle longblaster.

Holding the Uzi in both hands, J.B. swung around again and fired another burst.

"I see five of them, right now," he said, pulling back.

"Got it."

Ricky knelt. He paused, took a deep breath and crossed himself. Then he leaned out from cover of the giant steel plate, shouldering his longblaster.

It thumped. J.B. was impressed by just how much noise the carbine didn't make, between the fat sound suppressor shrouding the barrel and the big subsonic .45 slugs it fired. Ricky and his uncle had done an ace job building it.

J.B. was a man who just naturally admired craftsmanship in weaponry when he had a moment to himself to do so. As he did now.

"Okay," Ricky said, ducking back as bullets stormed past. "Four."

"Got it."

J.B. held up a finger for the kid to wait. The shooting subsided. The Armorer leaned out promptly to loose another brief spatter of 9 mm rounds.

As he returned to cover, he signaled Ricky to take his turn. With laudably machine-like precision the youth did. His carbine spoke.

"Three," he said, putting his back to the dozer blade again.

"Ace," J.B. told him.

Shots started to come from the east—down the block north of the gaudy and even from the half-gutted gaudy itself.

J.B. pivoted. The two remaining sec men were hightailing it to his left to put the mass of the dozer between them and the shooters. The Crazy Dog on his bike turned and accelerated down the street, only to jerk, throw up his hands and go down in a grinding crash with his machine.

As he did, a loud report rolled in from the south. Ricky glanced that way.

"It's Ryan!" he said. "Sniped him from the street, just a block down. Now he's running to join the others on this side of the street. They're firing up the Dogs!"

J.B. nodded as he heard more blasters crack.

As if wakening to its danger belatedly, the engine's subterranean grumble rose to an angry bellow.

"Follow!" J.B. shouted, darting around the blade into the open as the bulldozer began to move forward.

Chapter Thirty-One

"Ricky!" Krysty cried in alarm.

But the kid was right on J.B.'s heels.

"He's fine," Ryan said. He raised his head from the Scout's ghost-ring sights to look for other targets. "Blade missed him by at least a foot."

Krysty, Mildred and Jak had taken up position in doorways and an alley on the same side of the street as the Library Lounge, at the far end of the half-block to the south. Ryan had lingered a few feet out to blast the fleeing Dog. Now he moved to the cover of the alley, too.

The Crazy Dogs and their sec men allies were mostly lined up behind the bulldozer, spilling back up the main street from the intersection. Most of them seemed content to watch the show from a point that made it hard for the gaudy's die-hard defenders to get a bead on them.

Until J.B. and Ricky made their move, that seemed to be the only fire directed at the invaders. For all their vaunted well-armed status, and the spirited way they'd wielded those arms in defense of themselves and their ville, the Super Dozer's onslaught seemed to have shocked them to inaction. All their weapons were small arms, and visibly produced no more effect on the monster machine than spit.

From a standing start J.B. and Ricky seemed to pose no more threat to the machine or its operator than a pair of early mosquitoes buzzing around outside the bulletproof cab. But the operator couldn't *see* them. That clearly worried him.

The dozer lurched ahead to try to crush them. To his relief Ryan saw J.B. and Ricky dart clear. Unfortunately that put them on the far side of the mobile yellow mountain that was the dozer.

The dozer ground ten feet forward across the street, then bucked to a stop. Black smoke chugged from the stack of the dozer's 12-cylinder diesel engine and its gigantic mass pivoted counterclockwise with startling speed. Realizing he had missed his quarry on his first try, the driver was trying to catch them and grind them beneath the broad treads.

Gunshots had started to crack out again from the west side of the street where the Dogs and Joker Creek sec men were. Then J.B. and Ricky burst back around the blade, running clockwise.

Somehow realizing that his prey had dodged, and which way, the dozer operator reversed the machine's rotation, which was not an instantaneous process, given the thing's tons of mass. That gave J.B. and Ricky a chance to circle again between blade and gaudy.

Once more the dozer's bulk sheltered them from shots from the on-looking invaders. Krysty popped a shot off at the Crazy Dogs from her 640, although at this range she'd be lucky to hit anything. That recalled Ryan to the notion of trying to lay down cover fire.

He sighted on a Dog standing astride his bike cranking rounds out from a lever-action longblaster and dropped him with a shot that went through his chest armpit to armpit.

What are they doing? Ryan wondered. *How can I help them if I don't know what they're trying to accomplish?*

The pair ran around the far side of the Super Dozer again. This time the machine backed as it pivoted counterclockwise, ramming its yellow stern into the building on the southwest corner of the intersection.

"Listen well, you blackguards!" a voice rang out. "Your time has come!"

HUDDLED WITH HIS back to the blade, Ricky looked at J.B.

"'Blackguards'?"

The Armorer shrugged. He had his Uzi slung and the backpack off. He was rooting inside.

Ricky looked back at the Library Lounge. The whole gaudy sagged noticeably toward the immense hole the dozer had punched in the front of it. The front of the second floor had actually split open; a wide crack showed in the floorboards. A figure all in black crouched in a window of the floor right above it, still a good fifteen or sixteen feet off the ground.

Her slim form encased in what looked like tight-fitting black leather, a black coat shrouding her shoulders, Dark Lady crouched like a panther in what had been a third story. She had a megaphone to her mouth and a furious look on what little Ricky could see of her pale face past the instrument.

Even in that flash glance Ricky thought there was something very different about the gaudy owner now. Not just her garb.

Nervously he looked to his left—northwest. The thick steel blade, twenty-four feet wide by eleven feet tall and bulletproof, protected them from invader bullets. *Most* of them.

But with the mighty machine oriented diagonally to the intersection, there was functionally no place he and the Armorer could find cover from *all* of them.

As best of a bad lot of alternatives, J.B. had picked the right front of the blade to hide behind when the dozer came to rest. That put them at the monster's northeast corner, which meant that coldhearts to the northwest had a clear view of them. And "view," of course, meant *shot.*

Fortunately that was the side. He and J.B. had cleared most of the enemy from there earlier during the bulldozer's gyrations. With a little help from Ryan and his Scout. Unfortunately several coldhearts had shifted that way hastily as the dozer slam-backed into the building across the intersection from the Library Lounge.

That meant there was nothing between them and a clump of heavily armed, pissed-off-past-nuke-red invaders but a few yards of air.

But the enemy wasn't paying the pair any attention. The coldhearts were completely distracted by Dark Lady's startling advent.

Like a dozing dragon coming awake, the bulldozer's tremendous diesel engine began to roar louder and louder. The whole fabric of the mighty machine vibrated against Ricky's back.

"What's she doing?" he shouted. "She'll get killed."

"Buying us what we need," J.B. said. "Get ready to run alongside this bastard."

With a splintering screech, the dozer lurched forward out of the building it had back-rammed as the operator put it in gear. J.B. grabbed Ricky's arm and towed him.

"Follow me!"

CROUCHED BEHIND THE tailgate of a horse wag parked in front of the frame building that occupied the half-block south of the Library Lounge, Ryan stopped sniping at the foe to watch the scene unfold in front of him, whatever the nuke it was.

With Ricky in tow J.B. darted up the street toward Ryan as the Super Dozer lurched forward. The big bastard engine gave it startling acceleration for its size, although nobody was going to confuse the yellow metal mountain with a jackrabbit anytime soon.

Ryan glanced at the coldhearts strung out along the west side of the intersection, ready to blast any who showed the least sign of opening up on the now-exposed pair. But the invaders were all staring at the woman in the window of the stricken gaudy.

The apparently doomed woman. The dozer diver clearly meant to ram the Lounge again, right under where Dark Lady was positioned.

The dozer struck the building. This time was nowhere near as dramatic as the first—it hit mostly the hole its first attack had made.

But Dark Lady did not passively wait for the charging behemoth to bring death to her.

She attacked.

As the machine plunged its blade into the heart of her home once more, she sprang. The dozer's front deck, between the blade and the guardrail around the engine, was actually not more than a couple of feet beneath the window of the sagging third floor. She landed lightly on her feet, then crouched onto a pale hand to make clear she wasn't scraped off by the second floor of her own headquarters.

But the dozer stopped. The engine roar dwindled.

Dark Lady straightened. She'd thrown away her loud-hailer. But she didn't need it to make her ringing challenge heard.

"Now you'll find out," she shouted, reaching both hands across her chest beneath her long coat, "what it means to trifle with a *fully trained Combat Librarian!*"

"Are those really a thing?" Ryan heard Krysty call to Mildred.

"I don't know, Krysty," the freezie replied. "I know a lot, but I don't know everything!"

Just as the coldhearts snapped out of their own temporary inaction and began raising their blasters, Dark Lady's hands came out of her coat. Each one held what Ryan was flat astonished to recognize as a Micro-Uzi: a foot-long miniature cousin of the very machine pistol J.B. had strapped over his back. Each flashed fire as Dark Lady ripped off short bursts, alternating left and right, with a professional precision Ryan could only admire.

Meanwhile J.B. had darted back to the side of the dozer. He heaved the backpack on top of the right-hand track. The return rollers held the giant loop of segmented metal plates well above the top of his fedora, which he used his recently freed hand to clamp to the top of his head as he raced balls-out for the street that ran down the gaudy's south flank.

After a quick, befuddled glance, Ricky followed.

Ryan shouldered his Steyr. He fired as soon as his front sight lined up on a sec man aiming a shiny-chromed blaster at the fleeing pair. The man spun down to the street as Ryan's 7.62 mm round ripped through him.

Ryan wasn't sure where he'd hit him. He also didn't care. He jacked the action and looked for somebody else to shoot.

The bulldozer's engine roared again. The driver started to back up as if he could somehow get away from the slim and vengeful woman in black, spitting two-fisted fire on his very own front deck.

From the corner of his eye he saw J.B. grab Ricky's sleeve and drag the kid with him into a forward dive to the street. They hadn't quite made the corner. Apparently J.B. had more pressing concerns.

Those concerns became obvious when the contents of the backpack he had chucked onto the track detonated in an eye-searing white flash. A heartbeat later the savage crack of C-4 plas-ex going off hit Ryan hard in the ears. He actually felt the concussion wave on his face.

Mostly backed from the ruined gaudy, the dozer suddenly began wheeling to its left. There wasn't much else it could do. Ryan saw that the right-hand track was broken right above where the arm that moved the blade forked into upper and lower supports.

Dark Lady had hunkered down, bracing herself against the engine railing with a right hand still filled by Micro-Uzi. The front of the dozer had protected her from the force of the blast.

Now she leaned out to open fire on the coldhearts once more, as J.B. and Ricky scuttled on all fours the rest of the way around the side of her HQ.

Frantically the dozer driver reversed direction. That only resulted in the huge machine pivoting back right into the front of the gaudy again. Ryan saw Dark Lady duck to avoid being decapitated.

As she did, he saw her let the full-auto handblaster she held in her left hand fall to hang by a short lanyard from her slender wrist. Her right thumb hit the release and dropped the mag of her right-hand weapon. Her left hand plucked a fresh magazine from the harness she wore under her coat and slammed it home. Then she switched off and repeated the operation.

Ryan grunted. *Neat trick,* he thought. He shot the crown of a tall Crazy Dogs' woman aiming an SKS at the gaudy owner.

And Combat Librarian, he amended, whatever *that* was. Apparently their training worked, though.

It finally dawned on the dozer driver that his invincible machine was functionally now a gigantic yellow paperweight. Unlike a tank, it didn't mount any blasters. Its only tool was its tremendous mass—and its ability to move it.

Now it could only turn this way and that in place, which was the same as not being able to move at all.

Even with their main cannon and auxiliary machine guns, Ryan knew the armor-wag crew would lose its grit when its mobile fortress turned out not to be so mobile anymore.

The dozer operator freaked out. He yanked open the door of the sealed cab, which had undoubtedly been locked, and tried to dive out.

Unfortunately he found himself looking up at a very vengeful Dark Lady, who now stood on the broad steel step beside the cab—and up the barrels of her full-auto handblasters.

Which blasted a quick burst each. A spray of bright red liquid suddenly painted over the inside of the windshield on Ryan's side.

The Super Dozer's engine died away to a subdued dragon purr.

Dark Lady ducked back around the front of the cab as a fusillade broke out belatedly from the intruders. Most of them had gone to ground when J.B.'s track-cutting charges had cracked off—the woman Ryan had just chilled had been an exception.

More blasterfire ripped J.B.'s and Ricky's way. The two ducked farther back up the street to get out of the line of fire.

Lining up another shot, Ryan frowned. Morale was a funny thing. At a time like this, it could go either way. Seeing their almighty weapon neatly trumped, they could either panic the way the operator did, or they could get double-pissed.

Unfortunately, it looked like they had picked what Mildred would have called Door Number Two.

And there were still *dozens* of the bastards. Ryan heard

a familiar voice, now lacking its former electronic amplification but needing it even less than Dark Lady had, roar out, "Never mind the dozer! Boys and girls, we got the taints! Chill them all!"

Ryan looked. But there was no sign of Trumbo. The traitor sec boss of Joker Creek was clearly canny enough to exhort his troops from behind the safety of the now-stationary bulldozer.

Motorcycle engines rose to a triumphant and expectant howl. The Dogs and their allies prepared to attack.

Ryan raised his piece and aimed. There was no running now. They would just die tired. The only course he saw was to chill as much as he could before he himself got chilled.

From the west came a rip of full-auto fire.

Chapter Thirty-Two

The big Dog Ryan was drawing down on had just started his ride rolling forward. He slewed the bike to his left and stared back up the main street in what even through the iron ghost-ring sights Ryan thought to recognize as shocked surprise.

Another snarl of blasterfire rang out. A sec man near the biker dropped, thrashing.

By then Ryan had corrected his aim. The Crazy Dog leaned down over the bars of his big machine as if to accelerate away. Before he could, Ryan had shifted aim a fraction again, drawn a breath, let it partway out, caught it. *Squeezed.*

The Scout boomed and bucked. The Dog jerked as the speeding 7.62 mm round shattered a vertebra between his shoulder blades and tumbled to bring Hell to his heart and lungs. From the exaggerated spray of blood out the far side of him as the longblaster came back down, Ryan reckoned it had to have made a big exit wound.

The motorcycle fell. Another sec man raced north to south across Ryan's field of vision, frantically shooting a six-gun-style blaster to the west. He stumbled as red burst from his thigh and went down.

"It's a trap!" Ryan heard Trumbo holler. "Everyone for himself! *Clear out!*"

Like flocks of frightened birds, the invaders broke north

and south as if suddenly stone desperate to get away from the main street and the gaudy itself, where J.B. and Ricky had joined their fire to Dark Lady's.

In passing, Ryan decided the slightly built gaudy owner had to be stronger than he thought to hold up that much ammo.

He saw Trumbo speed past on a bike with double exhaust pipes. Ryan snapped a shot at him but missed. The sec boss simply kept going, south. He was getting out of Amity Springs, just as he'd advised his fellow coldhearts to do.

In a moment the intersection, so far as Ryan could tell, was clear of Dogs. At least functioning ones; half a dozen wounded lay in his line of sight, some stirring feebly and moaning, others flopping like landed fish and wailing.

Her twin machine pistols held at the ready, Dark Lady stepped out from behind the cover of the now-dormant Super Dozer.

Ryan had been focusing on the Dogs and sec men as they fled past. He had decided not to waste any more cartridges on them unless any of them showed signs of turning back to the fight. But they didn't need his help to keep their minds right. Whatever was coming down the main street at the shattered Library Lounge had well and truly impressed them.

Now from the corner of his eye he saw a young Crazy Dog with short blond hair and a batwing mask over his eyes—whether war paint or tattoo, Ryan knew no more than cared—suddenly rear up. He aimed a big double-action blaster at Dark Lady from thirty feet away.

Something to her right had caught her attention. He had her dead to rights.

Once more a blaster ripped on full-auto, this time from so close the echoes hammering back and forth between buildings stung Ryan's ears almost as much as the shots themselves. This was no 9 mm handblaster like the pair the gaudy owner carried.

The coldheart's chest exploded red. His blaster hand jerked up. His chill-shot cracked off into the merciless blue of the cloudless early morning sky.

He fell on his face with the floppy finality that told Ryan he was never getting up on his own.

Into the mouth of the intersection came a startling double apparition. It was Sinclair, the wag yard owner Ryan had last seen apparently getting crushed under a barrier wag overturned by the dozer. His face was a mask of sweat-stuck grime, from which his eyes blazed like beacons of vengeance. His coat and shirt were gone. A rough bandage had been wound around his upper torso. It was red-drenched with blood.

He held his BAR in his right hand. A lengthy sling held the barrel up at waist-level shooting position. His left arm was slung over the shoulder of the stocky, crazy-haired, Asian-looking carpenter named Coffin. The coffin-maker held the wrist in place.

"Feed me," Sinclair called in a feral croak. He dropped the magazine from the well of his Browning. With his right hand Coffin pulled a fresh twenty-round magazine of out of the canvas pouch he wore open on his chest and stuffed it into the longblaster.

They continued to shuffle forward. The wag yard owner's left leg didn't seem to be working well, but on they came, into the intersection in front of the sagging, groaning gaudy.

Behind them, the blond kid named Billy scuttled forward and snagged the dropped magazine.

Behind him came the people of Amity Springs, armed and looking very dangerous indeed.

KRIS HELD AN ax two-handed above her head. The ax descended with a wood-chopping sound.

The wounded biker's shrieks of agony stopped.

Krysty winced.

She knew the whys and wherefores. These people were prosperous and seemed decent. Even kind—as they could afford to be.

But these were still the Deathlands. It was still a brutal wolf-eat-mutie world. And when it came down to survival they were as hard and harsh as they needed to be.

Just like their unofficial baron, the Dark Lady. Though they didn't show it, she thought, in quite such an unexpected fashion.

Kneeling over an injured male entertainer who'd been carried from the perilous ruin of the Library Lounge, Mildred glanced up at the sound. Or likely the cessation. She nodded once with what seemed grim satisfaction, then returned to tending the young man's wounds.

Ryan stood nearby. He held his Scout in both hands and kept his lone blue eye scanning constantly for new danger. He and Krysty were nominally keeping watch—and also catching their breath. Jak had vanished into the Library Lounge, where he was helping a crew led for the moment by Mikey-Bob hunt for survivors. That surprised Krysty more than a little; the young albino generally seemed much more about taking life than preserving it, but then again he also felt a strong instinctive attraction to challenge and danger. With the invaders routed, for the moment, anyway, rescue was the most dangerous game in town.

Dark Lady knelt near another entertainer, a young woman whose eyes stared skyward through a mask of grit-crusted blood. She shook her head and shut those eyes with thumb and forefinger. Then she stood and faced Ryan and his group, who had been standing nearby discussing the situation.

"What will you do now?" she asked.

Despite the gleam of moisture in those black eyes, she presented a very different persona than Krysty had seen from her before—even when she was efficiently and ruthlessly chilling the Crazy Dogs who'd delivered the ultimatum in her gaudy. Then she had seemed little more than a person defending what was hers, although admittedly in more proficient fashion than anticipated. Now, with her coat off and her Micro-Uzis slung under each arm, she looked every inch the trained and seasoned blaster.

"Go after our friend Doc," Ryan said.

"Now? Just the five of you?"

"If need be."

"Old Diego's probably going to be in a vindictive kind of mood once he hears about this," J.B. said, polishing his glasses on his handkerchief. "Baron Sand isn't in charge up at Joker Creek anymore. Rules've changed."

"We can't."

Krysty looked over. Sinclair sat on a coverlet with a cup of water in his good hand. He refused other care while the worse injured required attention.

"We've done what we could," the wag yard owner said. "A quarter of the ville lies in ruins. People have lost loved ones—or had them hurt bad and in need of care. The Lounge is a deathtrap waiting to collapse. We simply can't do more to help you, son."

"Some of us are willing to try," Kris said, walking up with her ax over her shoulder. The head dripped red.

"No, Mrs. Kennard," Dark Lady said sadly. "He's right. If you folks can only wait a day, or better two, then yes. Right now we need to look to our own."

"So do we," Ryan said in a raspy voice.

"You'll throw your lives away," Sinclair said.

His erstwhile assistant, Coffin, was currently helping shift people out of the gaudy. Even though only the living were being brought out now, more than a few of those would become his customers soon. Like the hapless young woman Dark Lady had just bid farewell to—Trixie, Krysty remembered her name was.

"There's still dozens of the bastards left," Sinclair said. "Who knows how many for sure? And they got that nuking fortress of Sand's to anchor them. I know you people are ace at what you do. But against odds like—"

"Wait!" Dark Lady called sharply.

At first Krysty thought she had thought of some reason to contradict her former rival—and current ally, it seemed.

Instead she rapped out a command. She was looking past Ryan and his crew toward where a knot of ville folk gathered around another injured Crazy Dog.

This one was a sandy-bearded man whose once-white shirt was soaked with blood on the left side beneath his open black leather jacket. The right leg of his oil-, sweat- and road-grime-befouled jeans was also shiny with fresh wet. Despite at least two wounds, though, he had hauled himself up to prop his back against the building whose corner the dozer had taken out.

"Might as well chill me, too," he called.

Dark Lady walked toward him. From the way she stiffened, and the black light that flashed in her eyes at that epithet, Krysty thought sure she was about to give him what he asked for.

Instead she wrapped her arms tightly across her chest, beneath her small breasts.

"You seem in a loquacious mood," she said, walking up close to him. Out of striking range if he decided to make a suicide strike with a knife, Krysty noted.

She nodded at the Amity Springers clustered around the wounded man. They backed off. Reluctantly, Krysty thought.

Ryan and Krysty were following. Mildred kept at her work. "If that fancy-ass word means you think I'll talk to you," the man said, "why the nuke not? There aren't any secrets about what I got to say."

"What, then?" Ryan demanded.

"Well, we're taking over," the coldheart said.

"Joker Springs?" Dark Lady asked.

He laughed, then winced at the pain that caused, then laughed again.

"For starters," he said. "Diego and the rest of the boys and girls are back there now teaching the peasants who's boss. And having themselves some fun with that freak show of that fat-ass Sand's. Sorry to miss out on that part."

"My sympathies," Dark Lady said dryly.

He laughed again, then turned aside to spit blood. It mildly surprised Krysty he hadn't tried to spit it at Dark Lady. But he no doubt realized the range was too great for that.

"Oh, well. Can't win 'em all. And you bastards can't win at all!"

"Meaning what?" Ryan said.

"Meaning Diego's put out the word to some of our brother and sister clans. The Suave Monks and the Skull-Shaggers. People like that—like us. We're taking over the Basin. We'll get Joker Creek beaten into line. Then we'll come back here and finish the job proper. And after that we'll take down Río Piojo, and have ourselves an empire!"

Dark Lady looked at Ryan. He looked sternly back.

"Then we can't hang around licking our wounds." Mikey-Bob's voice boomed from behind.

Krysty turned. The two-headed giant had emerged from

the wreckage. Both his heads were coated in dirt and sweat. Jak followed him.

"Looks like nobody's left inside who's still breathing, D.L.," Bob said wearily. "A stiff breeze'd blow this kid away to look at him. But he can sniff out survivors like an old bloodhound."

Jak came up dusting his hands together.

"And you're wrong," Mikey said to his brother. "We need to hunker down."

"He's right," Sinclair said, shuffling up to join the others.

Coffin had emerged from the half-destroyed gaudy, as well, and was once more serving as the red-mustached man's support. Krysty realized he likewise figured the only ones left inside were his clients. And they had infinite patience.

"Now it's obvious," the wag yard owner said. "We have no choice but to concentrate on shoring up our defenses against the storm to come."

"Speak for yourself, Mr. Sinclair," Kris Kennard declared. "Plenty of us are willing to march right on over to Joker Creek and settle this for good and all. One way or another."

While much of the ville's population was involved with rescue and aid missions of their own, the confrontation with the shot-up captive had begun to attract a growing crowd.

Now they raised a many-voiced growl of agreement.

Sinclair shook his head. "There are too many of them to overcome by storm, anyway. We have no choice but to get ready to defeat them here, protecting what remains of our homes!"

"Good luck with that," the Crazy Dog coldheart said, sneering. "The storm Diego's raising will wipe this rat hole right off the Basin slicker than that triple-stupe dozer ever could. He's a magic bastard, and he's got a plan."

Krysty thought he was miffed at losing center stage.

From somewhere came a rising growl of engine noise. Ryan stiffened. Krysty found her snub-nosed blaster in her hand without conscious intent. Around them the knot of ville folk gathered around the wounded coldheart lost their sullen looks in favor of varying degrees of alarm and readiness.

Billy came running out the mouth of the main street. "It's Mr. Dix and Ricky!" he cried excitedly.

A moment later the Crazy Dogs' machine-gun wag rolled into view and stopped. J.B. and Ricky got out of the cab.

"Your shot just busted the tire," J.B. said. "Nothing structural. And they had a spare."

Dark Lady and Ryan exchanged glances again.

"I believe this shifts the odds in our favor," she said.

"What about Sand's castle?" Bob said. "It'd take that dozer to make any impression on it."

"Say! What about it?" his twin asked, brightening. "You're some kind of mechanical wizard, Dix. You even got you a likely sorcerer's apprentice. Can you fix that tread?"

"In a few days," J.B. said, "and with the proper tools. It's not like changing a tire on a wag, friend."

"I have some more blocks of C-4 plas-ex," Dark Lady said thoughtfully. "And blasting caps."

"Hope you don't have those stored together," J.B. said. Then he smiled. "But if that's the case, I believe we can do business."

"You're willing to blast the playhouse down on top of your own pal?" Bob asked.

J.B. chuckled. "Oh, I don't reckon your boss has enough plas-ex for *that*. No, not much danger there. But I bet we can knock a nice new door open."

"He knows what he's doing with plas-ex!" Ricky proclaimed. "None better."

"Kid's right," Ryan said.

"It's insane!" Sinclair exclaimed.

"Much as I hate to agree with the man," Bob said, "he's right."

"Bullshit!" Mikey roared. "Did you just give me sole proprietorship of our balls, or what?"

"Listen, you dark-haired son of a bit—"

"Enough," Dark Lady said.

She didn't raise her voice, but she didn't need to. A single finger upraised in the giant's direction and both twins instantly shut up.

"I find I have come to agree with Mr. Cawdor," she said. "The news that the Crazy Dogs expect imminent reinforcement changes the situation quite dramatically. Win or lose, we cannot remain passive."

"Dark Lady, please—" the wag yard owner began.

"I'm sorry, Mr. Sinclair," she said. "I know you have the ville's safety at heart. Nobody could possibly doubt that, given what you did today. And you have my gratitude for rallying the counterattack that saved us."

Stubbornly, Sinclair shook his balding head. "All I did was get myself up and go after the bastards," he said. "Couldn't've done that much without Mr. Coffin's help. The rest—that was the ville's people themselves."

"So much the braver, then," Dark Lady said. "But I for one refuse to wait."

She turned to Ryan. "Lead us, Mr. Cawdor. I shall follow. And anyone who wishes may, as well."

"It won't be easy," Ryan said. "For one thing, we still have to get close enough to blow a hole in that adobe fort. And there're still a large number of Crazy Dogs and that fat scumbag turncoat bastard Trumbo's sec men who'll have something to say about that. Even with the M-60's firepower on our side, plenty of people marching over to Joker Creek with us won't be marching back on their own legs."

"I'm in!" Kris declared, brandishing her bloody ax.

"So am I," said Stuart Marquez, a young wag repairman who had lost his wife to the intruders.

Other voices joined in. Not all the assembled ville folk agreed, but plenty did.

Krysty grieved for the losses to come, though her heart was gladdened that they'd have help rescuing Doc.

"What about you?" Dark Lady said to the wounded coldheart. "Are you willing to surrender and give me your parole not to escape, if I give you your life in return?"

"Hell no!" the wounded coldheart snarled. "If I can get my pins under me, I'll fight you, with my teeth and bare hands if I got to. And if not, I reckon I'll just sit by and drink and laugh while I watch hundreds of the rastiest, nastiest, coldest bastards and slavers to ride the West rape your bony ass to death. So you might as well just chill me, bitch!"

"As you wish," Dark Lady said coldly.

Like smooth lightning, she withdrew her right-hand machine pistol. It stuttered deafeningly.

The quick pulse of 9 mm bullets smashed the coldheart's face into itself in red ruin like a blow from a sledgehammer.

"I really dislike the word *bitch*."

Chapter Thirty-Three

"It was a trap," Doc heard Trumbo exclaim breathlessly from the salon. "They took out the dozer and shot the rest of us to shit. I was lucky to bring anybody back alive."

He knelt with his ear pressed to the bottom of a heavy glass, which in turn was pressed to the thick wood of the door. Beside him knelt Baron Sand, similarly equipped. It had given Doc a quite thoroughly childish delight to discover she knew the same trick of amplifying speech through a solid barrier.

"I notice you showed a lot of skill and initiative in bringing your own fat ass back without any new holes in it, Trumbo," the biker baron Diego said dryly.

Beneath the muted conversation, Doc heard the pops and ripple of blasterfire. And screams. Fortunately these were nowhere near as close as Doc and the baron had been forced to listen to for too long a time before.

The people of Joker Creek, it seemed, were not accepting their new overlords with the grace Diego seemed to expect. Or at least not with the alacrity.

"Believe me...Baron," Trumbo said, with only the briefest of pauses before the honorific. "You're lucky to get anything back at all. The bastards are *heeled*."

"Yeah. Well. You can quit shivering before you lose control of your asshole and shit down your leg. I reckon I'll need all the bullet magnets I can get here right directly.

Anyway, if the bastards do make a play here, we'll have the machine-gun wag to teach 'em the error of their ways."

"Uh, about that, boss," said a voice Doc failed to recognize. It was a man's baritone, and not decidedly firm at the moment.

"Yes?"

"We, uh, we lost the 60-wag back at the ville. Got shot right to glowing nightshit, it did."

"Did it now?"

Diego's voice was silky. It had dropped so far in volume Doc could barely hear it. Its sibilance reminded Doc of a braided silken lash sliding nude pink and shiny over in…happier times.

Despite their deficit in years, by any clock or calendar one cared to specify, the dear baron had certainly expanded Theophilus Tanner's repertory of experiences. Especially sensual ones.

"And who's the highest-ranking member of the crew I sent out to make it back here still breathing?"

"Uh, that'd be me, Baron," the same shaky baritone said.

Transmitted through the hollow glass, the blaster shot stung Doc's ear and made him jump upright. It would have been loud even muffled by the door. As it was, his ear rang cruelly. Clearly, the Crazy Dog chieftain's Desert Eagle was of some colossal caliber.

More deliberately, Sand straightened. She had set her glass on the floor by the door. Now she massaged her ringing ear.

"I think we've heard all we need to," she said. "We need to prepare."

"For what?"

"To depart."

"What? You mean we have had the means to get out of here all along?"

"Of course," she said with a smirk that under the circumstances he could only find fatuous. "I'm a con artist—a bunco steerer, as I believe you would say, in that charmingly anachronistic fashion of yours. You don't think I made preparation for any manner of covert departure?"

"Then why have we not departed before this?" he demanded. "Or—to be more realistic, I suppose—why have *you* not departed?"

"I won't leave you, dear heart. When I go, you go with me."

"But why?"

"I won't lie and tell you I've fallen in love with you. Well, more than just a little. But men of your quality are beyond rare in our decayed age. I value that."

He furrowed his brow. He longed to believe her. After all, it would be so easy for her to try to play on my vanity, he thought. And, honesty compels to admit, more than likely succeed.

"Allow me return to my original question," he said, aware he was probably blushing and wishing to skate past the fact. "Why not escape before, if you were able to? Why did you stand by and listen while your friends suffered at the hands of Diego and his Crazy Dogs?"

A look of pain so profound he could not help but take it as genuine racked her face.

"Yes," she whispered. "I listened. And it tore me up inside. I won't be so fatuous as to say I felt their pain, nor anything as poignant as they went through. But I felt my own pain."

He remembered, then, that tears had streamed in rivers down her face, and she had pounded her fists on the wall until he expected her to leave bloody marks. He regretted having asked the second question.

"Escape to where?" she asked him. "More to the point,

to what? Would it have helped my people if I joined them in their torments in the flesh, do you think?"

"Baron, I'm sorry—" For the first time it struck him he still had no idea as to her first name.

She waved his apology to silence.

"Trumbo knows how devious I am. And Diego, for all his studiedly uncultured manner and somewhat rough-and-ready approach to personnel management, is the opposite of triple stupe."

"Indeed."

"So they'll be keeping careful watch lest we slip away. Sadly, my escape preparations failed to include digging a secret escape tunnel out of this bedroom. It was always my plan, but it kept slipping down the to-do list. Curse responsibility! I should have known better than to try to play the role of lord of the manor in real life—"

She shook her head. Outside in the front room Diego was loudly berating. Trumbo, mostly, it appeared; but also his Dogs and the world in general. He seemed affronted at his associates for having both failed and lived. But as indicated, except for the hapless ranking leader, he seemed disposed to allow them to live long enough to die gloriously in his service.

"Anyway. My escape options require waiting upon opportunity. Your friends are going to provide a most splendid one in the form of a diversion. And I expect, sooner rather than later."

"They shall come for me," Doc agreed. "Just as Ryan promised. But you seem to expect their imminent arrival. Is that realistic, so soon after repelling the Dogs' attack?"

"Your friends seem to be of decisive bent," she said. "And also—we overheard Diego and Trumbo talking about how Diego sent up the Bat Signal for every coldheart and villain this side of the Rocks."

"The what?"

"You're not familiar with comic books? From before skydark, you know."

He shook his head. "I know of the phenomenon. Nothing more."

"Never mind. Your one-eyed, wicked and undoubtedly wonderful Mr. Cawdor will have learned reinforcements are expected. Unless all the fallen Crazy Dogs and my traitorous former employees, may plutonium eat their guts, got themselves thoroughly chilled—well, would you say it's a safe assumption that your man will have both thought to ask the question *and* gotten an answer?"

Doc wiped a hand down his face. "Yes. He may have but a single eye, but it overlooks little. And his methods in interrogation, as in most things, tend to be both cunning and abrupt."

"All right, then. They'll be here. So will Dark Lady, if I know the minx, and if she survived. And because I do, most intimately, she did and she will. So—"

She cast a glance at the bed, which lay unmade inside its decadent silken canopy. Regretfully, she shook her head.

"We should have a few hours before your friends come to call," she said. "But you're nothing if not resourceful devils, the lot of you. We don't know for sure when they'll arrive. And we dare not get caught with our proverbial pants down."

She gave him a grin. "And speaking of which—don't you think it's time you put yours on, Doc?"

WHEN THE BIZARRE procession came in sight of the farms and neat small homes of Joker Creek, the first thing Krysty saw, riding in the bed of the machine-gun wag, was a half-naked woman running up the road toward them.

A trio of Crazy Dogs on motorcycles pursued her,

whooping and laughing so loud Krysty could hear them a couple hundred yards off, even over the snarling of their bikes. They were clearly playing with her, allowing her to move ahead before sprinting after her.

Behind them, a dozen fires burned alongside Joker Creek. For what it was worth, at least two were black—meaning gasoline, meaning most likely Crazy Dogs' machines. Houses or sheds or crops would burn with brown or white smoke.

One of the Crazy Dog riders led the rest by perhaps twenty yards. He accelerated now, running up on the helpless woman.

"Stop the wag!" Krysty shouted.

The driver was Stuart Marquez, the brown-haired young artisan widowed in the attack on Amity Springs. Though he mostly worked with horse-drawn wags, he showed enough ability handling the Dodge for J.B. to trust him to drive it. Krysty's loader was the shopkeeper, Kris Kennard, who had also lost her husband to the Dogs. She had a blue bandanna tied around her short red hair, and a quietly determined manner.

The wag stopped. Krysty was already lining up her shot.

She was no trained machine gunner, and this was a long shot to make safely. But this wasn't her first time shooting one, either. And she felt the fleeing woman had more at risk from her not shooting, so—

The pedestal mount sucked up most of the recoil, but the heavy black blaster's steel butt plate vibrated against Krysty's right shoulder in a most unpleasant fashion. She was glad she'd learned to shoot the potent weapon in short bursts.

She managed to keep this one to three rounds. Fire and shock made the very air dance in front of her eyes, but the lead rider and his machine went down.

The following pair braked in alarm. They had either assumed the machine-gun wag approaching openly down the road from Amity Springs was still on their side, or had been preoccupied with their sadistic game.

Either way, it was too late. Two quick bursts put them down, as well.

Kris showed her a grin and a work-reddened thumbs-up.

"Go ahead, please, Stuart," Krysty called. "Slowly."

"Yes, ma'am."

The truck accelerated to the walking pace at which it had driven the whole way from Amity Springs. Daring a quick glance back, she saw Dark Lady and Mikey-Bob, trailing by ten yards, gesture for the party of thirty or forty ville citizens to follow them toward Baron Sand's domain.

They're so well armed, Krysty thought. *And they seem as determined as Kris is. But will they be enough—even with us to help them?*

"Krysty!" Kris exclaimed.

She snapped her eyes forward.

No doubt exhausted, the Joker Creek woman had stopped as soon as she realized she was no longer pursued. She stood now panting, her heavy bare breasts riding up and down above the ripped remnants of a peasant dress. She was no longer young, nor slender. But a strenuous farm life had clearly kept her in strong shape.

But now a coldheart suddenly sprang up and grabbed her from behind. Krysty guessed it was the first one she'd shot. He pressed a silver handblaster up under the hinge of the woman's jaw.

"Come ahead, you bastards!" he shouted. "Come on! I'll blow her head off! Then I'll chill you. This is the Dogs' Pound now. You don't come to attack us here!"

From the streamward side of the ditch a shadow seemed

to flit behind the Crazy Dog. It was mostly dark, but snow-white at the top.

Suddenly the coldheart's blaster arm was seized and thrust skyward. It cracked a futile shot into a midafternoon sky that showed a few scattered wisps of red-green clouds.

Then a big blade punched through his neck, left to right. Something torqued him counterclockwise, away from his victim, who dropped shrieking to her knees.

Blood fountained as Jak pushed the blade of a big trench knife out through the front of the Dog's throat.

Before the man dropped Jak twisted his blaster neatly from his dying hand. He waved it jauntily at Krysty, then he disappeared back into the tall weeds of the ditch, which had already grown well green with spring.

Krysty smiled. Her menfolk had gone ahead of the rest, meaning to infiltrate the settlement.

Mildred had remained in Amity Springs to tend to the many people wounded in the Crazy Dogs' assault. Ryan hadn't batted his eye at her decision. Mildred was an ace hand with a blaster, and triple good in a fight. But in this battle, one blaster more or less wasn't going to tip over any tables.

The wag continued to roll forward. Krysty heard the crackle of blasterfire from the houses ahead. Though probably less well-armed than the people of Dark Lady's ville, Sand's subjects did have blasters, and they weren't reluctant to use them in defense against the invaders. One-sided though that battle would undoubtedly prove.

Or would, had it not been for Ryan, Dark Lady, and their respective people.

Dark Lady sprinted out ahead of the slow-rolling pickup truck to bend briefly over the woman Krysty had rescued. She was slumped on her knees, sobbing into her hands. Dark Lady hastily examined her, then signaled that she was uninjured. As the wag passed, the slim woman in black helped the other to her feet and off the road.

Targets began to appear. No doubt making too much racket of their own, the marauding Crazy Dogs were initially unaware their blaster wag had returned—and turned on them. They were involved in kicking down doors, engaging in firefights with locals, and of course, victimizing those they had already subdued.

Krysty chilled them. It was almost appallingly easy. From the dozens of coldhearts in view she could pick out the easiest shots and blast them, with minimal danger to the locals.

Meanwhile she thought to hear shots in the distinctive voice of Ryan's Scout carbine, and occasional bursts of what she suspected was J.B.'s Uzi. She guessed her four male friends were putting their own pressure on the Dogs.

Being caught between cross fire was one of the greatest fears felt by anybody in battle, Krysty knew. Although a close second was being helplessly blasted by somebody with unmatchable superior firepower, which was also the Crazy Dogs' case. In short order all the coldhearts in sight were retreating to Baron Sand's playhouse. Some were actually reduced to fleeing on foot.

When they were still a good three hundred yards out, well in among the farm dwellings, Krysty called for Stuart to halt the wag.

Dark Lady came up alongside the vehicle. Mikey-Bob came with her like a vast, dumpy shadow.

"Good placement," the gaudy owner said with a brief approving nod. "You can support us from here."

Krysty grinned. "And the defenders forted up in the house will have a hard time hitting us at this range."

Plus she thought the machine-gun barrel could use some time to cool off, even though she'd been quite careful to keep her bursts brief. They had found no further spare barrels, either in the Crazy Dogs' wag or in Dark Lady's recovered arsenal. Not that Krysty had the first notion how to change barrels if she *had* a replacement.

Dark Lady nodded. She signaled for her followers to spread out and advance to either side of the road. They set out, working from cover to cover.

Both heads of Mikey-Bob met Krysty's eyes and nodded, as well. Then the two-headed giant was off, sticking with his mistress like a dog.

Krysty kept her eyes peeled for targets. Kris worked as loader as if she'd trained for the job, keeping the belts of linked ammunition from kinking as she fed them to Krysty, inserting new ones in the loading tray when the big blaster ran dry. She did her tasks with a calm and stolid determination, plus a set expression that might be mistaken for a smile. At a distance.

One thing they had was ample ammunition. Linked cartridges in the appropriate caliber were something Dark Lady had found in the lost lab's armory, though Krysty's reluctance to risk overheating the blaster kept her expenditures frugal regardless. She heard shooting from the ragged bunch of Amity Springers as they skirmished forward. Some of them showed a tendency to clump together, at which point she saw either Dark Lady or Mikey-Bob, who had taken opposite sides of the road, would hurriedly get them to break it up.

"Uh, Krysty?" It was Stuart, their driver. He had his head out his window and turned to look back at her.

"Yes, Stuart—?" she began.

From the right-hand corner of her eye she saw a form step out from behind a lean-to-style shed, just twenty yards down the road on the right.

An AK-47 bellowed on full automatic.

The truck quivered to ringing impacts. The near side of Stuart's head erupted in gore even as he tried to yank it back inside.

He seemed to melt into the cab. The wag started moving forward, picking up speed.

The sec man continued to blast his whole 30-round magazine into the wag. A bullet smashed a fist-wide chunk out of the rear window and whined past Krysty's left hip.

The redhead started holding down the big blaster's trigger even before its muzzle brake swung to bear on the blaster man.

He did a brief dance of death as a volley of rounds sleeted through him, scarcely slowed by flesh or bone.

As he fell, a familiar, terrifying tang went up Krysty's nostrils and seemed to clutch at sinuses, palate and throat with taloned fingers. *Gasoline!*

"We're on fire!" she heard Kris scream.

Chapter Thirty-Four

"So it begins," Baron Sand said, with a single crisp nod. "Is there still a guard on the window, dear heart?"

The baron was dressed in a loose white shirt, khaki cargo pants, and moccasins with thick leather soles. Given her flamboyant nature, Doc was mildly surprised she possessed an outfit more practical. Nonetheless, if he had learned one thing from his forced—if far from fully onerous—association with the Baron of Joker Creek, it was indeed to expect the unexpected.

"There is, regrettably," he reported.

"Very well," she said. She uttered a short laugh. "Riskier this way, but I admit I prefer it. I hate to bore, but if I must, I prefer to bore from within!"

Turning away from the window and stepping back to avoid chance discovery by the guard, although the man seemed preoccupied by the firefight raging on the building's far side, Doc shook his head.

"How can you think of wordplay in such a situation as this?"

"What better time?" she asked in a tone of manic flippancy. "If we cannot play, how can we truly be said to live? Now, do be a dear, and help me."

He had dressed, as well, in his usual clothes. The baron went to kneel beside her big bed. He hunkered down beside her as she began rummaging beneath.

"Here," she said, handing something back to him.

To his surprise it was a slim length of steel, like a fencing epee without the bell guard, and with the tip filed to a lethal point. As he took it and experimentally hefted it, he realized that was precisely what it was.

"And here," Sand said with satisfaction. She pulled back and reared up, brandishing—

"The key to the lock that keeps us pent in," she declared. "They were fools to think they could restrain me that easily. But of course, that's our gain, is it not?"

Her eyes were bright. Her cheeks were flushed. Under most circumstances those signs would have presaged another bout of wild rapacious sex. Instead she contented herself with standing and kissing him quickly but hard on the lips.

"Do you trust me?" she asked.

"Absolutely not."

"Smart man," she said. "But I knew that. And in this case, you *can* trust me. Although I'll not ask you to take it on faith. Rather, let that fine brain of yours calculate how rare the ways are in which I could gain from betraying you, under such circumstances as we find ourselves in."

He nodded. It already had. If anything, the baron was showing a lack of wisdom in trusting *him*.

"No hidden blasters?" he asked.

She shook her head. "Never really got along with them."

"But don't you want a weapon, as well?"

She smiled and handed him the key. "Oh, I'll have one."

The one she chose made his eyes widen.

She took up station beside the door.

"Key in lock," she directed softly. He obeyed.

"On three, unlock and throw the door open *fast*."

He was puzzled, but he understood the instructions and nodded to indicate so. He went ahead and thrust the sharpened epee into his belt to use both hands.

"One, two—*three.*"

The key turned. He turned the latch and flung the door outward as fast as he could.

"Hey!" the sec man on guard exclaimed.

Doc followed Sand closely as she stepped quickly into the hall and turned toward the sec man. He was young, unshaved, and as Doc saw in a flash, bleary-eyed. He appeared to have been leaning against the wall taking a nap when the door was so rudely flung open.

Now he gaped at the baron and reached for the long-barreled shotgun leaning against the wall beside him.

In her hands Sand carried a chamber pot. It held the various wastes they'd excreted during the course of a day or night; the sec men swapped it out with a similar one once every morning. It was white with blue figures of Rococo gentlemen and ladies in wigs disporting themselves. Its lid fit well enough to contain the more mephitic vapors. At least until it was inevitably opened, in the course of its intended employment.

Now Sand upended it neatly over the guard's head. It actually came down over his eyes like a helmet.

As he choked and gagged, she deftly plucked the shotgun away from him and stepped back.

"Stab him," she said.

Doc did. He thrust the hapless young man as justly through the heart as he could. He was rewarded with the man folding promptly.

The pot hit the floor with a clatter. It didn't break. By that time somebody was firing shots from a handblaster out a front window, while the shooting outside had grown to a veritable storm. Nobody seemed likely to hear that additional slight noise above everything else.

"Follow me," she said. He noticed she had managed not

to get a drop of the chamber pot's contents on her. Fortunately, neither had he.

She led him swiftly down the hall away from the front room. And then to his amazement, stopped at the door of what he knew to be a storage closet.

A WEIGHT CAUGHT Krysty in the midriff and flung her bodily right over the side of the pickup's bed as the wag picked up speed.

She landed on her back. The air exploded out of her as the weight landed full on her.

Right beside where the sec man had stepped out with his AK, the truck nosed into the ditch on the opposite side. It whoomped into a ball of yellow flame.

"I'm sorry, dear," the weight atop her said. "I hope you're all right."

"Can't...breathe."

"Oh. Right."

Kris sat up, still straddling Krysty's hips. But without her substantial weight pressing down on her, Krysty's lungs began to work again. She sucked down deep breaths as the woman adjusted her bandanna atop her short red hair, dusted herself off and stood.

"Let me help you, dearie," she said, extending a hand down. "It's the least I can do, since I threw you there and fell on top of you."

Krysty took her hand. It was strong and callused. Though Krysty was tall for a woman and exceptionally well-muscled, the sturdy shopkeeper simply pulled her to her feet with a single grunt of effort.

Despite their situation, and the death of poor Stuart, Krysty couldn't help but laugh. "Thanks. But I'd say saving my life made up for everything just fine!"

Kris looked down the road. The Amity Springs' people

seemed to have taken up positions behind the buildings nearest the big house. Return fire was coming from the playhouse's outbuildings, including the barn, as well as the giant structure that Krysty realized had to have concealed Sand's monstrous bulldozer.

Her heart soared as she saw Ryan lean around the corner of a stout adobe home and fire a shot at the main house.

"I suppose we'd best get going and join them," Kris said, "before they have all the fun without us."

Kris scuttled quickly off the road to the right, to get out of line of the fire coming from the baron's house. As bullets cracked over Krysty's head, she hastened to join her.

"I need a weapon," she said, crouching by the body of the man who had blasted Stuart and their truck. "I'll take his. He's not using it. And he has spare magazines."

Krysty pulled her own handblaster and came up to crouch behind the same shed that had concealed the sec man.

"Do you know how—" she began.

Straightening with the assault blaster in her right hand, Kristen ejected the magazine, slammed home a new one and racked the slide to chamber a round.

"You were asking?"

"Never mind," Krysty said.

A SMALL WINDOW—too small even for his spare frame to wriggle through, Doc noted with regret—let shade-dimmed afternoon light into the closet. It was stuffy and crowded with mops, brooms and shelves with dusty containers and bolts of brightly colored cloth. A tang of cedar used against moths tended to make the atmosphere more oppressive, rather than feel fresher.

At the rear of the closet Sand had her back turned to Doc and was bent over. Her shoulders worked.

He heard a click. Sand stepped back, raising what he had taken to be somewhat roughly finished dark wood paneling. Instead it was a hidden hatch.

"A secret compartment?" he said, amused.

She turned and gave him a smile and a shrug. "Of course."

"Of course," he said. "What is in there?"

"Your personal gear," she said, turning and presenting him with his LeMat in its holster. He accepted and donned it. She laid his swordstick across her palm, handle toward him, and bowed.

"I thank you, madam," he said, bowing back. He picked it up.

"You're welcome," she said. "And don't call me madam. That's my opposite number's job. And what is also in here—" she stepped to one side and gestured into the hidden hutch with both hands "—is my store of the ready."

He was about to ask what that meant, then he saw: stacks of notes, clearly the jack of the area. Metal boxes. A few small items, clearly scavvied late-twentieth-century technology whose purpose even he could not divine.

"Why are you showing me this?"

She shrugged. "You know what they say—you can't take it with you."

He turned to her in horrified surprise. Notwithstanding the fact she had been first his opponent, and then his captor, he had come to harbor...positive feelings for her. For her lively intelligence, her wit, her remarkable insight and remarkably insouciant view of life as much for her enthusiastic and skillful sexual charms.

And now, of course, they were allies. Although he realized she had as much as told him she was not to be trusted, and that could change at any time.

Still, he didn't like the import of her words.

"Surely you are not planning to—"

The closet door opened behind them.

"I thought I heard talking in here," a squat familiar figure said.

"Son of a bitch!" With the startling alacrity of which she was capable despite her size, Sand sprang past Doc, grabbing at the dead door guard's break-action single-shot scattergun leaned against a set of shelves.

Trumbo's blaster sounded like Thor's hammer striking the Anvil of the Gods in the tight closet. A flash filled the room. Sand screamed and grabbed her arm and fell against the wall.

"Quit sniveling," the turncoat sec boss said. "I just winged you. You've been a naughty girl, Baron. Diego is gonna want to punish you. For that you gotta be alive."

He looked past her at Doc, who stood with swordstick in hand.

"I got a score to settle with you, you oldie nuke-sucker," Trumbo said. "But I don't reckon I'm gonna get a chance to pay you back proper. So I guess I can settle for shooting you in your skinny old belly."

He extended the handblaster toward Doc, who prepared to spring at the sec boss. Death meant less to him than the bitter disappointment that it came at the hands of such a man.

The beefy hand that held the blaster down on Doc exploded amid a roar that made the early shot sound like a baby's wet fart. Trumbo shrieked insanely and held up what now looked like a bundle of bloody, twisted sticks. Blood sprayed from a severed artery.

Doc whipped the blade free of its ebony sheath. He launched himself into perhaps the finest balestra-and-lunge of his life.

The tip of his sword entered Trumbo's screaming mouth.

The steel encountered brief resistance from his soft palate, and then more pronounced but equally brief resistance from bone before it punched into the cranium and skewered the medulla oblongata.

The scream shut off as the traitor lost control of the muscles of his larynx and his breathing. His heart shut down. His eyes rolled into his head. He dropped straight down amid a cloud of stench as his loosening bowels filled his pants.

Sand dropped the empty blaster with a clatter. "Justly struck, dear heart. Help me up."

Doc did. Despite the blood beginning to drench the right sleeve of her shirt from the upper arm down, she required little assistance to regain her feet. She swayed once, and leaned back against the shelves.

"Oh, no," she said, fending him off with her left hand. "I can meet my fate on my own two legs. Rad-blast, I've almost forgotten what it feels like to be shot. Not an acquaintance I'm eager to renew."

She glanced down at her wounded arm. "Seems to've missed the bone. I suppose I should feel gratitude when life serves me a fresh cherry tomato atop the latest shit sandwich."

She knelt by the reeking corpse of Trumbo, which lay on its face mostly on the floorboards inside the closet.

"Your wound—" Doc began.

"Help me get this befouled husk out of sight first," she said. "Or worse than he will follow."

Doc did. With three hands and much grunting, the man's deadweight was dragged into the storage closet. Fortunately the blood that had leaked from him had all fallen inside the door.

When it was closed, the small already-close space filled immediately with the ripe reek of his voided bowels. Doc set his jaw against the stench and reminded himself he had known worse. *Much* worse.

Sand leaned back against a shelf and closed her eyes.

"You'll find linen bandages on the third shelf of the hutch, my dear," she said. "Please help me bind the wound. Quickly. We haven't much time."

Fussing like an old hen, to his own distress, Doc complied. Sand bore the wound and his binding of it, which of necessity was rough and ready, with a stoicism that surprised him. Although by now, he thought, why should anything about this woman surprise me? Whatever else she is, she truly is remarkable.

He straightened. "Had we met under other circumstances," he said, "I think you might have made a boon companion for Ryan Cawdor's merry band."

She laughed lightly. "I suspect that's as great a compliment as I've ever received. Thank you, though you must believe me—it isn't true."

She grabbed him, kissed him deeply, then broke away. Sand looked at him with pale-green eyes moist and shining.

"One thing you must remember," she said, laying her left hand over his heart.

"Yes?"

"Dark Lady is my sole heir and successor. I hate to inflict such a curse on poor, dear Eleanor, but she must bear it with her usual stoic bravery."

"Whatever do you mean, Baron?" he asked.

Through the closed door he heard a fresh spate of blasterfire erupt from the front of the house. A group of men ran past the small window shouting instructions to one another.

"I mean—"

She thrust hard against his sternum. Taken totally off his guard, Doc went flying back to sit hard inside the secret compartment. The shelves dug into his back.

"Farewell, you lovely man! You should be able to release yourself in a matter of minutes."

Before he could sort out the feelings that boiled within him—of betrayal, of concern—and give them voice, she slammed the door.

He heard the sound of the lock being turned.

Chapter Thirty-Five

Ryan ducked back around the wall of the farmhouse nearest the playhouse. Bullets cracked through the air that his head, shoulders and Steyr Scout had recently occupied.

He'd seen his target go down—a man firing a bolt-action hunting rifle from the corner of the big building where Sand had kept her gigantic yellow ace up her sleeve. Now he was just glad the farmers of Joker Creek tended to build their dwellings to the same sturdy standards as their baron's more pretentious place.

He glanced across the road to where J.B. leaned out and loosed a 3-round burst from his Uzi toward the house. The Armorer ducked back into cover as more bullets sought him.

He looked over, caught Ryan's eye and shook his head.

From the other end of the house where Ryan sheltered came a roar of a powerful automatic blaster. Dark Lady pivoted back around to safety, holding Sinclair's big BAR up in front of her. She had stripped off her black sweater to reveal the black sleeveless garment, probably a T-shirt with its sleeves cut off, she had worn beneath. A thin, gray trail of smoke wisped from the Browning's muzzle toward the clear afternoon sky.

She showed Ryan a grin. "Bonnie Parker was said to be a skilled hand with one of these," she called. "She was a small woman like me. I take inspiration where I can find it, Mr. Cawdor."

"Bonnie Parker?" Mikey asked. The giant stood next to her. While both twins refused to use a blaster, their enormous shared body had willingly carried a whole mule-load of fresh magazines and boxed cartridges for their comrades.

"The twentieth-century outlaw," his brother said, sneering. "Of Bonnie and Clyde fame. Don't you read?"

"Same as you," the better-looking but grumpier head conceded. "I just don't like to clutter my head with every scrap of useless trivia that happens to leak in through my eyes."

From behind came sporadic blaster shots—and the occasional scream. Though less well equipped than the Amity Springers with blasters and bullets, Sand's subjects had already demonstrated that they had them. They were certainly more than amply supplied with shovels, axes, hoes, rakes and other farm and labor implements that would serve as brutal, effective weapons when applied to the human form with sufficient fury. The sec men and Crazy Dogs who had been busily brutalizing the peasants when the rescue column arrived were finding that out much to their sorrow as they were hunted down one by one.

Ryan wasn't triple thrilled to have armed foes on the loose behind his back when he was fighting, but it wasn't as if they had any choice. They all knew it was just a matter of time before some of the brother coldhearts Diego the Dog had summoned to join his nascent empire would arrive. And if they caught Ryan, his companions and Dark Lady's contingent between hammer and anvil—well, they'd get pounded to purple mush about that fast.

He heard the vicious crack of Jak's Colt Python handblaster echo down the road. He was leading the clean-up of stray Dogs. That reassured Ryan that the odds of taking a slug in the spine were as low as possible. Nobody loved the sport of hunting more than Jak, and few did it better.

J.B. fired another burst at the big house, then ducked back to reload his machine pistol. Ryan saw Ricky duck around the other end of that house from loosing a shot from his fat-barreled DeLisle blaster.

The Armorer shook his head. "No way this works," he said. "We're just burning ammo. We've got to blow the wall."

Dark Lady's stock of plunder from the buried whitecoat lab included enough C-4 and blasting caps left over from the cutting charges J.B. and Ricky had used to immobilize the monster dozer to make up two satchel charges. One lay next to Ryan, the other between J.B. and Ricky. Each carried easily enough plas-ex to blow a man-size hole through even a wall as heroic as the playhouse's.

The problem was getting close enough to deliver them. The distance was too much for even Mikey-Bob to hurl one and get it close enough to do any good. As big as they were, the charges needed to be lying hard against the thick adobe, or they'd waste too much energy pushing empty air to do the deed.

And with the large number of blastermen holed up inside the main house, and especially giving flanking fire from the outbuildings to both sides, trying to dart across the nearly fifty yards of open ground to the playhouse was a sheer self-chill.

Ryan went to a knee, then leaned out around the side of the farmhouse. He saw a blaster-flash from the window to his right of the front door. He got a flash picture through his scope on its lower setting of two-power: a dark, mustached face grimacing over a longblaster. He triggered a quick compressed surprised break. Letting recoil help spin him back under cover, he wasn't sure if he'd hit or not.

As he slammed a fresh 7.62 mm cartridge into the Scout's receiver and locked the bolt, he saw a figure running toward him. It was female, trimly but amply curved, and had a head of blazing red hair.

She threw her back against the sun-heated wall beside him.

"Bad news," she said. "Kris says her lookouts report spotting a party of bikers down the road. Mebbe a quarter mile out. No more than five or six, and they seem to be coming cautiously. But who knows how many they're scouting for?"

"Yeah," Ryan grunted.

It was triple-bad news—the worst, short of spotting a no-shit relief force of dozens of the bastards bearing down on them. As it was, he couldn't be sure that wouldn't follow.

He gestured Dark Lady over. A couple of her people took up her place hopping and popping from cover as she ran up.

Her dark eyes widened as he gave her the bad news.

"We've got to get into the big house and triple fast," he told her. "They jump us from behind, we're chilled."

"That's it," she said, slinging the Browning Automatic Rifle. "I'll carry a satchel charge myself."

"No, you won't."

Her eyes blazed.

"Normally it'd peel no skin off my ass if you got your stupe self chilled," he said. "But we need every blaster we've got, especially if we have to fort up inside the playhouse and stand off a bunch of new coldhearts. And your chances of making it close enough to blow the wall range from *jack* to *shit*."

For a moment she stared at him with a wild fury that set him back on his heels. Her face, already pale, had gone a paper-white as pure as Jak's, meaning she'd gotten an adrenaline dump that usually presaged an attack *right now*. He braced to cold-cock her—if you could do that to a woman—with a steel butt plate across the jaw.

But then she frowned and sucked in a deep breath. Spots of color returned to her cheeks as she controlled her rage.

"You're right," she said in a voice that was almost calm. "I let my feelings get the better of me."

Ryan let out a breath he hadn't realized he'd been holding.

"Which leaves us the problem of—"

"Dark Lady!" called one of the two shooters who had taken her place at the far end of the farmhouse, a tow-headed kid named Buck. "Come look!"

Dark Lady ran that way. After a quick shared glance, Ryan and Krysty followed.

They joined the gaudy owner and peered around the corner of the house. Though the sound of blasterfire from the defenders had increased, Ryan didn't hear the crack of bullets passing nearby, nor the whine of tumbling ricochets.

He and Krysty stood behind the shorter woman to lean around themselves. At first he saw nothing of interest from the sturdy adobe sheds between the house and the creek, then noticed an absence of coldhearts popping out to shoot at them.

Then motion took his eye up the Joker Creek arroyo that cut the face of the bluffs that walled the north side of the valley. A lone figure was scrambling up the dirt road, just wide enough to let one wag pass, that ran alongside the creek to the top of the cliffs.

From its size and shape, and the short yellow hair, there was no mistaking Baron Sand herself. She was making heavy going of it, stumbling on the steep road, catching herself with her left hand. The reason wasn't double hard to make out: the right sleeve of her white shirt was bright red with clearly still fresh blood, as was the bandage he could just make out tied around her biceps.

Bullets kicked up dust around her. She continued a tripod scrabble to the top with desperate determination.

From the back of the house Diego's voice roared, belling with fury. "Cease fire, you mutie-lovers! I want her alive! Chill her and I'll peel the hide off you and let you watch me run it up a flagpole before I let your miserable ass die!"

The blasters stopped. Instead a handful of sec men started up from behind the outbuildings in pursuit. Ryan heard engines snarl to life from behind the main house, and then half a dozen Crazy Dogs' bikers joined them.

The traitor sec men blocked the road. On such a steep slope, not even big V-twin engines could accelerate the heavy sleds fast enough to bull them out of the way.

But Sand was clearly doomed. Exhausted, she flopped to the road, turning to land on her well-cushioned rump still a dozen feet from the top.

She kicked herself to the roadside, into a shallow space overhung by sandstone cap-rock.

"All right, you coldheart pricks!" she cried. "Come and get me, and be damned to you!"

They did. Gunning their engines impatiently, seeming to be as much pushing their bikes with their boots as riding them, the Crazy Dogs followed the sec men up to seize her.

As the first got within ten feet of her, Sand raised her left hand. It clearly clutched something small and solid.

She raised her middle finger. It seemed to Ryan she clenched her thumb and other fingers in the same moment, though as far distant as she was, he wasn't sure what gave him that impression.

Both walls of the cut erupted in dust and smoke, and a thunderclap rolled down past the houses and out across Baron Sand's domain. Ryan saw big chunks of rock tumble into the cloud.

It began to settle almost at once. Where Baron Sand and

her pursuers had been was now a mound of khaki earth and jumbled sandstone blocks. The rear tire of a single motor-cycle stuck out the lower end of it, still spinning.

"Cassandra!" Dark Lady screamed. She darted from cover to run up the road toward the baron's rocky bier.

But her giant shadow was right behind her. With a long-legged step, Mikey-Bob caught her from behind before she'd gotten ten feet. His massive arms unfolded her and picked her easily right off the ground. She kicked furiously and tried to slam the back of her head into one of his, but to no avail.

Blasterfire burst angrily from the playhouse and its satellite structures. Ryan jerked back behind cover, pulling Krysty with him as bullets cracked by.

He saw Mikey's black-haired head jerk, then it lolled lifelessly down the slope of his shoulder.

Making tough going of it, the giant carried Dark Lady back behind the farmhouse.

"Here," Bob said. He thrust Dark Lady toward Ryan. He caught her as well as he could with his left arm.

"Mikey!" she cried. Ryan saw that the left-hand head had taken a slug through the left eye. Blood and aqueous humor streamed from it like tears.

Dark Lady writhed free and threw herself against the giant's chest. He patted her clumsily with his right hand.

"Gotta…go," Bob said. His speech was slurred as if his tongue had swollen to fill his mouth. "Love…you."

He kissed her upturned forehead, then he pushed her toward Krysty, who holstered her handblaster and grabbed Dark Lady in a bear hug from behind. Dark Lady did not fight her.

"I love you, too!" she cried through a torrent of tears.

Dragging his left leg, Bob limped along the back of the house to where a satchel charge lay. It had been assembled in a scavvy backpack, incongruously bright and cheerful blue and yellow. He scooped it up and held it to his chest.

"Take care of her," Bob said to Ryan and Krysty.

"Are you going to do anything stupe if I let you go?" Krysty asked.

Dark Lady slumped. "No. We always knew one could never survive without the other."

Ryan followed him as far as the street end of the house. Suddenly seeming to grab complete control of his massive, failing body, Bob pulled himself up and rounded the corner with a defiant roar.

"I'm on my way to Hell! *Who's coming with me?*"

Ryan wheeled around the corner, longblaster shouldered. The playhouse's front windows flickered with fire. Some of the shots had to be hitting the charging giant.

He ignored them. Laughing, he ran at a lumbering, inexorable pace. Ryan shot a man in the window left of the door; he was leveling a 12-gauge. Then he ducked hastily back, slinging the Scout, as Bob ran full-tilt into the closed door.

The satchel charge went off with a thunderous blast. A cloud of dust and debris shot down the road past Ryan's sheltering corner. He imagined he saw a tree-trunk-size leg spin end over end through the rolling explosion.

Then he was around the corner and sprinting toward the playhouse. He pulled his SIG in his right hand and his panga in his left.

J.B. appeared at his right side, running as fast as his shorter legs could carry him, blasting from his slung Uzi with his right hand, clamping his fedora to his head with his left.

From the far end of the farmhouse Ryan heard Dark Lady ripping bursts from the BAR and keeping them short with expert precision. Clearly, she was not one to allow her loved ones to die in vain.

Or unavenged.

As he neared the big house, Ryan saw that the doorway had been blown out to about three times its original width. A figure appeared in the midst of it, coughing and waving at the smoke. Ryan gave it a quick double-tap from his handblaster and it fell.

He charged into the late baron's front room. It was still full of smoke and dust and the eye-searing fumes of detonated plas-ex. He saw shadowy figures and fired into them.

The fog thinned enough to allow him the beginnings of vision of his surroundings. The spiderweb swaths of cloth had been torn down; the outsize satin cushions shoved to the walls. Some of these smoldered, adding to the choking, obscuring smoke.

A figure loomed to his left. He slashed toward the shadow bulb of the head with his panga. He felt it contact bone, felt bone crunch. The figure grunted and fell.

"Ryan?" he heard J.B. call from behind him.

Before he could answer, another shadow flew out of the still-thick smoke swirled toward the rear of the house. It caught him by the upper body and slammed him to the floor. His right elbow struck the tile on the funny bone. His blaster popped out of briefly flaccid fingers and clattered away.

Foul, stinking breath filled his nostrils.

"Cawdor!" he heard Diego snarl from inches away, even as his dark hate-twisted face resolved from the gloom. "Now I chill your sorry ass!"

Chapter Thirty-Six

Kneeling with the tip of his sword stuck into the closet lock, holding it gingerly with fingertips of both hands to avoid cutting himself, Doc felt and heard the tumbler disengage. Holding the blade in place with his right hand, he turned the knob with his left.

He let out a long sigh of relief. He had had his concentration well and truly shattered by the earth-breaking concussion of a few moments before. But somehow he had pulled his scattered wits together quickly and actually completed his task.

The door began to open. It admitted the sound of shots and screams from the front of the house, and also a welcome draft of fresh air.

He pulled the door in just far enough to make sure the catch wouldn't reengage. Then he struggled to his feet. His knees creaked. He had had one propped awkwardly on the prostrate body of Trumbo. The stink of the man's excrement was so thick he could almost see it. It made his head swim and his stomach churn.

A few moments before the explosion, Diego's bull-bellow of rage had alerted him to Sand's escape. Through the small window he had witnessed the poor woman's last instant of life before she blew a section of the bluff down on her—and her pursuers.

I wish that I had never doubted her, he thought, finally

straightening. He thrust the ebony sheath of his sword through his belt and withdrew his LeMat.

Before undertaking to pick the lock, he had closed the secret compartment again. There was no reason to make plundering the baron's wealth easy on the villains, should they bring him down, as by all odds they would.

He extended the second and third fingers of his sword hand to grasp the door by the open end. Then he stepped back and to the side, pulling it open as far as Trumbo's corpse would allow.

And found himself staring into the black eyes of Trumbo's lieutenant, Lobo.

For some reason Doc did not fire at once into the huge, dark face. "Stand back, my man," he said instead.

The black eyes flicked past him to Trumbo's bulk.

"No trouble, man," the immense Indian said in a voice like a cannon ball rolling downhill in a wooden barrel. "My debt's paid. Not my fight now. I'm out."

He hawked and spit carefully past Doc. The glob landed with laudable precision on the back of Trumbo's round, balding head.

He stepped out of the way and gestured with a dinner-plate hand for Doc to pass. Nodding politely, Doc stepped past him and headed toward the sound and smoke of the fray.

FROM THE VIOLENT motion of the right side of the coldheart lord's body, Ryan guessed Diego was about to stab him.

He rolled hard to his own right, managing to twist in Diego's one-armed embrace.

The point of his knife slammed into the synthetic butt stock of Ryan's longblaster. He felt the weapon bounce against his back.

"Squirm," Diego snarled. "I like it better that way!"

Ryan flung his head back hard. He felt Diego's nose squash between the back of his skull and the coldheart's face. Blood squirted down the back of his neck.

Likely the Dog had had his nose broken before, but Ryan's reverse head butt made his grip slacken slightly. The one-eyed man twisted free, rolled clear and sprang to his feet.

Around him figures were struggling in the murk. There was still too much smoke and dust in the air for anyone to be able to shoot for fear of hitting a friend.

Diego scrambled up. He laughed at Ryan. Blood had given him a red beard dripping from his big chin.

"That the best you got?" he taunted.

"Talk big, chill small," Ryan said. He transferred the panga to his right hand.

Diego swept his big bowie knife back and forth between them. Ryan simply knocked it aside with his heavier blade. As he rolled his wrist over for a backhand strike at Diego's neck, the Crazy Dogs' leader grabbed his forearm with his left hand.

Ryan pivoted his hips to the right, yanking his arm out of his enemy's grasp while powering a straight right fist into Diego's face. The coldheart's head snapped back.

Ryan kept after him, bringing the panga up and around for an overhand stroke. As quick as a striking sidewinder, Diego whipped up his knife to parry high with a ring of steel on steel.

The one-eyed man pressed forward. He fired a left uppercut into Diego's gut. He felt a bit of softness, then muscle as hard as an oak plank. But Diego lost some air and leaned forward. The biker boss grabbed Ryan's knife arm as it relentlessly pressed the broad machete-like blade toward his forehead.

Ryan fired three quick shovel hooks into Diego's short ribs. He felt bone break; Diego grunted.

And brought his right knee pounding up into Ryan's groin.

There were men who could absorb a full-on shot to the nuts and keep on coming without batting an eye. Ryan had delivered ball-mashing blows to a few of them—and been lucky to escape with his life. Especially the first time, when he was totally shocked that his opponent kept coming.

Ryan was not one of those men. It felt as if his lungs and his guts were suddenly trying to come out his nose. He doubled over and dropped to his knees.

"Ace," Diego said. "You got something for me to cut off."

He aimed a savage backhand slash for Ryan's face. The blade whipped toward his one good eye.

Ryan couldn't breathe, but his will, as tough and hard as vanadium steel, saved him—along with the hard-wired human reflex to protect the eyes.

His right hand flew up and across the body. He managed to control the instinctive strike a last fraction of a second, turning what would have been an attempt to knock Diego's knife arm aside with his own to a crosswise cut with the panga.

What slashed across Ryan's face was hot blood, not cold steel, as Diego's hand was severed just above the wrist.

Diego followed through with the blow, but his eyes got wide and locked in shock and horror on Ryan's.

But the biker chief was no soft touch. He sprang back as Ryan thrust himself to his feet, jumping back from a disemboweling slash.

Then his left hand came out from the small of his back holding a small hidie semiauto handblaster. With a wordless hawk-scream of triumph, he thrust it toward Ryan's face.

The Deathlands warrior hacked that hand off.

Diego reeled back toward the hole where the door had been. Right outside the blown-out front wall a motorcycle snarled to a stop, a dozen feet behind the Crazy Dogs' chieftain. The coldheart didn't glance back.

"What are you gonna do now, One-Eye, chill me?" Diego demanded. He held up his spurting stumps. "I'm unarmed. Get it? Unarmed?"

Something dark and thin flew through the gap above his head to drop down in front of his face and settle around his upper arms and chest.

"Uh-oh," he said.

In the yellowing afternoon light starting to slant in between the farmhouses of Joker Creek, Ryan saw a slim, black-clad figure with bare pale arms forking a Crazy Dogs' bike. Then with a roar of a powerful engine and a squeal of tires on hard-packed earth, the motorcycle spun and sped back down the road.

Diego bellowed as the lariat jerked him backward out the gap. He hit hard on his back and his booted heels flew up. And then he was being dragged, by one of his own gang's bikes, bouncing, rolling and howling, through the ville he had thought to conquer.

WHOEVER THE SCOUTING party of half a dozen motorcyclists was, the sound of the firefight in Joker Creek had made them cautious.

Perhaps more to the point, they weren't stupe enough to have been lulled into a false sense of security by the sudden cessation of the shooting. Or most of it, at least.

They came cautiously, in a loose vee, spread out across the road into the ditch on both sides.

Among the fields and houses ahead of them, nothing stirred.

The leader, a big guy with a face full of seams and a

grizzled pale beard, stopped his Harley a few feet shy of a dark form sprawled on the dirt track in front of him. He signed the others to a halt. Dropping his kickstand, he swung a boot off and walked up to examine the vaguely manlike figure.

He stuck out a boot and prodded one end with his toe. It was the head, lying facedown. It rolled to one side.

Dark Lady hadn't dragged the Crazy Dogs' boss far behind the Crazy Dog motorcycle she had commandeered. But she had made it count, zigzagging the stolen bike to bounce him off the maximum number of hard adobe corners on the way to the ville's outskirts.

And even then, he might have bled to death before he felt every one.

Watching through his Leupold glass at the maximum magnification, Ryan could tell from the dismounted biker's body language that he recognized what Dark Lady's vengeance had left of Diego the Dog. He turned his head to shout something to his men.

That was all Ryan saw of the scene for an instant, as the Steyr kicked his shoulder. The sound of its blast was loud in the front room of the ville, even though he was sitting in the darkness just inside the gaping hole.

When the longblaster descended again, Ryan saw the grizzle-bearded man toppling backward with blood spurting from his blown-out throat.

From the right window Dark Lady fired a full magazine of rounds from Sinclair's borrowed BAR. None of them struck any of the surviving riders as they hastily turned their bikes and rode back the way they had come as fast as they could go.

"*Nuestra Señora*, I hope they weren't just innocent travelers," Ricky said from somewhere right behind Ryan.

"Me, too, kid," Ryan said. "Hate to waste a bullet."

FOR THE EIGHTEENTH time Ricky Morales, bringing up the rear of the trudging party with his friend Jak, turned to walk backward.

A mile west down the road toward its meeting with the Río Piojo, and eventually the ville of that name at the Basin's west end, the glow of the lights still burning in Amity Springs in the small hours wasn't bright. But it was still clearly visible.

The folk back there were busy: tending the wounded, saying goodbye to their dead, and figuring out how to rebuild their shattered ville. Not just one but two: the people of Joker Creek had added their voices to Doc's account of Baron Sand's last oral testament, to request that Dark Lady should rule them, too.

Mebbe the not-baron of Amity Springs will call herself the not-baron of Joker Creek, too, Ricky thought.

"I still don't understand," he muttered resentfully, turning his face forward again, "why we had to get out of bed in the middle of the night and go running off across the desert."

"You know what they say about a baron's loyalty, kid," Mildred called back.

She walked just ahead of Doc. The old man walked in front of Ricky and Jak. From the curious slump to his shoulders and the way he walked with his head down, Ricky guessed his mind was wandering through the mists that sometimes filled it, to the exclusion of the outside world.

"Still," Mildred said, shaking her head, "I got to admit it strikes me as a little raw, running out on Dark Lady like this without even saying good-bye. I judged her all wrong. I feel like I never got a chance to make amends."

"Deal with it," Ryan called.

He strode in the lead with his head up despite what had to be a major case of the wearies and his longblaster in his hands. There had been no further sign of Diego's promised reinforcements since the battle of what was now the day before. But Ricky knew what their one-eyed leader would say if asked about his current state of high alert; he hadn't lived this long taking things for granted.

"Anyway," Ryan said, "what makes you think she expected anything else?"

"What do you mean, lover?" Krysty asked. She walked a step behind him on his right. "She did ask us to stay and help rebuild the two villes. Or help defend them, at least."

J.B. chuckled. He walked right behind the lead pair, cradling his Uzi in his hands.

"She paid us," he said.

"Why not stay for a while and do that, Ryan?" Mildred asked.

"Like Trumbo's big Indian told Doc back in the playhouse," Ryan said. "It's done. Not our fight. And we have a redoubt to find."

A sick sense of dread crept into Ricky's belly. He glanced back at the lights of Amity Springs. Their amber glow had grown perceptibly fainter, or so he thought. It seemed in danger of flickering out forever.

"You don't think they have a chance to hold out against what's coming, do you?" he said.

He wasn't sure he spoke loudly enough to be heard from the front of the procession, really, but he should have known better. "As long as they got somebody like Dark Lady on their side," Ryan said, "sure. They got a chance."

"But a good one?"

He shrugged. And, never looking back, kept on walking.

* * * * *

The Executioner

Don Pendleton's

HARD TARGETS

A missing-persons case escalates into Mafia war...

While investigating a missing-persons case, Mack Bolan's brother Johnny uncovers a link between the Buffalo police department and the Mafia. But when he's forced to kill one of the cops moonlighting for the mob, the stakes suddenly go through the roof. Both sides want him to pay—in blood. But they're not the only ones looking for payback. The Mafia don is about to get a lethal message—delivered personally by the Executioner.

GOLD EAGLE ®

Available December wherever books and ebooks are sold.

TAKE 'EM FREE
2 action-packed novels plus a mystery bonus

NO RISK

NO OBLIGATION TO BUY

James Axler
Outlanders®

WINGS OF DEATH

A legion of flying monsters spawns terror across Africa...

An old enemy of the Cerberus warriors unleashes Harpy-like killers
on the African continent, hoping the blood-hungry winged beasts
and their love of human flesh will aid in his capture of a legendary
artifact: the powerful staff wielded by Moses and King Solomon.
Except, the staff's safe in Kane's hands, and with the murderous
rampage spiraling out of control and an exiled prince bent on
unlocking the gates of hell, the staff is all that stands between the
rebels and Africa's utter decimation.

Available February wherever books and ebooks are sold.